TAKE ME

Steamy Secrets, Book Three

DIANE DEMETRE

LUMINOSITY PUBLISHING LLP

Take Me
Steamy Secrets, Book Three
Copyright © November 2019 Diane Demetre

Paperback ISBN: 978-1-9993066-6-3

Cover Art by Poppy Designs

DEDICATION

For all the men who love, laugh and live with passion.
Heroes one and all.

QUOTE

---

*The dancer's body is simply the luminous manifestation of
the soul*

— *Isadora Duncan*

CHAPTER ONE

____

AIDEN WINCED WHEN THE surly Spaniard threw her to the ground where she struck the timber floor with a thud and collapsed like a rag doll. But none of this brutish treatment diminished her extraordinary poise or beauty. Her long, ebony hair fell forwards covering the exquisite sculpture of her face, and her dark eyes flashed with fury as she struggled to escape. The ferocity with which the man treated her, triggered Aiden's instinct to save the beauty and give the beast a good thrashing. But this wasn't a time to intervene, to play the hero. This was tango, and it was obviously being performed by a pair of Spain's leading exponents of the dance.

Trying to find shelter from an unexpected downpour earlier this evening, Aiden had accidentally stumbled upon this local club, this *peñas*. He'd heard about such clubs in whispered conversations between the locals over the past days, but no one would give up their locations. Tourists weren't generally welcome. Even the concierge at Aiden's hotel had proved elusive as to their whereabouts no matter how much money Aiden had discreetly offered. So ever resourceful, he'd decided to conduct his own investigations. Tonight, the heavy deluge had proved an unexpected blessing. For on his hunt in the backstreets of Seville to find a *peñas* and trying to evade the slapping rain, he'd spied a couple staggering from a hole in the stone block wall. He'd squeezed into the space the happy couple left in their wake before the door slammed behind them and was finally rewarded for his search.

Now with damp jeans, sodden shoes, and wet hair, he leaned against a wall on the far side of the club, mesmerized by the fiery, violent performance taking place on the small stage in front of him. A cluster of equally passionate musicians playing the guitar, flute, violin and a strange-looking accordion, drove the tempo onwards matching the fervour of the couple performing onstage. The exotic woman slithered to her feet then turned with a venomous snarl to her partner. When she hurtled towards him, she found her assault blocked by his strong arms which spun her away at alarming speed. Then in a final show of male dominance, he dragged her to him and with chest heaving, threw her into a back-breaking arch across his bended knee. Having conquered her and with a thrust of his chin, he raised his arms overhead on the music's impressive crescendo. The prior hush of the club broke into cacophonous applause, cheers and stamping feet. Aiden jammed his thumb and forefinger into his mouth and showed joined in the appreciation with an ear-piercing whistle. The sweat-lathered couple rose like a pair of indestructible Phoenix and with haughty pride, took their well-deserved bows then made grand, graceful exits from the stage.

A small table became vacant close to where Aiden stood so he slid into the setting, nearly knocking the candle jar over. His sharp reflexes meant he could grab it before the molten wax snuffed out the flame and spilled on the floor. Steadying the jar on the rickety timber table, Aiden plonked down into a similarly unsteady chair, and a buxom waitress swooped in to take his order.

God, he loved Spanish women. At least what he'd seen so far. Sex, sex, sex seemed to be all they oozed. Stunning, big-breasted and round-hipped, their bodies were designed for pleasure and pleasuring. And that's just what Aiden intended on doing. Judging by the sultry, come-hither look on the waitress's face, he'd be in for such an opportunity tonight.

Sipping on his icy beer, which his pouting waitress delivered in double-quick time, Aiden scanned his surroundings more closely. The entire space appeared to be suspended in a time warp dating back to the mid-nineteenth century. Hewn from rugged, grey stone, the walls, ceiling and floors formed a shadowy den in which the venue operated, giving it a cool, otherworldly atmosphere. Like most clubs and despite the no-smoking signs strategically stuck on the walls, the air hung thick with the smell of stale cigarettes, body odour, and alcohol. There were no ashtrays for the customers and since he couldn't see any tell-tale signs of glowing cancer sticks wedged in patron's fingers, he suspected the staff smoked before and after trading hours leaving the rank smell. Lit in a vermillion hue, the place burned with a devilish glimmer, more subtle than the garishly bright illuminated sign above the bar. Sevilla Flamenco it proclaimed, in coloured LED chaser lights, some sections of which no longer worked. Behind it, a small variety, but a large number of glasses hung in rusty racks strung on old beaten timber planks roughly drilled into the stone ceiling above the bar. With its clutter of wall posters and paintings, flamenco memorabilia, and dusty stage curtains, the entire space resonated with decades of dance, passion, mystery and more-than-a-little neglect. While Aiden continued his reconnaissance, his eyes fell upon the waitress once more. This time, she lounged at the bar, wiping glasses and demonstrating her sexual stroking skills on each item, her eyes twinkling with mischief. Lifting his empty beer bottle for another, he nodded in wry amusement, and she rushed to fill his order.

Bending down further than needed, she pushed her blushing bosom toward Aiden and placed his *Corona* with a slice of lime, on the table. "*Buena nochese, señor,*" she said with a flutter of her mascara-laden eyelashes and a glossy, red smile. Aiden guessed she couldn't have been more than twenty, but her overt sexuality befitted a more mature and experienced woman.

Aiden's lips curved upwards enjoying her unmistakable flirting. "*Buena nochese, señorita.*" He flashed her one of his easy-going champion smiles, the waitress swooned, and Aiden chuckled. Although nearing twenty-eight years of age, Aiden still couldn't fathom the effect he had on women. He'd never tried to be swoon-worthy or the James Bond type of lady-killer. Sure, he'd been brought up to respect and appreciate women. His mother, Julie had made certain of that, and his father Roger was naturally charismatic and a real ladies' man. So maybe it was in his genes, and he'd inherited his father's charm? He didn't know. For years his mates ribbed him and jostled to be his wingman whenever they went on the prowl. "Like moths to a flame, Ace. You burn hot, man," was their catch-cry. At times, Aiden had been embarrassed by how easy it was for him to attract the opposite sex, but now he'd given up trying to understand the attraction and enjoyed his God-given gift.

"My name is Theresa." The waitress slipped into a chair at his table, flaunting herself unashamedly at him.

"Good to meet you, Theresa. I'm Aiden." He offered his hand into which she placed hers, giving a gentle but firm squeeze.

"Where do you come from, Aiden?" With her layered black-frilled skirt falling between her splayed legs, plump breasts bursting from the red bustier and her tanned skin shining with a thin film of perspiration, Theresa was a thing of lusty beauty.

He pushed his chair back a little and smiled. "I live in Australia." He noticed Theresa glance at his crotch with a cat-like twitch of her lips, and settling in for the game, Aiden bracketed his hands behind his head.

"Someday I will go to Australia," Theresa said, twirling her long, dark locks in her fingers. "Perhaps you will take me?"

These young Spanish women aren't backwards in coming forwards, he thought.

"Theresa, get back here. You have work to do." The stern baritone voice rumbled from a middle-aged, beer-barrel of a man standing behind the bar. With his round torso trying unsuccessfully to break free of its black, bibbed apron and the cardinal cap bald spot on his head glistening under the lights, he reminded Aiden of a jolly cartoon character, except the death stare his beady black eyes burned at the waitress belied his cheerful appearance. "We haven't closed up yet, Theresa. Come on, you have to finish cleaning."

Theresa screwed up her nose, leaned forwards to Aiden and growled. "That is my papa, Domingo. He and Mama own this place. I hate it here." All the sensuous beauty disappeared from her young face. She scraped the chair backwards obeying her father's command. "You want another beer, Aiden?" she asked with none of her previous customer service charm.

"But aren't you closing up?" Most of the other customers had left, the band was packing up, and Domingo didn't seem thrilled with Aiden's ongoing custom.

"It's okay. You have time for another beer. Forget about papa." Her hand flew up in disdain then perched obstinately on her hip.

"Yes, thank you, Theresa. Another beer, please." He shot her a sympathetic smile, and she softened once more.

With the sullenness only a foiled daughter can muster, Theresa returned to the bar making sure her rapid Spanish curses, spoken loud enough for her father to hear, hit the mark. Accompanied by finger-pointing and theatrical arm-waving, Domingo continued chastising his daughter as he shuffled her back to her duties while giving Aiden the evil eye.

"I'm telling you, you did it wrong, Carla!" The roar of another man's displeasure interrupted the family dispute behind the bar.

Following the voice to its owner, Aiden recognized the man as the tango dancer. Tall, lean, strong and obviously self-important, he carried himself with the air of one who's used to others doing his bidding. Opposite him, his female partner stood, chin to chest. Although petite in stature she matched his spirit and determination. Not backing down she yelled up at him. "Just because you're the famous Rafael Flores doesn't mean you never make mistakes. I'm also famous don't forget, and you are the one who did it wrong." She jabbed her finger into his chest for good measure.

A pocket rocket, Aiden thought. He liked women with fire and was keen to see how this battle would play out.

"I do not make mistakes, Carla. Here. This is how it should have been danced." Rafael threw his bag onto the stage. Grabbing Carla's hand, he twirled her from one side to the other, counting out the beats in clipped speech.

She propped, stamping her foot. "No. No. No. That is wrong. Here." Likewise, she grabbed Rafael and threw herself under his arm, twirling and counting the beats.

"My God, you are impossible!" Tearing himself from her grip, he snatched up his bag and marched off the stage.

"Me, impossible?" Carla screamed at his departing back. "You come back here, Rafael Flores. I'm warning you." With a toss of her head, she hauled her bag onto her shoulder and stormed after him, cursing in an endless tirade.

Aiden lost sight of them when they stomped past the other side of the bar. But he did hear the door only slam once, which meant Rafael must have waited for her, and they left together. *Ah, the passion of the Spanish,* he thought and drained his beer.

Strolling to the bar, Aiden returned his empty bottle and fished out his wallet. "Are those two always like that?" he asked Theresa, nodding towards the door.

"Yes, they are dancers and lovers. Always in love and always fighting." She shrugged and tallied Aiden's account, giving him the bill.

"Are they dancing again tomorrow night?" He counted out the money from his wallet.

"Yes. Tomorrow night they do flamenco." Theresa's eyes began to shimmer as she nuzzled across the bar, pushing her fleshy breasts towards him. "Perhaps you will return?"

"Oh yes, Theresa. I'll be back." He placed an extra fifty euro on the bar. Theresa spied her sizeable tip and quickly tucked it into her bustier, checking over her shoulder that her father didn't see. Aiden patted her hand. "Start a travel account so you can come to Australia. Okay?"

With a coquettish flutter of eyelashes, she said, "Okay." But Aiden doubted the money would see the inside of any bank. It'd be spent within the week.

CHAPTER TWO

BY THE TIME AIDEN arrived at Sevilla Flamenco the following night, Theresa had reserved a table for him right at the front of the stage. Sporting a knowing smile, he realized the sizeable tip he'd given her yesterday had secured him a front-row seat. Like last night, the *peñas* groaned with locals chatting, drinking and flirting. Handsome men and voluptuous women touched and caressed each other, their fingers sliding in and out of clothing, their mouths interlocking and tasting. In darkened corners, women secretly exposed their nipples for their lover's fingers to tweak, while men grabbed their woman's hand, rubbing it up and down on their growing cocks under the table. The sexy rhythms of the music mixed with the customers' lascivious laughter made Aiden's crotch twitch. The intoxicating blend of sounds and shadows swirled around him, while the spice of perfume and raw sexuality cloaked the stale air Aiden remembered from the night before.

Leaning over, he looked down the corridor to the restrooms. Because of the dim lighting, he thought the walls had come to life, but they were plastered with bodies dancing and gyrating against each other. Barely able to contain their wanton desires, women thrust their hips into their men's crotch, while their partners devoured their necks like hungry vampires. This erotic display seared silhouetted images into Aiden's mind and stirred his cock, now eager to join the party. He readjusted himself discreetly while reassessing his previous night's appraisal of the club. This place didn't time warp to the mid-nineteenth century. It more aptly resembled Sodom and Gomorrah. A seething mass of barely controlled human sexual display, Sevilla Flamenco warranted an X-rating. No wonder the locals didn't want foreigners in.

When Theresa slipped past him, he caught her wrist, pulling her to him. "Is it always like this here?"

She cocked her head, giving him a puzzled half-smile. "Like what?"

"Like everyone here needs to get a room."

She threw her head back and laughed, giving Aiden a chance to admire her young, taut throat and décolletage. "Passion is in our blood. Most of us descend from gypsies. Wait for the flamenco. Then you will understand." Theresa bent down and whispered, "Perhaps later I will show you more." Theresa thrust her bosom toward his face, smiled a salacious promise and sashayed away.

Since he was the only blond-haired, blue-eyed person in the club, Aiden stood out from the sexy Spanish crowd like the proverbial, but no matter. Theresa's flirtatious attention and VIP treatment had marked him as someone to be trusted, so the foreplay ritual proceeded around him unabated.

Aiden spied her before most of the other patrons. He calculated she must have only been about 1.6-metres tall and by the look of her taut, strong body, weighed no more than fifty kilos, but she filled the stage with a powerhouse presence. For a moment, he forgot to breathe. Poured into a figure-hugging, blazing red gown with circles of heavy frills fanning out from her knees to the floor in a train, Carla paraded onto the stage. With her black hair slicked into a low bun adorned with a crescent of red flowers and enormous gold hoop earrings dangling from her petite lobes, she presented herself as austere and untouchable. Again, the air locked in Aiden's chest. She kicked her leg sending the frills into a voluminous cascade and then took centre stage, her back to the audience. The deep V cut of the gown exposed the fine, muscular structure of her back, each vertebra a knuckle of perfect alignment slicing down her spine. A slight shimmer of perspiration already coated her cinnamon-brown skin and Aiden licked his lips. Once the frills settled, her bare sinewy arms snaked overhead, reminding him of a cobra ready to pounce. The crowd hushed, and the guitarist began slow and steady, picking at the strings, setting a pensive mood. Full of control and strength, Carla unfurled her arms, leaning back, back, back. Then as the other musicians clapped their hands in a staccato percussive beat, she gathered her ruffled skirt exposing the most amazing footwork Aiden had ever seen. Over the next five minutes Carla's performance strategically built in speed, passion, and intensity until Aiden thought he'd explode from sheer excitement. That she could fire off such repetitive, rapid shots of sound using nothing, but her heels and feet astounded him. He could all but taste the perspiration running down her face, arms and back, as the incongruence of the scowling, obsessive determination on her pretty face moved Aiden further to the edge of his seat. Just as Carla struck her final pose, he sprang to his feet panting, his heart racing, as if he'd held his breath throughout her entire performance. Giving her a standing ovation, he let out a couple of ear-splitting whistles and joined the audience in calling out *Olé*. His effusive enthusiasm caught her eye, and Carla shot him an appreciative smile with a nod of thanks.

When she floated from the stage, Rafael entered commanding the space. Stripped bare to the waist and wearing only tight-fitting black pants and heeled boots, Rafael was the perfect male counterpart to Carla. A slender, supple specimen of the male species, his muscles stretched long and lean. His face bore the same intense expression as Carla's, and whenever his shoulder-length hair, the colour and shine of onyx dropped over his face, he speared his fingers through its unruliness and tossed his head. A male singer began to cry a painful lament, and the clapping commenced once more. With arms outstretched like a matador holding his cape, Rafael clicked his fingers in time, and his feet stamped and drum-rolled a variety of rhythms too complex to decipher. Sweat poured from his trim dancer's body as he spun, clapped, ground his hips and flicked his bedraggled hair from his face. Like a bird desperate to take flight, Rafael pushed against gravity, expanding his chest, stretching his arms, reaching and reaching until with a double kick of his legs, he stopped upright in the sign of the cross with a loud self-satisfied yell. Again, Aiden sprang to his feet, his hands burning from applause and cheered with the rest of the audience. Obviously satisfied with his performance,

Rafael strutted from the stage, casting a pompous stare and cautious twitch of a smile at the boisterous foreigner.

During the next few hours, Carla and Rafael performed once more, and Aiden racked up a sizeable bill in *Coronas*. Seeing the band begin to pack up, Aiden stood to pay his account and invite Theresa back to his hotel for a nightcap. She'd just told him her papa had gone home unexpectedly so Aiden didn't want to waste any time. The thrill of flamenco and the passion it stirred in him, coupled with the overt display of sexuality by the *peñas* customers had his body yearning for closure.

Rising from his table, he heard Theresa say, "Aiden, this is my older brother Marco. He plays the bandoneón in the band." By the case Marco was holding, Aiden figured it was the whining instrument that looked like an accordion. "And this is Pascual and Felipe and Raúl." As Aiden said "hello" to each of the young men he noted by their cases, they played the flute, violin, and guitar. Not that he'd remember. Names and faces were something he tried to memorize but adding instruments was a new level of difficulty.

Theresa tapped him on the shoulder. "Aiden, this is Carla Armando and Rafael Flores." Aiden turned his gaze to the couple. Close up, Carla was breathtaking, and Rafael oozed some quality Aiden hadn't witnessed in a man before. He was at once, a man's man but also exuded a deeper enigmatic element.

Carla thrust her diminutive hand forwards, a gleaming smile lighting her face, "*Buena nochese,* Aiden."

Aiden engulfed her hand in his. "*Buena nochese,* Carla. I loved your dancing." She accepted the compliment with humility, downcast her eyes and fluttered her thick black eyelashes. Meanwhile, Rafael stood by watching the exchange, an inscrutable expression on his face. Used to assessing his sporting and professional rivals with a cursory glance, Aiden noted Rafael was dressed head to toe in black. In a ponytail, his hair was as tightly restrained as his demeanour.

"*Buena nochese,* Rafael." With a warm grin, Aiden offered his hand which Rafael accepted politely in an unenthusiastic shake. Undeterred by Rafael's icy exterior, Aiden continued, "I do a lot of sports, surfing, climbing, rafting and things like that, but I've never seen anything like you. You're fit, man. I'm in awe."

With a flinty stare, Rafael eyed Aiden while everyone waited through the ensuing silence. Aiden held his ground. He stood eye to eye with the dancer and although Rafael didn't have his muscle bulk, he displayed the same strength of will as Aiden.

"*Gracias*, Aiden. That is most kind of you."

Aiden thought he heard a collective sigh escape the group, but he couldn't be sure. "Listen. How about I fix up this bill and you all come back to my hotel for a few drinks?"

Theresa shot Marco a silent plea and on receiving his approval, nodded vigorously at Aiden. The other musicians murmured in agreement while Carla glanced sideways at Rafael, who waited a beat then nodded with a shrug. "*Gracias*, Aiden. *Sí,* we will join you."

~ ♥ ~

ALTHOUGH AIDEN INVITED EVERYONE back to his hotel, it was Rafael who led the entourage back to Casa del Jardín. Not that Aiden minded. Hanging out with the six performers and the gorgeous waitress was the highlight of his trip to date. He'd been keeping a low profile since arriving in Seville, and aside from brief sexual liaisons, he'd not mingled with anyone. After the hotel's heavy metal door closed behind them blocking out the noise and bustle from the Santa Cruz barrio, the old town district, the group strolled through the open loggia of the seventeenth-century palace now converted into a swank hotel. A variety of plants flung themselves with careless abandon from the balconies, arches, and patios, their cool greens contrasting with the warmth of the ochre painted stucco walls. Having just finished work, the performers chatted loudly unconcerned with the lateness of the hour. Their excited voices mingled with the clip-clop of their shoes on the worn flagstone flooring and echoed around the towering archways. Aiden tried his best to quieten his rowdy new friends who reluctantly obliged, if only for a few subdued minutes. Cloaked in the amber glow embracing the pillars and arches of the old architecture, they drifted past the courtyard's burbling central fountain towards the stairs. Aiden took the lead and they followed him up to the third floor, along the narrow balcony and waited until he opened the door to his room. "Well, here we are. Make yourselves at home while I raid the minibar." They trekked inside the exclusive well-appointed suite, nodding approval. The musicians dumped their instruments and settled onto the lush carpeted living room floor. Carla and Rafael scanned the room, obviously impressed by its elegance and then sequestered one of the buttery-coloured leather couches.

Spying the king-size bed with its cushiony mattress, Theresa investigated further into the suite. "Ooh, Aiden, this is a wonderful room." With a gleam in her eye, she bounced her hand on the bed, unaware of the threatening glare Marco directed in their direction. Aiden knew any chance of getting Theresa into his bed had been well and truly thwarted by her brother's menacing presence.

Aiden returned to his hosting duties. "This is all I have. Come help yourselves." He placed all the miniature spirits, soft drinks and a couple of bottles of red on the hand-made parquet dining table with a mixture of glasses and cups. Amid smiles and chit-chat, the musicians seized the spirits, while Theresa poured glasses of merlot for Carla, Rafael and herself. Watching them settle in quelled some of Aiden's thoughts of home. He missed his family and mates, but tonight, not so much. When Felipe and Raúl slipped around the armoire and disappeared from general view, Aiden wandered around to check they weren't smoking in his non-smoking suite.

"Here," Felipe offered Raúl a small blue pill just as Aiden appeared. "Aiden, do you want one? I have more?" With his doe-shaped eyes and soft full lips, Felipe's femininity was undeniable. Aiden suspected Felipe's secretive liaison with Raúl was more than two blokes having a quiet chat. Raúl tongued his pill and took a hefty gulp.

"What is it?" Aiden asked, a slight frown creasing his brow.

"*Viagra.* Want some?" Felipe swirled his glass and slurped.

"Why would I want to take *Viagra*? I don't have any trouble getting my cock up?"

"Maybe not. But with *Viagra,* you have trouble getting it down and that's the way we like it." Felipe made a furtive grab at Raúl's crotch, and his lover giggled like a schoolgirl.

Nodding his head, Aiden shot them a big, fat smirk. "I see. Well, you fellas have fun. Just not in my bed. Right?"

"*Si,*" they replied in unison. With the first, sharp hit of the spirits and the prospect of their every-ready cocks titillating them, Felipe and Raúl wandered out onto the terrace to explore.

Aiden poured some red wine into the last remaining cup and sauntered over to Theresa, who'd squeezed in on the couch with Carla and Rafael. Smiling down at the three, Aiden said, "So who's who in the zoo around here?"

Three quizzical stares met his question, and he tried again. "So, who is everyone? I know Marco is your older brother," Aiden said to Theresa, "but what about everyone else?"

"Raúl is the youngest of my four younger brothers," Carla explained. "We're all second cousins." Her elegant hand included the three of them on the couch, "While Felipe and Pascual are just our friends."

"God, that must get confusing." Aiden shook his head trying to picture the family tree. "Kissing cousins is what we call it in Australia." Again, Aiden received a confused look from them. They reminded him of the three monkeys — hear no evil, see no evil and do no evil, but he couldn't fathom who was who. "Anyway, it doesn't matter." He waved his free hand in the air in a relaxed manner.

Theresa sprang to her feet and snuggled under Aiden's outstretched arm. Her warm, sultry presence triggered an immediate response in his groin, and he visualized her fleshy body underneath him in his bed.

"Theresa, your brother is watching," Carla hissed behind her hand.

Theresa leaned forwards to peer around Aiden and spotted Marco scowling from the other side of the room.

"Oh, I'm sick of Marco always stopping me from doing what I want." Theresa tossed her long, black hair and tugged Aiden closer.

In a low rumble, Rafael said, "Theresa. Stop this now. We are guests in Aiden's suite, and you are making a fool of yourself." He glowered at his impetuous, young cousin, and she deflated at his reprimand.

"I'll get us some more wine." Aiden freed himself from Theresa's grip, strode to the table and reached over for the bottle, just as a determined hand grabbed his wrist.

"My sister is a virgin. I would like to keep it that way." Marco's loosely veiled threat reverberated off Aiden's ear, prompting the corded muscles in his neck to tighten.

"Listen, mate. If you have anything to say, I suggest you talk to your sister. Talking to me like this is going to get you into a whole new world of hurt." Aiden straightened to his full 1.9-metre height, his chest deflecting the threat. He drilled his guest with a steely stare until Marco, who was no match in stature or determination to his host, released his grip and retreated. A nasty snarl remained imprinted on Marco's face as he stalked over to Theresa. Seizing her by the forearm, he spat his displeasure and dragged her to the door.

When Aiden approached them, another hand clasped his wrist, this time in a soft, appeasing grip. "No Aiden. This isn't your business. Theresa is strong. She will get her way." Carla looked up at her host, a protective smile gracing her lips.

God, she was beautiful. Dangerously so.

"Let go of me, Marco." Theresa snapped her arm free and hissed at her domineering brother.

"You come home with me now, or I will tell Papa." Marco's intimidating tone sounded grossly out of place in the seductive atmosphere of the luxurious suite.

"Tell him what? That I stayed and had fun? Ha! Tell him what you want. I don't care." True to her passionate nature, Theresa stamped her foot, snapped an about-face and marched over to stand beside Aiden and Carla.

"I think the young lady has made up her mind, Marco. Maybe it's best that *you* leave." Aiden took one pace forwards. Not that he wanted to get in the middle of a sibling argument, but he wasn't going to stand back and allow Marco to bully Theresa any further.

Marco's eyes flamed. "You lay one finger on her, and I'll kill you."

"You have my word, Marco. I won't lay one finger on your sister." Theresa shot Aiden a petulant pout, but he waved his hands in self-defence. "Hey, I'm not getting myself into some family dispute over your virginity. I left Australia to get away from trouble, and I'm certainly not looking for any here." He redirected to Marco. "You have my word. Not one finger." Squinting at Aiden, Marco deliberated on the promise of his host.

"We'll make sure she's okay, Marco. You can go home." Carla walked over and kissed her cousin on both cheeks, soothing his manhood, his responsibility, and the situation.

"Very well, Carla. Come on, Pascual, let's go." Bending, he collected his bandoneon and Pascual, his flute. With a wooden nod, Marco mumbled *"Gracias," and* they departed.

Theresa shimmied over to Aiden with a pout. "Not one teensy-weensy finger?" she teased, slinking her hips from side to side.

"Theresa!" snapped Rafael, his voice deep and sonorous.

Carla clapped her hands, turning to Rafael. "Come on, Rafe, show me that step you keep saying I get wrong." She dragged him from the couch and fumbled with her phone finding the music. Rafael acquiesced, but it was obvious Theresa's petulant behaviour tried his patience.

"Come on, Theresa. I'll show you the view from the balcony." Aiden gave Carla an appreciative glance and bustled Theresa outside.

No sooner had they passed the threshold than they spied Raúl and Felipe, the latter leaning back against the railing with his cock shoved to the hilt in Raúl's mouth.

"Oh sorry, fellas," Aiden said loud enough to stop the action, while Theresa giggled beside him.

Felipe fumbled with his zipper while Raúl simply feigned a demure smile and licked his lips.

"I think we need another drink." Felipe reached for his glass.

"I don't. I just finished mine." Raúl rose to his feet, making it obvious what beverage he alluded to by the swipe of his tongue.

Aiden noticed their cocks still bursting from their jeans and wondered if this *Viagra* scene might be worth a try. Theresa squeezed his hand and he nearly lost himself in the dark pools of her dewy eyes. "You're too beautiful for your own good, Theresa."

"Maybe?" She pushed Aiden into the dark corner vacated by Raúl and Felipe. "You may have made a promise not to lay one finger on me, but I didn't make a promise. Raúl thinks he's very good at giving head jobs, but mine are better." Before Aiden could speak, she'd unzipped him and was on her knees.

"I don't think this is such a good idea, Theresa. What if Carla or Rafael come . . ." He broke off his remonstrations the moment she engulfed him in her hot, sweet mouth.

Muffled, she replied, "It's not them who I want to come. It's you." She twirled her tongue around teasing the head of his cock and he surrendered. She may have been a virgin, but there was no doubt in Aiden's mind she'd wrapped her mouth around many cocks in her short, young life. She played him like a virtuoso. At times she deep throated him all the way to the base of his shaft then returned to peck at his knob. Licking and lapping at him, driving him to distraction she toyed with him. As he placed his hands on her head, groaning in appreciation, she reminded him of his promise. "Not one finger, remember?"

"Yes of course," he moaned. His hands withdrew, and he leaned back on the balcony, letting her suck at his manhood. Feeling the familiar rise through his muscles, his body burned with rigidity, and he exploded into her accommodating mouth.

"Oh, God," he sighed as ripples of pleasure surged through his cock.

"Mmm, your cum tastes different to Spanish cum. Much sweeter." Still on her knees, Theresa zipped up his fly then stood to face her conquest.

"Theresa, we're going soon," Carla called the warning from within the suite.

"Okay," Theresa replied in the voice of an innocent youth and not of a woman with extraordinary fellatio skills.

"Thank you, Theresa. That was amazing." Aiden flashed a grateful smile.

"You are welcome. I like giving head jobs." She all but skipped a two-step.

"Well, you're very good at it. Pity I made that promise."

"Yes, it's a pity. So here. Let me lay my fingers where yours should be." With that, she hitched up her skirt, slid her fingers into her panties and along her wet cleft. "Taste a virgin, Aiden." She slipped her glistening fingers into his mouth and the taste of sweet, dripping juices called his cock once more to attention.

"You're so fuckin' hot, Theresa. No wonder Domingo and Marco don't want to let you out of their sight." All he wanted to do was pull her to him and devour every inch of her body. Suck her and fuck her all night long.

"Theresa!" Rafael's impatient voice sliced through the air.

Readjusting themselves, they returned indoors to find the other four ready to leave.

"Thank you, Aiden. I must apologize for Marco, but brothers can be very protective." Carla reached on tiptoe and kissed Aiden's cheeks.

"That's okay. No harm done." He breathed in the exotic scent of Carla's perfume and gave her trim waist a slight squeeze. Offering his hand, he said goodnight to Felipe and Raúl whose excitement to leave demonstrated the *Viagra* still worked. With instrument cases in hand, the two musicians said hurried farewells and departed before the others.

"Have you seen much of Seville?" Rafael collected his dance bag.

"A little. Mainly the tourist sites. Tomorrow I wanted to do something different, though."

"Sevilla Flamenco is closed on Sundays. Perhaps you would like to join Carla and me, and we can show you what we do on Sundays to relax?"

Surprised, but delighted by the invitation, Aiden said, "Sounds like fun. Why not? I'd love to join you. *Gracias.*" He extended his hand which Rafael grasped in a slightly more enthusiastic handshake than before. As an afterthought, Rafael glanced at Theresa then back to Aiden, "Theresa won't be joining us, though."

"That's a shame, but we understand. Don't we, Theresa?" Aiden beamed one of his champion smiles at the waitress who reluctantly nodded, producing one of her famous sullen pouts.

"Yes. I understand," she conceded, obviously miffed at not being included.

"We'll collect you at nine-thirty in the morning. Bring your bathing costume. *Duerma bien.*" A cool smile wavered on Rafael's lips as he said goodnight.

"Sleep well, Aiden." In contrast, Carla's smile pulsed with warmth. Still playing chaperone, she hooked her arm through Theresa's, ensuring her young cousin wouldn't loiter.

Aiden dashed in front of them and opened the door. "*Duerma bien,* everyone," he said, pleased with the evening. Aside from Theresa's great head job, the promise of spending tomorrow with local celebrities added a sweet note to the night.

Aiden closed the door, stripped off his clothes and took the least number of steps he could to drop into bed. It was a balmy night, so he left the balcony doors open, preferring the sultry temperatures over the chill of the air conditioning. These first few days in Seville had proven an apt antidote to the chaos he'd left behind in Australia. Maybe things would settle down there, and he could return soon? It wasn't a decision he'd need to make yet, though. His open ticket and substantial savings allowed him to ponder his future without restriction for a while longer.

His thoughts swirled to tonight's events. What a passionate, fiery lot the crew from Sevilla Flamenco were?

Fortunate for everyone that Marco decided to back down. Aiden never liked trouble, but he certainly never shied away from it. *They all need to take a chill pill, instead of that bloody Viagra,* he thought, smiling to himself. Granted, he could appreciate the advantages of the little blue all-nighter. Not having had a serious relationship for some months, he'd been indulging in more than a few casual nights of crazy sex and lusty women. Sowing his wild oats was what they called it. And now being in Spain, he intended to scatter himself around like a thistle on a breezy day. But as much as the thought of tasting and testing untamed Spanish women appealed, he knew the casual sex scene couldn't fill the emptiness lurking within. All his mates were engaged and settling down. And he was fast becoming the odd man out. He wanted to find the right partner, settle down and get married, but he just couldn't find the woman who'd stick.

As sleep crept in to interrupt his self-enquiry, his eyelids closed. The memory of Theresa's outstanding head job caused a stirring in his loins, and his face creased into a contented smile. But instead of picturing Theresa's voluptuous body bucking beneath him, it was Carla and her cool, polished manner who accompanied him to peaceful dreams.

CHAPTER THREE

THE RISING HEAT OF the Andalusian's summer's day reminded Aiden of the Gold Coast. Back home the heat was more humid than dry, but today's bright sunshine, mounting energy, and promise of adventure felt similar. He loved summer. Nothing suited him more than the surf, sand, and the rays, toasting his WASP — White Anglo-Saxon Protestant — skin to a bronzed, nut brown. Spain's sunny clime was one of the reasons he chose to hide out here rather than another faraway place. Having risen early this morning, he jogged a quick five kilometres through the barrio before shaving, showering, and breakfasting.

Ever punctual, he waited outside the hotel for Rafael and Carla before the appointed time, hoping punctuality was a trait they too possessed. It was. After brief "Hellos," they set off in silence. The Santa Cruz barrio was a rabbit-warren of laneways and hidden courtyards, most of which Aiden had spent time exploring since his arrival. Now with Rafael in the lead, they navigated the narrow passageways and endless opportunities to get lost, eventually coming to a stop in front of a nondescript building.

"We're here." Rafael nodded at the doorway.

Glancing left and right Aiden noticed there wasn't anybody around, which was odd because the barrio usually teemed with people. How they'd managed to arrive in an empty laneway divorced from the crowds was unfathomable. Aiden tried to get his bearings but failed. If Rafael and Carla left him here alone, he'd merely wander around the pedestrian circuitry until he came upon someone who could point him in the direction of his hotel.

Note to self — swat up on orienteering skills.

In front of him stood vast, henna-washed stone exterior walls and massive carved wooden double doors, pinned with giant iron nails. No sign identified this as a special building, so unless you knew differently, it could have been just a private residence. Like a local Aladdin, Rafael pushed on one of the doors which opened effortlessly under his touch.

"This is how we relax," he said in a grand manner, allowing Carla and Aiden to enter the dark, cool space inside.

"These are the Arab baths and hammam spa," Carla explained. "Here we relax the mind, body, and soul."

It was like entering the cool, dark womb of the Mother Earth. All of Aiden's senses ground to a standstill as the outside world disappeared behind the soundless closing doors. Gone were the brightness, chaos, and frivolity of a busy Sunday morning. Instead, a shadowy silence of peace engulfed them.

"We have an hour and a half booking so let's begin." Rafael nodded at the receptionist who obviously knew his VIP status and allowed them entry.

As they padded down the lantern-lit corridor, serenity rolled over them like an endless ocean wave, drowning them without resistance. Subtle ambient background music and distant falling water were the only sounds Aiden heard, intensifying the sense of escaping normality and venturing into the unknown.

Carla tugged at Aiden's sleeve and whispered, "This is a restored sixteenth-century palace. It has three thermal pools of different temperatures, massage and steam rooms." Aiden nodded thanks for her commentary and returned to scanning the architectural features unfolding before him. Overhead, dark latticework hung suspended from distant ceilings, while the corridor walls, coloured in the same henna hue as the exterior walls, funnelled them further into the palace's interior. Instead of being illuminated by sunlight, the walls were warmed by the soft glow of candlelight and the aromatic smell of incense and fragrant oils wafted on the cool air. Scattered on the floor, Moroccan-style lamps lit their way to the well-equipped changing rooms.

"See you back here shortly," Rafael said to Carla before she disappeared into the ladies changing rooms. He then turned to Aiden. "Follow me."

Aiden followed him into extravagant changing rooms complete with lockers, private changing booths and enough top-end men's products to keep a stable of male models happy for a year. Within minutes they'd changed, stuffed their feet into spa slippers and slung thick towelling bath sheets over their shoulders and waited in the corridor for Carla to join them.

"This is amazing." Aiden spoke in a hushed voice, respecting the aesthetics of the baths.

"*Si,*" Rafael replied, a cheerful smile lifting his face.

It was the first unaffected smile Rafael had given him, and Aiden suspected his host enjoyed the privacy and anonymity the baths afforded him. Some of Rafael's severe exterior softened in here, much like the palace itself — hard and impenetrable from the outside, yet gentle and quiet on the inside.

"Where to first?" With her dark, glossy locks coiled on top her head and her towel thrown casually over one shoulder, Carla appeared beside them, seemingly oblivious to her beauty. Even the thick oversized fluffy robe, which concealed her dancer's body, couldn't hide the enticing line of her neck or poise of her posture.

"We go to the thermal baths." All business once again, Rafael led the way. Leaving the cocoon of the corridor, they stepped into a cavernous chamber with ancient pale brick walls forming a beehive effect around and above them. A deep luxuriant pool engulfed most of the floor space, its underwater lights adding a soft, ethereal glow. Flanked by hewn sandstone walls and ledges on which perched more candle-lit lamps, the entire space hummed with the promise of peace and pleasure. Not quite the adventure Aiden had expected, but one he nevertheless committed to enjoy.

"This is the first bath. It is body temperature warm. The next bath is very hot, and the last bath is freezing cold with ice dripping into it. Very good for the tone of the skin." Rafael rattled off the details like a tour guide, discarded his towel and slippers, and slithered into the pool.

"Sounds good to me." Aiden did likewise and joined Rafael in the warm waters. By the time he sunk onto the sitting ledge, Carla was folding her towel in a neat bundle before joining them. With Rafael's eyes already closed, Aiden stole a lingering glance poolside at the beautiful flamenco dancer. Barely covering her copper-coloured skin, the tiny pieces of black fabric of her bikini proved fortuitous for Aiden. There was nothing of her, not an ounce of fat. Like a creation of God, she was exquisite. With her sculptured muscles, perfectly proportioned limbs, delicate throat, and neck, gentle fingers with manicured nails dipped in red nail polish and breasts plump like ripe fruit, Carla Armando was flawless — and with her back to the pool, Aiden was granted an uninterrupted view of the tightest, most enticing arse he'd ever seen. Although just covered by her bikini, its shape and roundness beckoned to him as did the slight curve of her cleft between her legs when she bent forwards. With a deep sigh, Aiden closed his eyes. It was the only way he knew to stop his cock from misbehaving, but it was too late. Carla's image had been seared into his mind's eye and was dancing provocatively for him.

It was most unlike Rafael to invite a stranger into their private Sunday sanctum. That had been the first thing Carla had said when they'd left Aiden's hotel last night. Not that she minded. She thought Aiden was a nice young man, but she couldn't understand why Rafael had made the invitation. Neither could he. Doing strange things was becoming his new *modus operandi*, with the accompanying confusion a close second. Rafael expelled the thoughts from his mind, inhaled, controlled his exhale and relaxed. Normally full of fire and frustration, he surrendered to the calming effect of the tranquil water. He loved how it caressed his skin, stripping away his stress, seducing him to believe everything would work out. How he wished the hammam still had bath boys who would help you bathe and . . . Perhaps he'd invited Aiden as a buffer? Between Carla and him? But threesomes seldom work. Someone is inevitably left out. Maybe Rafael longed for it to be him?

~ ♥ ~

THE NEXT HOUR SLINKED past in slow motion. With no other people invading their time in the baths, Aiden settled into a comfortable silence with his two new friends. From the comforting warmth of the first bath to the scalding heat of the second and the invigorating freeze of the third, the three amigos finally retreated to the steam room. With fresh towels laid beneath them, they lounged like rock lizards in the sweltering heat, unwilling to move. Fresh blistering steam pumped into the room mingling with the sweat dripping from their bodies. The heat was nearly unbearable but intoxicating. It challenged them to test their physical limitations before succumbing to the inevitable and retreat.

"This morning has been terrific. Thanks, Rafael." Aiden lounged on a bench with thick, hot mist swirling around him.

"I thought you'd enjoy it. Not many tourists know how to find this place, so it is something now you know. *Si?*"

"*Si.*" Aiden felt the most relaxed and rejuvenated than he had in a long time.

"So, what is it you do for work, Aiden?" Rafael shifted position to recline against the wall.

"I'm a corporate lawyer."

"Are you a good lawyer?" Carla asked with more than casual interest in her voice.

"I guess I'm too good a lawyer."

"What do you mean?" Rafael dragged his legs around and stared at his guest.

"To cut a long story short, I found discrepancies with some transferable shares and investor ownership on a deal I was working on. The client tried to buy me off, but I wasn't having a bar of it. So, I exposed their dirty, little plan. Now they're awaiting trial, and I'm taking an extended holiday until things cool down a little. These guys have some influential and rather nasty associates. So, I thought sunny Spain would be the best place for me to hang out a while."

"Oh, Aiden, that's awful," Carla said. Even through the steam, Aiden could see her big, brown eyes blinking in sympathy.

"Yeah, but there's nothing I can do at the moment. Just lay low. Anyway, I haven't had a holiday in years, so I figure I'll make the most of it." Switching the subject, he asked, "When do you two dance again at the club?"

"The club is closed now for a few weeks for renovations," Carla said. "So, we're going to Granada to dance . . ." She waited a beat, then shot a sharp look at Rafael. "And to confront Rafael's wife so he can get a divorce and marry me." The triumphant determination in her voice shattered the previous easiness of their conversation. Aiden could almost feel Rafael's skin prickle at Carla's remark. Telling Aiden their personal business wasn't something he thought Rafael took too kindly to even though Aiden had told them about his situation.

"Carla," Rafael hissed with unconcealed disdain.

"What?" she snapped back. "Aiden is a lawyer. He understands legal things. Maybe he can help us sort this out with Leta."

"Aiden is our guest. He's not here to listen to you whine about my wife, divorce, and marriage."

The emotion rushed from her throat. "I don't care. And I don't understand, Rafe. Why won't she divorce you? Why? You never talk about it. Why?" Her last plea broke into soft sobs, proving to Aiden this was a subject they'd fought over many times before.

"Enough, Carla." Rafael's voice rose in impatience.

Aiden strained to see through an untimely burst of steam and realized Rafael was making to leave, probably with her in tow. "It's all right, mate. Every couple has their ups and downs. I won't say anything. Whatever you tell me is confidential."

"Thank you, Aiden, but Carla shouldn't have said anything or asked for your help." Although his voice still reverberated with barely controlled anger, Rafael made no further movement to leave.

"I'm sorry, Rafe." Carla sounded like a little girl, pleading with her father to buy a long-sought-after toy. "It's just that I've been waiting a long time. I want to get married and have a baby, and I thought maybe Aiden could help us, rather than using local lawyers." The mist in the steam room began to dissipate, giving Aiden a better view of the couple sitting on the opposite bench. Wooden-faced, Rafael sat bolt upright showing his partner no sympathy. Just like the first time he'd seen him throw her to the floor in the tango, Aiden wanted to give Rafael a clip around the ear — to lighten up a little and see her point of view. But again, this was no time to interfere. Still, his heart ached for Carla. She looked so small and broken next to her partner, not the determined, feisty dancer she was only moments before.

Just as suddenly the mood changed again. Rafael softened with lightning speed and turned to Carla, caressing her cheek. "*Mi pequeña luciérnaga,*" he cooed in a conciliatory tone. "We'll sort it out with Leta when we go to Granada, I promise." When she lifted her face, he glanced a mollifying kiss across her lips.

Like a flash, cynical fire danced in Carla's eyes. "You liar!" she shrieked. "I don't believe you."

"How dare you!" Rafael jumped to his feet, towering above her in righteous indignation.

"You've promised me before and see, I am still unmarried." She flashed her naked wedding finger at him as spiteful evidence.

"But, *mi pequeña luciérnaga . . .*" In another peace-making attempt, Rafael pouted and opened his hands in submission.

She slapped them away. "Don't you, my little firefly, me. You better get this divorce worked out with Leta or it's off. It's all off — our partnership both professionally and personally." Her threats lashed Rafael, stoking his anger and making him visibly wince.

"Do not threaten me, Carla Armando." The deliberate rhythm and rumbling growl in his voice unsettled Aiden. He'd heard men reach this tipping point before, and he prepared himself if Rafael went to hit her. "We will talk about this at home. Not here." Rafael glowered at her, collected his towel and with an insulted *harrumph*, snapped a turn and left the room, steaming.

The silence in his wake was even more oppressive than the sudden burst of fresh steam into the room. Aiden watched Carla disappear behind a cloud of mist, waiting for her to speak. Based on what he'd witnessed, he figured this passionate tug-of-war was a regular occurrence in their relationship. Still, he was pleased it hadn't escalated. No matter where he went lately, he found himself in the middle of disagreements. Maybe his Midas touch had joined Elvis, as his mother would say, and left the building. The door opened, and Aiden shuffled over, making room for the newcomer.

A calm, familiar voice spoke. "Aiden, if you're not doing anything, why don't you come to Granada with Carla and me, as our guest?"

Floored by Rafael's unexpected return and invitation, Aiden blinked and tried to collect his thoughts to reply.

"Oh, Rafe, that would be wonderful. Please, Aiden, please come." Carla's bright voice swam through the mist. "I'm sorry about before. Rafe and I need a break and going to Granada will be a wonderful way for you to see more of Spain, and we could do with the company of someone new, like you. And maybe you could give us some legal advice . . .?"

"Well, I don't know much about family law, especially in Spain, and it's very nice of you but . . ." Aiden didn't know whether to accept the invitation or run as fast as possible. This pair certainly ran hot and cold, but they were entertaining to be around. "I've already booked a place on the Costa Del Sol for a few days to do some surfing. I leave tomorrow. When did you plan on going to Granada?"

"Oh, we don't need to go for another week yet," Rafael said, still propped at the door.

"Are you sure? I mean I'm a bloke you've just met. For all you know I could be some serial killer . . ."

Carla crossed the room and perched next to him. "But you're not. You're a lawyer."

Aiden found her logic amusing and beamed a broad smile at her, his eyes racing over her elfin face. She squeezed his thigh, returning his smile with a dazzling one of her own.

"Well, there is one other thing." He paused and they waited. "Tomorrow I planned to pick up my new Ferrari . . ."

The conversation stalled for a beat before Rafael said, "Very nice. May I ask as to which one?

"A red Alonso Barcelona 27 convertible." Although his new car was the top of the range, he wasn't one to flaunt his financial ability to make such a purchase.

A slow, appreciative whistle escaped Rafael's lips. "Very nice indeed. But why are you buying a Ferrari here?"

"Because if I buy it here and stay for six months, I can ship it back to Australia and not pay any duty on it. If I bought it in Australia, it'd cost me twice as much. So, since I'm here on an extended holiday for a while, I thought I may as well take advantage of it."

"I see," Rafael said in a thoughtful tone.

Even though he couldn't make out Rafael's expression clearly, Aiden thought he heard a hint of respect in the Spaniard's voice. Rafael moved from the door and flicked out his towel to sit beside Aiden. "So, I'd planned to collect the Ferrari in the morning and drive down to the Costa Del Sol. I'd be happy for you both to join me for some sun, surf, and sand, but it's a convertible two-seater?"

"That's okay. Carla can go with you, and I'll ride my Ducati down. It needs a good run." Rafael sounded enthusiastic at the thought of suiting up and hitting the road.

With his need-for-speed peaked, Aiden turned to Rafael, keen to know more. "Ducati, eh? What model?"

"The latest black Diavel. Carbon version of course." A touch of smugness crept into Rafael's reply for which Aiden couldn't blame him.

It was Aiden's turn to whistle in appreciation of Rafael's choice of machine. "Another Italian beauty." He nodded in admiration. "Seems we both have the same good taste in Italian engineering." The two men shared an approving smile and chuckled at how clever they were.

Carla leaned forwards trying to break up their newly established boy's club. "If you two have finished slapping each other on the back . . ." She rolled her eyes at both of them and gazed at Rafe. "Why don't we go to the coast with Aiden and then onto Granada from there? It'd be a good break for us."

"*Sí,*" Rafael said. "Sounds like fun." To Aiden, he said, "And since we both appreciate precision craftsmanship, we are now friends. You can call me Rafe."

Being given permission to call him Rafe meant Aiden had chiselled a sizeable chink through the dancer's armour. Nothing like a bit of Top Gun talk to bond a couple of fellas together. Ensuring he didn't miss the moment, Aiden added, "And you must call me Ace."

"Very good." Rafael offered his hand and with a solid shake, they sealed the deal as Carla clapped in approval.

CHAPTER FOUR

____

LISTENING TO THE SWEET voice of the satnav emanating from the dashboard, Aiden steered his prancing new horse around the corner. Just as Carla promised, up ahead stood her twin brothers, Gerado and José guarding the one parking spot left on the street. Like most other cities in this part of Europe, street parking was at a premium and fights for ownership could often turn violent. Having the two burly men standing sentinel on the street ensured Aiden could park his gleaming new toy safely. The Ferrari burbled up to the men whose agape mouths dripped with envy.

"*Buenos días,*" they called out, ogling the car. "You must be Aiden."

"*Sí. Buenos días.* And you're Gerado and José?"

The twins looked to be in their late twenties. Both were strong, handsome fellas and their strikingly similar facial features and body shapes distinguished them as identical twins. The one in the black T-shirt introduced himself as Gerado and José wore blue. At least they wore different coloured T-shirts which gave Aiden some chance to remember who was who. He chuckled to himself when he noticed they both wore Ferrari caps. *Perhaps the closest they'll ever come to owning any authentic Ferrari product,* he thought. Aiden appreciated his good fortune and reversed the car in and leapt out rattling the keys.

"I'll take you upstairs to Carla, and José will protect the Ferrari." Gerado's voice resonated with an odd mix of excitement at being the designated leader and of disappointment at having to leave the Ferrari under his brother's care.

Aiden threw the keys to José. "Here you go, José. Look after her for me."

A massive grin lit José's face as he stared at the sacred keys. "*Sí.* I will look after her." He all but clicked his heels and saluted before returning to stand sentinel over his prize. Aiden followed Gerado into the building and with one final glance over his shoulder saw José keeping the street urchins and young male admirers at arm's length away from the gleaming, red machine. *Good man*, he thought.

During the trek three floors up, Aiden noted the building was old but clean, and built in the Baroque style. The familiar crimson-coloured walls flanked the narrow stone staircase from which narrow corridors led to a series of apartments on each floor. Being mid-morning Monday, most of the hustle and bustle of families getting themselves off to work and school had died down, but the inviting smell of coffee still lingered, reminding Aiden he hadn't had his fix yet.

Gerado pushed open the door to 305. "Carla, Aiden is here to collect you."

With a quick scan of the room, Aiden realized how difficult it would've been for a family of father, mother and five children to grow up here. The gloomy under-sized living room with its tired drapes was barely big enough to fit the shabby couch and two wing chairs. Tucked off this room, an even smaller kitchen peeped around the corner, its overhead cabinets and counter a faded forest green. To Aiden's left, a corridor led down to what he expected were a few bedrooms and a bathroom. Although Carla and her eldest brother Estéban no longer lived here, the flat was still cramped with the twins, Raúl, and their father.

Carla pranced up the corridor, waving a purple velvet pouch. "*Buenos días*, Aiden. Thank you for coming. Rafe is getting a quick service on the Ducati, and I simply had to get these before we go to Granada." She reached up and kissed him on both cheeks.

"*Buenos días*, Aiden," another familiar voice called from the kitchen. It was Raúl. "I'm making coffee. Would you like one?"

Before Aiden had time to answer, Carla cut in. "We can't stay, Raúl. What if Papa comes home?"

Raúl ambled from the kitchen, a mug of steaming coffee in his hands. "But he's still at the bakery. He won't be home until lunchtime." With a silk gown thrown loosely around his lithe body and standing next to his older sister, he looked even more feminine than Aiden remembered. His deer brown eyes, pouting lips, and luscious eyelashes matched Carla's exactly.

"Okay. But make it quick." Carla grabbed Aiden's hand and led him around the counter. Gerado retreated downstairs to help José protect the Ferrari, leaving the three of them squeezed nearly elbow-to-elbow in the scullery.

"So why are you so frightened of your father coming home?" Aiden blew across his mug and sipped.

"Because Papa disowned me when I moved in with Rafe. He said I was nothing but a cheap whore living with a man out of wedlock." The anger and hurt in Carla's eyes made everyone stiffen, and the tiny kitchen contracted around them. "I'm not allowed back in my family home until I marry."

"Papa is an angry, unreasonable man." Resentment rose in Raúl's voice. "I was only two when Mama died, and Carla raised me." He shot his sister an affectionate smile. "She raised all of us really. Poor Carla was only twelve years old herself, and if it wasn't for her dancing, I don't know how she would've survived." He blew his sister a kiss, bringing a tear to her eyes. "As we grew up, Estéban was more like Papa — mean and pig-headed. He joined Papa in the family business at the bakery . . . Manolo's Bakery, Manolo, that's Papa's name. I think Papa got jealous when Carla fell in love with Rafael and wanted a life of her own. When she turned thirty, she told Papa she was moving in with Rafael, and he hasn't spoken to her since."

"That was nearly two years ago now," Carla said with bitter disappointment. Crestfallen, both sister and brother, stared into their coffee mugs in silence.

"So that's why you want Rafael to marry you so badly? So, your father will accept you back into the family," Aiden said, piecing together yesterday's heated exchange in the steam room.

"Yes. If I get married, all will be forgotten, and I can visit home. Papa is getting older, and I worry about him. But he is so set in his ways. He is so stubborn and so Catholic."

Aiden cocked his head in a silent question to Raúl.

"Oh no. Papa doesn't know about my being gay. Carla, Gerado, and José do, but not Papa or Estéban. Papa would throw me out too, and Estéban would give me a beating. I don't wear gorgeous silk gowns like this when they're home." Lightening the moment, Raúl performed a petite pirouette like a runway model, fluttering his eyelashes. Carla and Aiden couldn't help but laugh.

Aiden placed his mug on the bench. "Well, we better go then."

"Bye, Raúl. I'll see you in Granada." Carla hugged her brother tightly and kissed him.

"Bye, Carla. Have fun on your holiday with this very handsome Australian." Raúl hugged and kissed his sister while making doe-eyes at Aiden.

"Yeah right. See you in Granada, Raúl." Aiden shook his head in amusement at Raúl's unspoken inference.

The three of them headed to the front door when it suddenly opened. Expecting to see either Gerado or José, they halted in front of an older, stouter version of the twins. As if chiselled from stone and with a seething look of rage masking his once-handsome face, the man blocked their exit.

"Papa." Carla took a small step back into Aiden's chest.

From the corner of his eye, Aiden noticed Raúl tie his gown tightly and replace his former softness and frivolity with a stern expression and taller posture. Aiden realized Manolo Armando wrought demonstrable fear in his children, despite their adult status.

"Who is this?" Ignoring his daughter's greeting, Manolo demanded to know who the blond-haired stranger was standing uninvited in his house.

Aiden thrust his hand out. "I'm Aiden Bishop, sir. I'm here on holidays from Australia, and I was just helping Carla get some things. We were just going." Aiden's trademark champion smile lit up his face to match his likable, yet respectful manner. This approach had worked many times before in tight spots so he hoped it would work now.

With a disinterested snort at Aiden, Manolo resumed his attack on Carla. "What things? You took everything when you left here to go live with that faggot of a boyfriend, Rafael. How dare you come back here."

"How dare you say that about Rafael. Rafael and I will be getting married once he gets his divorce. It's just a matter of time." Carla's scorching rebuttal stoked the fire.

"Don't be stupid, girl. He doesn't love you. He's using you."

"Papa, leave her alone. She's a grown woman and can live her own life." Even though his voice trembled with fear, Raúl took his sister's side.

"You dare speak to me. Go put some clothes on. You look like a woman," Manolo roared at his quivering son, who backed up but didn't flee.

Carla stepped toward her father. "No, Papa. You leave Raúl alone. This is our fight. Rafael loves me, and I love him. Once we see Leta in Granada, it will get sorted, and we will marry."

Exasperated, Manolo threw his hands in the air, glaring at his youngest and eldest children. With another snort, he scowled at Aiden. "Are you going to Granada too?"

"Yes, sir."

"Maybe you can talk some sense into her. I can't."

"Papa." Carla stamped her foot and scowled even harder at her father.

"What is that? What are you taking from my house without my permission?" He pointed to the pouch Carla grasped in her hand.

"These are Mama's runes. She left them to me and now it's time for me to have them." Carla clutched the bag to her chest.

At the memory of his dead wife, Manolo's bravado visibly crumpled. His voice softened as a precious memory touched his heart. "I know she left them to you, but why now? And why sneak them away."

"Oh, Papa. I'm sorry. But it's a special time in Granada. You know that. It's time for me to connect with Mama's

Romani heritage." A brief cease-fire gave pause to the bitter feuding. In that instant, the past years of anger, resentment, and hurt seemed to dissipate, leaving the Armandos' silent, eyes downcast. Feeling like an interloper, Aiden also looked at the floor, wishing he was driving his Ferrari as fast and as far away as he could.

Manolo lifted his head and spoke in a calm, controlled manner. "Very well, Carla, you go to Granada to honour Isabella's heritage, and when you are done, we will talk again."

"Oh, thank you, Papa." Carla rushed forwards and crushed her father's neck in a tight hug.

He didn't respond, but neither did he push her away. When she stepped back, he looked directly at Aiden. "I don't know who you are, Aiden Bishop from Australia, but I think you are a good man. One to be trusted. I think my Isabella would've liked you. She had the gift, you know?" Manolo nodded thoughtfully at Aiden who had no idea what the older man alluded to, but he nodded as if he did. "Look after my daughter, keep her safe and make sure you tell her the truth. You understand?"

Aiden still had no idea what Manolo was talking about, but he certainly wasn't going to haggle over details. "Yes, sir," he said full of confidence. "Your daughter is safe with me." Aiden knew that part was true.

"Then go." Manolo stood back to allow them past. "And you . . ." — he cast an askance look at his youngest son — "go change."

"Yes, Papa." Raúl flapped a quick goodbye wave before dashing down the corridor to his bedroom.

CHAPTER FIVE

SCREAMING DOWN THE A-375, the Ferrari whined making conversation impossible. Even though she'd strangled her hair into a ponytail, Carla received repeated lashings from it across her face as the wind tossed it in every direction. With her elbow propped on the window ledge, she fought her long locks into submission, while Aiden and Rafael played cat and mouse on the motorway. She loved men, but when they turned into silly, little boys trying to outdo each other, she could scream. At least she was in a jaw-dropping red Ferrari rather than being a pillion passenger on the back of Rafael's Ducati. Not that she minded the bike. It'd been their relationship saviour on many occasions when their arguments became overheated. Either they'd both jump on the Ducati together to blow off steam or Rafael would take a solo ride, returning in a calmer, more agreeable mood. But what Aiden and Rafael were doing now was just plain foolish. Overtaking, accelerating, racing each other side by side on the motorway, giving each other the thumbs up. She gritted her teeth and rubbed the nervous perspiration from her palms on her cotton slacks. When they lost all common sense, boys and their toys infuriated her. Rafael could handle the Ducati, she knew that, and by the way Aiden drove, it seemed he also was more than competent behind the wheel of the Ferrari. So, there was nothing she could do, but sit tight and pray they'd arrive safely.

With Aiden's full attention on the road, Carla contemplated the current turn of events. Unlike her Catholic, God-fearing father, she believed God was a forgiving god and that everything happened for a reason, normally a good one. The altercation with her father this morning had at least cleared the air somewhat. That Papa even spoke to her, let alone asked Aiden to look after her was more than strangely optimistic. Aiden's easy-going nature seemed to captivate everyone, including her. She studied the handsome Australian behind the wheel of the Ferrari, thinking his strong, square jaw was more ruggedly masculine than Rafael's artistic, heart-shaped face. Where Rafael had a trimmed, light beard accenting his fine jawline, Aiden's face bristled with an attractive, unkempt stubble of a few days' growth. *A little rough around the edges*, she thought, *but most appealing.* And his fresh open-faced smile lit up the entire room as could Rafael's, but he seldom smiled much anymore.

Aiden's unexpected presence in their life must have meaning, a positive one. She just wasn't sure what it was yet. Maybe it was to help Rafael convince Leta to give him the divorce. Yet there remained a niggling feeling she couldn't shake. Why had she been so insistent he join them? No matter how much she mulled these questions over during the drive, she couldn't catch the tail of the tiger that stalked her mind.

"OH MY GOD, AIDEN. This is beautiful." Carla stood on the driveway, scanning the romantic Mediterranean villa they were holidaying in for the next week. The villa's walls shone brilliant white in the midday sun and created the perfect backdrop for the pots of sprawling red geraniums, positioned strategically along the orange brick pavers at the front of the house. Taking pride of place on a pillar near the front door hung a large timber sign etched in charcoal letters, Casa de los ángeles. When she read the sign, she smiled. A house of angels will be the perfect residence in which to relax and find peace over the next few days. "How on earth did you possibly find this place and book it at this time of year? It must be costing you a fortune."

"A mate of mine was doing a home swap with the people who own this place, but he was called away unexpectedly on business. The owners are in his home in Australia, he's in America, and we're here." A satisfied grin creased Aiden's face, and his eyes danced, mirroring the same azure sparkle of the pool peeping around the courtyard's corner. The three of them grinned like monkeys, well pleased with their new digs. They heaved their bags onto their shoulders and headed for the front door. Above them, the porte-cochère dripped with a twining bougainvillea, its fuchsia-coloured blooms a vibrant invitation in contrast to the heavy, wooden front door.

"Well, let's see if it's as good on the inside as it is on the outside." Aiden turned the key in the lock and pushed open the door. On stepping inside, the three of them gasped and gently lowered their bags onto the cool, terracotta floor. Also painted in brilliant white, the villa's interior walls and ceilings stretched to an apex high above the timber diagonal beams. The foyer vestibule opened before them, inviting them into a massive living room, kitchen and lounge area, complete with quality furniture and furnishings in bright beach colours. Vivid greens, blues, and yellows injected cheerfulness into the sophisticated villa's vast interior, while Moroccan style white pendant lights dangled artistically from the ceilings.

"Not bad. Not bad at all," Aiden said, nodding his head.

"This is indeed beautiful. You may be running away from bad people in Australia, Ace, but Spain seems to bring you good luck." Rafael clapped Aiden's shoulder.

"It's gorgeous." Carla removed her sandals and ran her toes along the decorative Moroccan ceramic floor tile border. From the other side of the room, dazzling sunlight flooded through a series of oversized glass sliding doors beckoning them to explore the enormous outside courtyard complete with a full-size pool, more potted geraniums and a privacy fence of olive trees. She padded across to the sliding doors, and when she slid them open, the entire villa bared itself like an oyster offering up its pearl. "I'll stock the fridge with our provisions and you boys sort out the rooms. Then it's pool time."

CARLA BREATHED A DEEP sigh of contentment. Within thirty minutes they lay prone on luxurious blue and white striped bath sheets atop elegant pool lounges, their faces to the sun like Aztec sun worshippers. Usually, she tanned topless, but with Aiden so close, she decided for more modesty. Beside them, glasses of crisp white wine struggled to remain cold, as spoonfuls of ice melted under the early summer sun. The pungent smell of blooming geraniums hung in the air mingled with the scent of coconut oil sunscreen. Like Marbella celebrities, their attractive faces wore designer sunglasses and their fit, young bodies were nearly naked to take full advantage of the bronzing sun.

"Pity it didn't come with a butler," Aiden said.

"I'm sure we can get our own food and drinks." Carla rolled her bikini top down further to minimize possible tan marks.

"Maybe we can find a young butler to hire for a week?" Rafael tilted his glasses upwards, giving the others a cheeky smirk.

"Or a young maid? Now that's more my style," Aiden said, thinking about Theresa.

Swinging her legs over the lounge and clutching her top, Carla fixed them with a stare. "Now listen here you two. We came away to relax and not constantly do boy-talk. So, if you don't mind . . ."

Not unlike a schoolteacher, Carla chastised them, but before she had time to finish her terms and conditions, Rafael said, "For God's sake Carla. Be quiet, take your top off and lie down. Ace won't mind you sunbathing topless. I'm sure he's seen plenty of breasts in his time on the beaches in Australia."

Carla opened her mouth to voice her objection at being told what to do but again was cut off.

"Yeah, don't worry about me, Carla. Take your top off. I've seen your dance costumes. You can't have strap marks when you're wearing them. I promise I won't ogle." Aiden chuckled at his own humour, and Rafael joined him in the joke.

Deliberately and without a word, Carla tossed off her bikini top and lay down, voicing an audible *harrumph*. The raucous chirping from the olive trees teased her into thinking that the birds on the branches were also male, and the whole joke was on her. She swore under her breath, willing the birds to be quiet. A gentle afternoon breeze freshened the air, and the leaves rustled as if rubbing their hands together with the expectation of a chilly night. Giving up her feigned indignation, a sanguine smile crept to her lips, and she relaxed deeper into her lounge. With the ice now melted in their glasses, the three of them drifted into heat oblivion.

~ ♥ ~

CARLA WIPED THE SINK while Aiden folded the tea towel and hung it through the handle of the oven door.

"That was delicious," he said. "I didn't know a pan of rice could taste so good. Thanks."

She accepted his compliment with a demure smile and continued in her kitchen duties. From the corner of her eye, she watched him store the crockery. Barefoot and dressed in a pair of scruffy blue jeans with a tight white T-shirt, Aiden possessed a magnificent body. One he obviously worked hard to maintain. She scolded herself for taking furtive glances, but she'd not seen a man of his stature or strength before. When he hovered beside her, he smelled of soap and a fresh, crisp, masculine scent, and she thought he probably tasted far more delicious than the paella she'd just served.

"I'm pleased you enjoyed it." She flicked her hair behind her shoulder and gazed up at him with a kittenish smile. She was flirting, though she didn't mean to. But he was so different to Rafe, kind and helpful. Hurriedly, she turned away, picked up her wine glass and swallowed a mouthful. What had gotten into her? She must pull herself together.

Aiden wandered into the living room. "So, Rafe, don't you blokes here help in the kitchen. Back home if the lady cooks we help clean up?" He reclined into one of the comfortable couches, his long legs stretched in front of him and gave Rafael a quizzical look.

Carla leaned on the kitchen bench watching the two men, wondering how Rafael would react to Aiden's remark. Knowing Rafe, he wouldn't be pleased.

Rafael dragged his attention away from whatever he was reading. "The kitchen is a woman's place, not for men. Sometimes I cook, but mostly it's Carla. She's a better cook than me."

"No argument from me on that one. But I'm talking about helping to clean up. Surely you can get off that tight dancer's arse of yours and give her a hand." Though Aiden shot Rafael a cheerful, mocking smile, his insistence for an answer was obvious.

Reciprocating with an even bigger grin and a voice dripping with sarcasm, Rafael said, "But there's no need for me to do that. You're here and seem very skilled with a tea towel." Like young sparring lions, they eyed each other off, the tension prickling between them with neither willing for the confrontation to turn vicious. Carla remained in the kitchen, out of the line of fire.

Aiden's voice remained even and casual. "I don't know Rafe. There's something not quite right here. One minute you're all hail-fellow-well-met and the next, you go into some dark place."

Carla had no idea what Aiden was talking about and by the look on Rafael's face he didn't either. Neither of them could understand Aiden's Australian slang at times. "I mean, how hard is it to help the woman you love?"

"It's not hard, but it's also none of your business." With the bluntness of a dull axe, Rafael smirked across at Aiden then returned to his reading.

"Well bugger me," Aiden said, with a resigned smirk. "Come on, Carla. Let's you and me go look at the stars."

"Enjoy." Rafael tipped his half-full glass to Aiden and returned unperturbed to his reading.

Aiden opened the sliding door for Carla to pass through, closing it soundlessly behind them. With glasses in hand, the two of them sauntered to the far edge of the pool courtyard and gazed into the dark distance towards the ocean.

"Is he always like that? A good bloke one minute, and a bit of a bastard the next?"

"Yes," Carla said. "He can be wonderfully loving and kind and then he turns into a selfish monster. I've learnt to live with it."

"But why? Why put up with it?"

"Because I love him," Carla replied in a matter-of-fact tone. Though she had asked herself the same question on many occasions. Maybe she'd just resigned herself to it.

Aiden stared at her, his blue eyes blasting through the clear night. "But there are hundreds of other men who'd kill to be with you, Carla. You're stunning. You're talented and kind and . . ."

She caught her breath and looked up at his abashed expression. *What is he doing?*

Aiden stepped back. "Sorry. Rafael was right. It's none of my business. I shouldn't be talking to you like this. Forgive me." Aiden took a hefty slurp of wine and focused skywards on the distant stars. After an awkward pause, he continued, "The stars look different here in the Northern Hemisphere, but just as beautiful."

Carla brushed up beside the tall, gentle giant beside her. "Everything here probably looks different to you," she said in a quiet, pacifying voice.

Aiden glanced down at her. "Yes, but beauty remains the same no matter where in the world I see it."

What was he doing to her? She'd never been complimented with such sincerity as she'd witnessed on Aiden's face. Aside from being the strong, rugged, outdoor type, the sort of man she'd never encountered before, he wasn't afraid of saying what he felt. Not that she expected this kind of attention. But there was a part of her that needed it. That soaked it up like a thirsty sponge. But she mustn't encourage his advances even though she longed to be treated the way Aiden had just done. Nevertheless, she was betrothed to Rafael and had suffered her father's wrath and rejection for him. She must nip this silly infatuation with Aiden before it grew into something they'd all regret.

KEEP LOOKING AT THE stars, you fool. Aiden had no idea what came over him. Sure, he found Carla extremely attractive, but being so personal with her like this when she was engaged to Rafael was inexcusable. Regardless of his opinion of their relationship, he had no right to interfere. Making matters worse, this intrusion was out of character for him. Normally he kept his nose out of his mates' business with their girlfriends. Though thinking about it, it wasn't Rafael's welfare he was concerned about. It was Carla's. Maybe it was the promise he'd made to Manolo to look after her? Perhaps that was making him overprotective of her? He'd promised her father to tell her the truth, but that didn't include offending or criticizing Rafael or their relationship. Whatever was going on in his head or his heart, he needed to be more careful and not compromise Carla in any way. *Or put her at risk.* It was this last thought that really unsettled him.

~ ♥ ~

BY THE TIME CARLA said goodnight to Aiden, washed the glasses and retired, Rafael had already gone to bed. On Aiden's insistence this afternoon, they'd claimed the master bedroom — a spacious, well-appointed bedroom with en suite, oozing with good taste and privacy. When she entered the bedroom, Carla paused and smiled in appreciation of Rafael, who was already sprawled on the king-size bed naked. Lithe, strong and deliciously demanding, he commanded their sex play with intensity. No matter how difficult he was, Rafael wove a spell over her. His brooding black eyes, expressive hands, and magnetic personality conspired to seduce her. Now as he reclined on the dozen or so pillows like a sultan, his presence called to her. She obeyed and walked to him in silence. With deliberate, sensuous actions, she peeled off her clothing, until she stood beside him, naked and moist.

"Carla," he purred. "You're magnificent." His hand reached over and slipped between her thighs, seeking her juice.

When he dipped one finger into her cleft, she faltered a little. Smiling his delight, he began to stroke her in a slow, even rhythm, opening her up for his pleasure. She moaned, her head lolling backwards. Her body needed satisfaction, needed penetration, needed a cock deep within, so she gave herself over to his insistent manipulations.

"Here, *mi pequeña luciérnaga*. Place your foot here." Rafael patted the bed and with her dancer flexibility, she lifted her foot onto the bed in one deft movement, exposing herself for him. The cool air nipped at her open folds and he continued his tedious torment, sliding his slick fingers from clit to anus. Backwards and forwards, relentlessly, he probed her but never penetrated her craving orifices. He just kept juicing her until she thought she'd collapse. His other hand joined in the torture and squeezed her breast, tweaking her nipple, punishing it. With his thumb rubbing her clit and his fingers refusing to satiate her, she flooded juices onto his hand.

"Please, Rafael. Please," she begged, pushing her yearning onto his hand, desperate for his fingers to relieve her.

"Not tonight, Carla," he replied in apology.

"But you never finish me with your hand or eat me, and I suck you all the time," she said, demented from the gnawing pain in her gaping maw.

"Very well. You don't have to suck me tonight," he crooned in a gentle voice.

At once, everything changed. He sprang up, and seizing her in a dancer's lift, flung her onto the bed, like an unwanted toy on the scrap heap. Her dark hair flew onto the pillows as she landed on her back, legs splayed. Closing her eyes, she held her breath and waited for the satisfaction she longed for. Instead, Rafael spun her over onto her belly, dragged her to her hands and knees and rammed his cock into her wet cleft. Carla groaned in pain and pleasure, but Rafael froze. This had become a ritual for some months now, the incessant teasing, the refusal to satisfy her with fingers or his mouth and the doggy-style fucking.

"Eat my cock with your cunt," he demanded, tugging on her hair.

Carla contracted her internal muscles until they pulsed. Only when she began this tempo did he continue. Rafael's hands found her soft breasts and tugged hard on them while he rammed his cock up into her. As he laid his weight on Carla's back, her strength and balance did the work for both of them, leaving him to rut her like a mad dog.

Although she disliked this sex play, her body's treachery couldn't be ignored in its demand for orgasm. With Rafael's cock engorged and hammering at her G-spot, she exploded in a frenzy of sensations while he pumped his essence deep within her. They both cried out in agonized gratification before collapsing onto the bed. After a few deep breaths, Carla wrestled Rafael off her and escaped to the bathroom. She didn't mean for the door to slam, but it closed with a louder sound than expected. Wincing, she stood rigid wondering if Rafael would charge in to admonish her. He didn't. Dropping heavily onto the toilet seat, she sat for a moment, catching her breath. She reefed off some paper, wiped herself and flushed it away. Standing at the mirror, she proceeded to remove her mascara and cleanse her face. Drained and tired was her self-assessment of her reflection. *No, there's one more word to add to that,* she thought — *stupid. Carla Armando, you are stupid.*

With a self-flagellating rub of moisturizer, she scowled at herself, shook her head in disgust and returned to the demon in her bed.

CHAPTER SIX

WHEN SHE HEARD SOMEONE knocking at their bedroom door, Carla groaned and reached for her phone. 7:00 A.M.

"Hey guys," Aiden called in a cheery voice. "It's a beautiful day about to happen, so up and at them."

She and Rafael weren't used to early starts, but with the delicious smell of coffee wafting into their bedroom from the kitchen, they crawled reluctantly out of bed. Carla threw on a red silk gown while Rafael slinked into a pair of shorts, grumbling. "I wonder if he's always this chirpy of a morning?"

Carla smirked. "We have many mornings to find out." Although still groggy, she found Aiden's happy voice a welcome change to the usual morning silence she and Rafael had fallen into.

Rafael slid onto a kitchen stool and hugged his mug of coffee. "Do you always get up at this ungodly hour."

"Yeah. I guess I've got used to it. What with work and surfing, my body wakes up early. This is the best part of the day." Aiden lifted his arms in the direction of the courtyard, where birds flitted about singing their morning song, and the plants seemed to grow taller towards the sun. The only thing missing, Carla thought, were fairies dancing around the garden holding hands.

She blinked from the sheer brilliance of Aiden's smile and the sunlight streaming into the villa. "Maybe so," she said, sipping her hot brew. "But we're dancers, we work at night. We usually sleep until mid-morning." She eyed Aiden as he leaned against the kitchen bench opposite them. Like a big, happy kid, his enthusiasm bubbled out of him, and she couldn't help but smile at his unfettered energy. She couldn't remember the last time she felt like that, but she knew she wanted to again.

Aiden slammed her with a massive smile. "Yes, but you're not dancing late nights now. You're on holiday. So, let's get started." He rubbed his hands together like a mischievous magician and stepped toward them. "The surf forecast is great with a south-westerly swell and easterly wind. I'm going to drive to El Palmar around the coast road, about two hours from here. Rent a board and jump some waves." He all but hopped from excitement, and Carla felt her heart miss a beat.

Rafael cocked his eyebrow and gave Aiden a sardonic smile. "Surfing?"

Aiden's wild blue gaze danced from one to the other. "Yeah, surfing. Come with me. You could take a beginner's class, Rafe, if you want to learn. I'm sure with your dancer's balance and body you'll be on your feet in no time."

Carla chuckled and elbowed Rafael in the ribs. "Come on. Let's give it a try. I'll take a class as well, and we'll see who gets up first?"

Obviously up for a challenge, Rafael smiled, and an amused glint sparkled in his eyes. "Very well. Surfing it is? When do we leave?"

"Now, if possible. It's going to take us two hours to get there, and I want to catch the best of the tide. I've made us a quick sandwich. You can eat it while you're getting dressed." He thrust an egg sandwich each at them.

Carla giggled. "Thank you." The entire scene reminded her of when she was at school in grade two and her young male classmate, Alejandro offered her his lunch in the hope of getting a kiss. Aiden's simple attempt at breakfast was a similar, sincere gesture. "Rafe and I will be ready in a few minutes."

Used to making quick costume changes, Carla and Rafael met Aiden on the driveway in no time, dressed and fed.

"Right. Let's hit the road." Aiden winked at Rafael whose face opened in a conspiratorial grin as he kicked over the Ducati.

"Listen, you two. Can we not do the cat and mouse this morning? Let's just drive safely down to El Palmar, please?" Carla hoped one of them would agree.

"Sure, Carla. Not a problem." Aiden opened the car door for his passenger. "Just an easy drive along the coast." With a chuckle, he glanced over at Rafael, who lashed his helmet tight. "You follow me," Aiden called to Rafael, over the burble of the Ferrari's engine.

A muffled reply emanated from the black leather-clad rider astride his machine. "Not likely." Like a horseman of the apocalypse desperate to be free, Rafael launched the Ducati on one wheel up the driveway.

Carla swore a litany of Spanish curses under her breath. "He can be such an idiot."

Dropping the clutch on the Ferrari, Aiden released the prancing horse with a cheeky wink at his passenger. "Can't we all."

Carla gritted her teeth, closed her eyes and hung on.

CARLA ENJOYED HER SURFING lesson, despite the mouthfuls of saltwater she gulped at the beginning. Due to her weight to strength ratio, she'd been able to at least stand and ride her board a few metres, before losing her balance. Now, she lounged beside Aiden on the sand admiring the broad set of his back and shoulders. With his steady gaze locked on Rafael as he struggled with his board, Aiden sat on the beach shading his eyes from the midday glare. "He looks a little nervous out there."

Carla followed Aiden's gaze. "I'm sure he'll be okay. He's not a lover of the sea so he's a bit awkward in the waves, but he's determined not to be outdone." She sat up next to him and studied Aiden's right shoulder. "What's that tattoo mean, Aiden?" She wanted to touch his moulded muscles but refrained. Platonic chit-chat with no physical contact was a safer option.

He glanced down to the image he had inked on his skin nearly seven years ago. I got this done as a twenty-first birthday present to myself. It reminds me of who I am and who's important to me."

"I don't understand." Intrigued, Carla studied it closer.

Aiden's gaze returned to the ocean and whether he was still watching Rafael or not, Carla didn't know. But she sensed his mood change to one more pensive.

"In the Chinese zodiac, I was born in the year of the snake," he explained.

"What does the year of the snake mean?"

"Well, snakes are supposed to be intuitive, hard-working and intelligent and at the same time we like to possess everything, and we're easily stressed."

"Well I can agree with some of that, but you certainly don't seem to be someone who gets easily stressed. That's more a quality Rafe possesses, not you."

"My ex-girlfriends would disagree with you on that one." A small muscle in his jaw flinched, and Carla felt his body tighten next to her.

In a lighter tone, she said, "And what do the two red roses the snake intertwines around symbolize?"

"The two great loves of my life. Firstly, my mother, Julie, who I think is the best woman I know."

"Why do you think that?" Carla had never heard any man call his mother a great love of his life. Here in Spain, sons respected their mothers but didn't necessarily think of them as the best woman they knew.

"I was an unplanned baby. Mum got accidentally pregnant when she was forty-four and despite everything, she still chose to have me. She gave up her career to raise me even at that late stage in her life. I owe her so much. She's strong, independent, intelligent, won't put up with any shit, a bit of perfectionist . . . Actually, you remind me of her, now I think of it." He fixed her in a penetrating stare, obviously considering this unexpected revelation.

Carla breathed in the salty smell of his burnished body and her skin tingled.

Aiden continued. "My mother is a beauty as well. But hers is a blonde, sophisticated type of beauty, whereas yours is a wild, mysterious one. You look like a mermaid flung onto the beach — that thick, black tousled hair falling over your shoulders and those jet-black eyes that any man could lose himself in . . ."

The hiatus lingered and the world seemed to shrink around them.

Oh, no. He's making me lose myself again, she thought. Carla swallowed and returned to the tattoo. "So, one rose is for your mother and what about the second red rose?'

"That's for the second great love of my life."

"And who's that?"

"I don't know yet. But it'll be for the woman I marry, when I find her." The force of will he exuded made her dizzy.

Carla shook her head free of the giddiness. "But why haven't you found her yet? You're a good man, Aiden. You have a good job. You're kind, sensitive, generous and very good looking . . ." Now she was complimenting him. She bit her tongue, realizing the admiration in her voice revealed too much of her inner longing.

"Seems I'm not every woman's dream man." He shrugged. "They get tired of my go-go-go personality. Seems I do too much — too much work, too much surfing, too much time with my mates and not enough time with them or taking holidays or relaxing. It's been the constant issue with all my ex's, but hey! I want to get the most out of life. I like a challenge. You're a long time dead. Right?"

Carla nodded thoughtfully. "Well, I hope you find the right woman to marry who understands your, how do they say it in the movies" — she rolled her eyes up, trying to remember — "need for speed?"

"I'm sure someday I will." Just as Aiden turned his gaze back to the ocean, he saw Rafael sink behind a wave. The surf instructor's arms flailed in the air, his strangled cries for help calling attention to his pupil's plight.

"Shit, Rafe's in trouble." Aiden sprang to his feet and dashed down the beach with Carla sprinting through the soft sand after him. He leaped over the smaller beach waves, and crashing into the surf, dived into the next big breaker. Carla stood on the water's edge watching him stroke hard through the roiling surf towards Rafe, who was being sucked out to sea. Powerless to help, she watched and prayed. Her heart thudded in her chest. The ocean currents swirled like a foamy washing machine around Rafe, sucking him under only to fling him like flotsam to the surface once more. Terrified, she stared as the same treacherous rip that had Rafe in its clutches, latched onto Aiden, sucking him out to sea.

Oh, God, she thought. *He's caught too.* Her hand flew to her chest in an unconscious effort to still her escalating heart rate.

Instead of fighting against the rip when it grabbed him in its murderous hold, Aiden surrendered. *Oh no. No. They're both drowning.* But as Carla stared harder, she realized he was using the rip's menacing force to swim faster toward Rafe. Aware of the commotion in the waves more people gathered on the beach to witness the drama, and Carla sprinted in the direction the two men were now being dragged. Halfway down the long stretch of white sand beach and about five hundred metres offshore, Aiden and Rafe bobbed like disappearing corks. Further and further they travelled, and she worried if they'd ever return. Squinting in the glare, she fixed them with an unwavering gaze, willing them to come back. Around her, a crowd of onlookers chatted and pointed excitedly at the disappearing men. She wanted to scream at them to be quiet, to go away or dive in and help them. But she said nothing. She swallowed the ferocious fear strangling her throat and burning her eyes. And she waited for what seemed an eternity before their heads dipped over more waves, this time coming closer and closer to shore. Before long, she could see their arms stroking through the churning surf propelling them onwards to the beach, to safety. Finally, and with Aiden's strong arm hoisting Rafe to his feet, they stumbled onto the beach, wrecked and wasted.

Carla dashed to him; arms outstretched. "Rafe, are you all right?"

He was bent over, spluttering and coughing briny seawater from his mouth. With a rough swipe of his hand, he pushed his tangled hair from his face, sighed and stood up. He looked shaken from the ordeal, but otherwise unharmed.

"*Si, si, mi pequeña luciérnaga.*" Crushing her in his arms, Rafe kissed the top of her head, murmuring, "My little firefly, my little firefly." Carla felt his body shudder from the shock. She buried her face into his chest and hugged him tighter, reassuring him he was safe. After a few moments, the panic passed, and their grip relaxed.

"Thank you, Aiden. Thank you." With misty eyes and arms still wrapped around her lover, Carla cast Aiden a relieved smile.

"*Muchas gracias*, Ace. *Muchas gracias.*" Rafe extended one hand while holding Carla firm with his other. "If you hadn't saved me, I would've surely died."

Aiden grabbed Rafael's hand and pumped it hard in both of his. "Not a problem, Rafe. What was I supposed to do? Let you drown?" His light-hearted chuckle broke the tension. "I've seen lots of fellas get caught in rips back home. There's only one way out, and that's to go with it." He shook his bedraggled blond hair like a golden retriever and laughed. "Damn. I've got water in my ear." He jumped on one foot while he tilted his head to the other side obviously trying to dislodge the unwelcome liquid.

"What on earth are you doing?" Carla giggled as she watched Aiden's strange antics.

"It's something I learnt to do when I started surfing. Come on. I'll explain at lunch. Time for food and you could do with a drink." Aiden eyed Rafael whose colour slowly returned to his face.

"We all could," Rafael said, and they scampered up the hot sand to the nearest café.

~ ♥ ~

While other beachgoers lazed, surfed and enjoyed nature's playground at the southern tip of Spain, Carla remained with Rafael at the café after lunch. Obviously, the thought of going back in, or near the water, still unsettled him because he declined to even venture back onto the beach. Instead, they sprawled on plastic beach chairs, reclining side by side, unwinding in the afternoon sun. Carla thrived in summer, her olive complexion tanning to a rich, chocolate brown, her thoughts deepening to a richer quality. Beside her, Rafael too soaked up the warm, comforting rays, his eyes closed. Together they recovered from the morning's drama. In contrast and like a kid making the most of his holidays, Aiden dashed back to the sea for another surf.

"See you guys soon." He grabbed his board underarm and disappeared down the sand into the waves.

They watched his departing figure, smiling at his enthusiasm. A slight breeze picked up, cooling the sun's bite and blowing away the residual stress from Rafael's near-fatal accident.

"I don't know what I would've done if something had happened to you." Carla gazed at Rafael and gave his hand an affectionate squeeze.

"To be truthful, I thought I was going to drown." His dark eyes locked on hers.

"Thank goodness Aiden was here, and he knew what to do. That surfing instructor had no idea." Carla clucked her teeth at the incompetence of the so-called professional.

They watched Aiden cut a dashing figure, whipping his board left to right on the sunlit polished waves. "Yes. He certainly saved me," Rafael said. "He makes it look so easy." Respect and admiration filled his voice. "Carla?" He turned to face her and took her hands in his.

"Yes, Rafe?" She spun around, mirroring his posture.

"Do you like Aiden?" Rafael's voice sounded oddly serious.

Without his domineering bravado, he looked troubled, like a child trying to solve a difficult problem. She'd not seen him so thoughtful or communicative before, and although she wanted him to be more forthcoming with his feelings, it worried her.

"Now that's a silly question. Of course I like Aiden. He's a good man, and he just saved your life," she said in a cheery tone, trying to lighten the intensity of the mood.

"No. I mean. Really like him. As a lover?"

Stunned that Rafael asked such a question, she scowled. "I don't know what you mean?"

"Neither do I," he said with a vigorous shake of his head. "I'm sorry. This whole incident has me crazy . . ." Rafael's voice trailed off to join the breeze.

"What is it, Rafe? Surely you're not talking about sex at a time like this?" Still holding his hands, Carla tried her best to be concerned for Rafe's welfare, but she needed a straight answer for her own peace of mind.

Rafael lifted his head, embarrassment splashed across his face. "No. no. I'm not asking whether you want to have sex with him . . . It's just that you two seem . . ." He pulled his hands away and rubbed them in short, sharp strokes on his thighs. "I don't know why I even asked that. This whole episode has got me thinking *loca*." Rafael pushed back his chair, and it screeched like an angry bird against the rough concrete floor. He lurched to the edge of the patio and gripped the railing, white-knuckled. His lips pursed shut, his gaze distant.

Carla rushed after him. She'd never seen Rafael act so strangely. His personality had become more unpredictable of late, but not like this. This possessed a sense of doom, of irrevocable consequences that were destined to happen. She touched his hand gently. "Rafe, what's wrong?"

He stared down at her with anguish in his eyes. "I'm not sure, Carla. Being so close to death makes you think about your life, about the decisions you make and about your future . . ." Again, he seemed to drift into melancholy while watching Aiden surf. She remained silent, afraid of what he may say next.

Suddenly, his death-like grip released, and his muscles relaxed. With an almost imperceptible pout, his contorted expression changed to one more tranquil, more resolved. Whatever haunted him seemed to vanish, leaving in its place the old Rafe — controlled, confident and master of all. "Forget about it, *mi pequeña luciérnaga*. Forget I said anything." With a ravishing smile and deep sigh, he scooped her in his arms. "I'll try to be a better man for you. I promise."

Relieved the confusion had passed, she buried her face in his chest, hugging his sun-kissed body. "Oh, Rafe. Thank you. It'd be wonderful if we could enjoy each other more. I'd really like that." She beamed up at him, hope filling her heart.

He gazed down at her tenderly. "Me too. I do love you. I'm sorry."

"Sorry for what?"

"For not being the man you deserve." Catching one of her wayward curls, he stroked it behind her ear, with a gentleness Carla had almost forgotten.

"Never mind the past. The future is all that matters. A fresh start." She crushed his torso in a tight hug and snuggled deeper into his embrace. He planted a soft kiss to the top of her head, and they held each other close looking out to sea. The constant crashing of the waves as they dashed to and from the beach was like an endless soundtrack, hypnotic and reassuring. Unconsciously they swayed together to its rhythm, holding on to each other and the promise of a new future.

Yet within Carla, another soundtrack played. Her gut instinct struck up its familiar tune — wanting to know more, wanting to know what troubled Rafe so much. She wished she could turn it off, change the insistent urging to find out. But no matter how much she tried to focus on a happy future with him, the niggling refrain of things not being what they seemed, would not be silenced.

THE DRIVE BACK ALONG the coast road to the villa proved uneventful, soothing in fact. Instead of racing each other, Aiden travelled safely behind Rafael the entire distance, alert to his mate's riding behaviour. By late afternoon, they arrived tired and pleased to be home. Rafael dismounted while Aiden and Carla stepped from the Ferrari.

"Look," Casa de los ángeles." Carla pointed to the large timber sign on the villa. "It's true. It's a house of angels. There certainly were angels with us today."

Aiden nodded. "Yeah, maybe you're right."

"I'm not a religious man, but maybe there were angels there today." Rafael walked over and wrapped his arm around Carla's waist.

"Without a doubt," she insisted. "The angels sent an Australian hero" — she shot a sunny smile at Aiden — "to look after my Spanish lover." She squeezed Rafael's waist.

"Come on. Let's get this gear inside," Aiden said, and they shared an intimate smile before they drifted indoors.

~ ♥ ~

THE NIGHT SHROUDED THE courtyard with ghostly faces of olive tree branches floating on the evening's comforting breeze. Muted conversations from neighbouring villas drifted across occasionally only to be lost in the acoustic guitar music emanating from Carla's phone. Entranced by the night, Aiden reclined on a pool lounge staring at the stars. On another lounge beside him, Rafael stretched out while Carla splashed languidly in the pool. A hot shower, hearty meal and generous glasses of Vega Sicilia Unico worked wonders, calming their spirits and stripping away any lingering anxiety from the day.

"Did either of you see that fella hanging around today at the café?" Aiden asked before swallowing another hefty slug of red.

"I didn't notice anyone in particular," Rafael said, sounding fully recovered from his surfing ordeal.

"Me either. Why? What's wrong?" Carla swam over to the pool's edge.

Aiden propped himself higher. "I'm not sure. Maybe I'm paranoid because of what happened with my job. But I could swear there was a guy watching us today. He appeared after we arrived at El Palmar and then on the drive home, I'm sure someone was following us."

"You've got my attention now." Rafael rolled over and eyeballed Aiden. "What did he look like?"

"I don't know. Like every other big Spanish bloke, I guess. A bit shorter than you and me, black hair, of course, strong jaw. He was acting cagey and turned away whenever he thought I was watching him."

"I wouldn't worry about it, Aiden. I'm sure it's nothing." Carla climbed out of the pool and grabbed a towel to dry off.

"I guess you're right. Just me being suspicious. Here, let's finish this." Aiden pushed to his feet and poured the last of the red wine equally among them. "Then we'll hit the sack and clean up in the morning."

"Sounds good to me," Carla said, wrapping the towel around her waist.

"Tell me, you're not going to wake us up early again." Rafael shimmied over to allow Carla to join him on his lounge.

"No way. Sleep as long as you want. After today's drama and all the sun we got, maybe we should have a day indoors tomorrow and chill out. What do you think?" Aiden's skin had copped a good dose of rays and was tinged a bright pink.

"Perfect," Carla and Rafael said, cuddling together on his lounge.

Rafael yawned. "I'll be asleep before my head hits the pillow."

"Me too," Aiden agreed.

"That makes three of us," Carla added.

But as an easy silence enveloped them, Aiden's mind couldn't stop piecing together likely scenarios to explain the appearance of the stranger at the beach.

CHAPTER SEVEN

BRIGHT AND EARLY THE next morning, before Carla and Rafael awoke, Aiden set off on a stroll through the neighbourhood. Sequestered behind wrought iron gates and skirted by lush moss-green, manicured lawns, luxurious homes lined the labyrinth of streets. Except no one seemed to live in them. He wondered why the residents even bothered having such spectacular houses if they never enjoyed them. Back home, everyone would be outside during summer, eating, playing and swimming. He missed the Gold Coast. The memory gave him an idea, so after lunch, a swim and a siesta, Aiden jumped in the Ferrari on a mission.

On his return, he strode through the house calling aloud. "Okay, you two. Tonight I'm cooking, and it's authentic Aussie barbeque." Before anyone answered, Aiden sensed that in his absence, the pair had had a disagreement. *You could cut the air with a knife* sprang to mind as he dropped the shopping bags on the bench.

With her head down, Carla appeared and shuffled into the kitchen. Barefoot and dressed in figure-hugging white jeans and singlet, her black hair cascaded in long tendrils covering her face and falling over her tanned shoulders.

"Hi, Aiden. I'll help you with this," she said in a meek voice. When she began to unpack the fresh produce, he noticed her flushed face, as if she'd been crying. Before he could ask if she was all right, Rafael rounded the corner. His posture and bluster immediately confirmed Aiden's intuition. Something was definitely amiss.

Hoping to lighten the mood, Aiden laid out his 'hunt' from the local butchery. "I'm going to make some real Aussie rissoles with this mince, and since I couldn't find any suitable snags, I bought these chorizo sausages. A little bit of both worlds, I reckon." He shot them one of his champion smiles. Carla did her best to reciprocate but failed and turned away.

Rafael remained stony-faced with a pitiful smirk barely escaping his tight lips.

Undeterred, Aiden forged ahead. "If you can make a salad, Carla?"

"Sure." She collected the fresh vegetables and moved away to another bench, her back to them.

"And, Rafael, if you could set the table outside please?" Aiden wondered if he was being overly optimistic in thinking Rafe would help at all.

With a growl, Rafael replied, "I need something to drink first." He stormed over to the wine rack in the foyer and grabbed a couple of bottles of red. Returning to the kitchen, he opened one roughly and poured nearly half of it into his glass. He swallowed large and hard. Grabbing the other bottle, he opened it. "I'll let this one breathe." With Rafael brooding and swilling wine in the corner with no offer to pour for anyone else, Aiden decided to continue with his one-man show. He found a grater and a bowl. Around him, he gathered his ingredients and into the bowl combined the mince, grated onion, carrot, garlic and seasoning making a firm mixture, which he rolled in his hands and flattened into patties.

"Now that's an Aussie rissole fit for a king," he said with pride, holding one of his creations in the palm of his hand. Carla turned around and murmured her approval, while Rafael snarled his appreciation from across the room.

Aiden shot him a sarcastic smile. "Glad my rissole hit the mark." Receiving no response, he set about making the rest and placing them on some greaseproof paper on a plate. Rafael topped up his glass and took his stormy mood outside.

Once he'd left, Aiden moved next to Carla. "What's going on? What happened between you two when I left?"

Soft sobs choked Carla's voice. "Oh, it's just silly. He wants to go out on his bike tonight and I told him, he's an idiot. After what happened yesterday at the beach, he needs to relax. Not go off into the night riding. He got really angry and—"

"But why does he want to go out? What for?"

"That's what I asked him. He never gives a reason."

"Bloody strange if you ask me." He paused and watched Carla's small hands tremble as she tore the lettuce leaves. "Are you okay, though?"

"Yes, I'm fine. I thought after his near drowning in the ocean yesterday, things would be different. I thought Rafe would be different. He was for a little while but then . . ." Her voice trailed off and more tears pooled in her eyes.

Aiden's heart melted just a little at being in so close to her beauty and fragility. Those soft, Bambi eyes of hers made his stomach churn — a similar sensation to hunger, but more emotionally intense. It was an odd feeling. One he'd never experienced before, and it unnerved him. Being commissioned by her father with Carla's safety triggered his protective nature and at times, especially now, he had to restrain himself from reaching out and bundling her to him. Thankfully, with his hands covered in the mince mixture, his urge couldn't be fulfilled.

Instead, he turned back to his duties. "Well, I can't work it out. Why he'd want to be riding off into the night when he has you here, is beyond me. Is there anything I can do to make it easier for you?"

"Okay, Ace, what now?" Rafael stood at the sliding door, malevolence masking his normally handsome face. The prickly atmosphere ratcheted up a notch. Aiden had no idea how long Rafe had been there or how much he'd heard, but his gut told him the conversation he and Carla just had was not exclusively between them. Underneath Rafael's restrained emotions, Aiden sensed a threatening quality, intimating that Aiden was venturing on shaky ground.

"Now I know why they call you Ace?" Rafael cocked an unforgiving eyebrow at Aiden, and the mocking tone in his voice did little to hide his displeasure.

Aiden knew exactly what Rafe referred to but chose to ignore his sarcastic remark for Carla's sake. "It's because I make a damn good barbeque. Even if I say so myself."

"Looks like you're good at a lot of things." Rafael prowled into the kitchen, his black eyes locking onto Aiden with an unmistakable message blazing from them. *Stay out of my affairs and leave her alone.*

Still trying to diffuse the situation, Aiden said, "How about you score the chorizos while I finish these off and put them in the fridge to cool before we cook?" Aiden handed a slicing knife to Rafael, who wrapped his elegant fingers around the grip with a sneer.

"Did you know I grew up on a farm, Ace?"

Carla glanced over her shoulder, a look of apprehension on her face.

Continuing with his tale, while sliding his finger along the blade of the knife, Rafael elaborated. "We had a farm on the other side of Andalusia, in Extremadura. My family has grown crops in the region for generations. When I was young, my father used to slaughter the wild pigs that roam there for our dinner table. It was awful. I watched him cut their throats. They'd scream forever. I hated it, and I hated him for making me watch. I didn't eat meat for years as a young boy."

AND IT IS BECAUSE of my father, I am the way I am, thought Rafael. God, how he wanted to relieve himself of this burden, of the secret he carried. For a moment, he contemplated telling Carla and Ace. But, how could he? He might lose everything. Carla would never forgive him, and he'd lose her love, his career, the life he'd worked so hard to achieve. No. He couldn't tell them, although he felt on some level Ace would understand. But it was a risk he wasn't willing to take. He had to stop behaving so irrationally. If he didn't pull himself together, Carla would leave him anyway. *But what good is fame and fortune when I can't be who I truly am?*

AIDEN NOTICED A LIGHT film of perspiration prickle Rafe's face. More conflicted than any man Aiden had ever met, Rafael could be at once menacing and miserable. The enduring horror from this boyhood ordeal ravaged Rafael's eyes, sparking Aiden's curiosity and empathy. Long-suffering seemed to describe Rafael best. *But long-suffering from what?* Aiden said nothing and waited.

"But there's one thing I learnt from Papa. I know how to use a knife . . ." A triumphant smile sprang to Rafael's face as he held up the knife twirling it with the proficiency of a butcher. "So, yes. I'm sure I can score the chorizos."

The frequency and rapidity with which Rafael changed moods left Aiden flabbergasted, wondering how Carla managed. Working with Rafael in a professional relationship would be hard enough but enduring his unpredictability personally must be beyond taxing. Perhaps this was what worried Manolo so much? Not that his daughter was living with a married man, not yet divorced. But that she was living with a man who suffered from bipolar disorder.

"Then stop talking about it, come stand next to me and do it." Carla beamed a sunny smile and reached out to Rafael, beckoning him to join her at the bench. With barely an askance look at Aiden, Rafael set up his workstation and whispered something in Carla's ear. Fluttering her eyelashes and nuzzling into his side, she nodded. Unable to decipher if Carla was peacekeeping by playing coy with Rafael or not, Aiden returned to his preparations. He understood Rafe's loosely cloaked threat to stop sticking his nose in where it didn't belong and to leave Carla alone. Hell, he couldn't really blame him, but he'd made a promise to Manolo and his concern and growing feelings for Carla strained at the leash. *You need to get your act together, mate,* he chided himself silently. Aiden fidgeted in the fridge to find space for the plate and glanced over his shoulder at Carla. For the first time in his life, Aiden felt like the third wheel and despite his self-admonition, a green-eyed monster stretched from a long slumber in a hidden cavern in his heart.

~ ♥ ~

Retreating to the barbeque, Aiden plied his culinary expertise. The sizzle and heat of the cooking meat permeated the courtyard, adding much-needed warmth to the previous chilly altercation. A glass or two of red pacified Rafael's temperament giving Carla and Aiden a chance to relax. By the time the mouth-watering aroma from the barbeque drifted upwards, escaping on the early evening breeze, a truce had been called, and the three housemates relaxed into familiar, emotionally non-hostile territory.

"*Buena nochese.*" A woman's voice called through the fence of olive trees. "Hello?"

Aiden placed his tongs on the barbeque plate and walked over to where the voice originated. An attractive, smiling face peered through the branches. "Hello. I'm Sofia, your neighbour."

"Hi, Sofia. I'm Aiden," he said, ducking to see her more clearly through a gap between the trunk and the lower branches.

"I was wondering if you could help me. My garage door is jammed, and it won't close. I don't have the strength to shut it." Her smile broadened to reveal perfectly capped artic-white teeth.

"I'd be happy to help, but we're about to have dinner. I could do it later?" He paused a moment to consider the thought racing through his mind. "Listen, why don't you join us? Then I can come over after dinner to fix your door."

"Are you sure? I don't want to interrupt."

"Not a problem. Walk around and come through the front door. It's open."

"Thank you, Aiden. I will. That is most kind of you."

Aiden found Carla and Rafael inside and proceeded to inform them of the extra guest for dinner. Carla sighed as if relieved she'd have some female company and Rafael nodded nonchalantly. "I'll set another place on the table then." Aiden returned to his cooking post leaving Carla and Rafael to attend to the last-minute details before joining him.

"Hello . . ." Sofia's bright voice rang out from inside.

Aiden lifted his head, and as their dinner guest came into view, he was struck by the Hollywood glamour of the woman walking through the villa. Figuring she must be in her mid to late forties, Aiden nodded at the discipline Sofia obviously had to maintain such a taut, fit body. Tanned to a deep chocolate brown, her skin shone with a layer of sparkling cream which flickered under the lights. The transparent lemon-coloured short, drawstring dress floating around her thighs and barely covering her precision implanted breasts, awoke Aiden's cock with a bewitching tickle. Vibrant red hair coiled on top of her head, while wayward tendrils escaped their captivity to frame her face which hinted at the pretty, virgin she once was.

Aiden called out, "We're out here, Sofia."

With long elegant strides, she stepped onto the courtyard and accepted Aiden's hand in a welcome shake. "I'm Aiden, and this is Carla and Rafael."

"Thank you so much for inviting me to join you for dinner and your offer to help me with the garage door afterwards. I'm here by myself so it's a little difficult when things break." She rolled her sea-green eyes in mock distress.

"Not a problem," Aiden said. "Here take a seat."

While Sofia, Carla and Rafael chatted, Aiden returned to the barbeque to plate up. From the corner of his eye, he studied their guest. A striking woman with strong bone structure and high cheekbones, she oozed a sexy, confident maturity. Her face glowed and her glossy coral lips contrasted the brilliance of her teeth. Expensive looking gold jewellery dangled from her ears, wrists and neck completing the perfect movie star look. Sofia, like Sophia Loren, thrummed like a sexual magnet.

"Here you go, everyone. Authentic Aussie rissoles with a few Spanish chorizos thrown in for good measure. Help yourselves."

"Smells delicious." Sofia aimed a deliberate smile at Aiden. "Are all young Australian men as good at cooking barbeque as you?"

"Sofia, he's good at a lot of things." Rafael winked at Aiden.

"Well let's hope you're as good at fixing garage doors then," she said.

"I'll do my best."

~ ♥ ~

Dinner passed easily enough with the four of them eating and laughing. Sofia had made a point of retelling her recent history, sprinkling the clues of her predatory nature like giant hunks of bread rather than dainty crumbs. Recently divorced, her husband cheated on her with a younger version, Sofia got the Costa mansion, he kept the Seville residence, and she got a sizable divorce settlement, which she was happily spending. Soon after dinner, Rafael and Carla politely retired for the night, leaving Aiden to fulfil his handyman promise. With the moon shining bright on the night's dark canvas, he followed Sofia back to her luxurious, celebrity-style home to play Tim the Tool Man.

As he suspected, there was no garage door that needed a man's touch. The only thing in Sofia's mansion that needed a man's touch was Sofia. Now standing on the marble surround of the Olympic size swimming pool, it was obvious the only tool Aiden was about to use was the one God gave him.

Like a serpent, she slithered out of her dress revealing her intoxicating nakedness. The moonlight cascaded down her back in a thin silvery streak and when she freed her hair, it fell over her shoulders in lazy, loose curls, shining in fiery streaks of auburn. Naked except for rhinestone-studded gold sandals, Sofia's hourglass figure with its trim waist and full hips cast a mesmerizing silhouette.

"Do you like to swim, Aiden?" she purred, glancing back over her shoulder.

"Absolutely," he said, an appreciative grin curling his lips.

"Why don't you join me then?" She didn't wait for a reply. Instead, she folded forwards, dipping down with the grace of a swan. Bent over, she slid one foot then the other out of her sandals while lifting her arse high in the air for Aiden's enjoyment. Riveted by her womanhood and what he was going to do with it, Aiden began to salivate. Not wasting any more time, Aiden peeled off his T-shirt, kicked off his loafers and shrugged out of his shorts. Left standing in his underwear, he grabbed his cock with a preparatory squeeze. Pre-ejaculate leaked through the cotton fabric leaving a sticky residue in his palm. *God this is going to be good,* he thought.

Unhurried, Sofia pivoted to face him. Tossing her hair back to expose her breasts, she posed, hands on her hips. She waited a long moment, giving him time to appreciate what was on offer. She padded slowly towards him, obviously giving him time to appreciate her full, buoyant breasts atop a flat, taut plank of a stomach and the soft, dark curls on her mons which were precisely waxed into the shape of a heart. *A cute touch,* he thought. Her muscular thighs were long, lean and cut. She reminded him of a female superhero — tall, masterful and drop-dead gorgeous. An imposing woman used to getting her own way. By the time she reached him, they stood eye to eye, the energy of an unspoken contest crackling between them.

"I see you approve." Her hand rubbed the dripping head of his cock through his underwear.

Aiden didn't flinch. "Absolutely."

"I notice absolutely is your favourite word. I adore acquiescent men. It demonstrates their willingness to please." She nibbled his earlobe and tweaked his cock harder. Aiden thought he'd explode, but still he didn't falter.

"Trust me. I know how to please women," he assured her, his pulse quickening.

"Show me." Quick as a cobra, she gripped his underwear and pulled it down to his ankles. He stepped out of his jocks and his eager cock brushed her cheek. Quick as a snake, her tongue flicked out, licked the head of it and then disappeared back into her wicked mouth. Aiden groaned. *She plays this game well,* he thought.

Sofia role-played handmaiden and led him into the pool, down four gently inclined steps. Once submerged to their waists in the cooling water, Aiden brokered the deal. "I know you enjoy playing cougar, and I'm sure you've had lots of younger men since your divorce . . ."

A glint of satisfaction sparkled in her eyes at Aiden's correct appraisal of the situation.

"However, let's see if we can't make this more interesting?" His hands slid over her hips but purposely refrained from any intimate touching.

"You have my attention," she said in a sultry tone.

"I don't intend to let you win."

"Excuse me?"

"By the sounds of things, you ended up winning pretty big in the divorce, and I'm sure you've broken a willing young man or two since then. But you won't break me. I intend to give you what you've never had."

"And what might that be, Aiden?" She batted her black, extended lashes at him.

"A real man." His smile revealed the Ace within and like a charm it worked.

Sofia's perfectly sculptured eyebrows shot up her forehead in delighted surprise. "And what does a real man do?" Her hand drifted down and cupped his balls, barely caressing them. The sensation was maddening, but Aiden showed no response.

He leaned into her neck. "I'm going to lick, eat and fuck you until you can't walk."

"I'd like to see that." The sarcasm and challenge in her voice spurred him on.

"Let the games begin." Clasping her face in his hands, he leaned in and snaked his tongue into her hot, welcoming mouth. He could taste the lingering saltiness of his pre-ejaculate mingled with her own intensely sensuous flavour. Dragging her closer, he plundered her savagely. She moaned and thrust her tongue deeper into his mouth. Driven by ravenous appetites, they unleashed themselves on each other. Living up to his promise, Aiden took control and thrusting his forearm between her thighs hoisted her up further out of the water.

"So how much abuse can these expensive tits take?" With her larger-than-needed fake breasts at face height and a scorching open snatch on his arm, Aiden teased Sofia's nipple until it puckered in a hard, tight bud.

She grabbed his shoulders for balance and thrust her breast into his mouth. "As much as you can give."

Aiden slurped and sucked on her tit, tugging at the nipple, testing her punishment threshold. His other hand pushed in the centre of her back, making sure she couldn't squirm away from the delicious torture. Obviously delighted, Sofia fucked his forearm, moaning.

In an act of contrition, Aiden twirled his tongue lovingly over the spoiled breast and glanced up at her. "Would you like more or was that too hard?"

Swivelling on his arm, Sofia pulled her breast away and offered the other. "More," she demanded. Again, he laved relentless torture on her other breast and nipple. Even his large hand had trouble encompassing her oversized tit, so he squeezed it hard, pushing as much as he could into his mouth. She squealed in delight. "Bite me, bite me." He bit down, hoping it wasn't too hard, but as she gasped, he felt her cleft splay open on his forearm. *She likes it really rough,* he thought. Having found Sofia's near lack of limits with sexual pain, he dropped her back into the water and wrestled her to the steps.

"*Mmm,*" she crooned, "the head job seat. Who goes first?"

"Let's pop you up here," he said with polite patience. He hoisted her onto the highest step and pulled her legs apart. "Perfect," he said. "You have a glorious vag'." With water lapping at her perineum, Aiden studied her exposed slit. He so wanted to drive his throbbing cock in there, but there was more fun to be had first.

With her snatch gaping, Sofia leaned back on the pool edge. "She loves being eaten, Aiden. I hope you're hungry . . ."

"Trust me. I'm starving." Aiden slipped lower into the pool, his face level with her yearning. He began with a clear plan in mind. Teasing her with his warm breath, he then licked her soft, fleshy folds with such precision, he felt her shudder and squirm. The more he tasted and took of her, the more he lost himself in the wanton desire of the older woman. Even as a young boy experimenting with sex, he adored the taste and smell of women. The sparkling jewel hidden between their legs lured him like a tomb seeker of treasures. Licking, sucking, tongue fucking, and peeling snatches open to please his women was one of his favourite past times. For him, giving great head was as much a turn-on as receiving it. Burying his face into Sofia's open and generous vag,' he ravished her. His hunger hadn't been satiated for nearly a week, so tonight he intended to have his fill. Aiden loved that the tongue, the strongest muscle in the body, was such a wonderful biological instrument for pleasure. Deeper and deeper he penetrated her, only to return to harass her clit until it burned beneath his lips. By the way she pulled herself further apart, groaned and thrust harder into his face, he knew she was enjoying his technique. Sucking harder to engorge her clit and tonguing her delicious folds with long, hard strokes, he unearthed the treasure. Sofia expelled a murderous scream, as sweet female ejaculate gushed into his mouth, nearly choking him.

"Oh God that's good," he groaned through slurping gulps.

"More," she moaned. "More. Finger fuck me."

Like a champion equestrian show jumper, Aiden mounted the step beside her and rammed three fingers into her loosened snatch. Unleashing his powerful arm muscles, he pounded at her, aggravating her G-spot and bringing her to multiple climaxes. Bent back across the edge of the pool, her plastic tits pointing to the sky and her burnished skin stretched tight over her elongated body, Sofia looked almost unreal — like an avatar of sordid sex.

Succumbing to the avatar's wickedness, he pummelled her flesh. The knuckles of his hand ruthlessly pounded against the bone of her pelvis until at last, she cried out, spent. He stopped and withdrew. His hand throbbed and by the heat coming from her vag', he knew she'd taken a beating. But obviously, one she wanted and enjoyed. Aiden smiled down at her, pleased he could be of service, but her eyes remained tightly closed, her body still quivering. As she lay prostrate with her legs languishing in the pool, her red hair strewn on the pale marble and her breathing laboured, she could've easily been mistaken for a woman in pain rather than in pleasure. A sly satisfied smile crept across her face, hardening Aiden's cock.

His balls throbbed in jealousy of Sofia's euphoria and demanded attention. Clutching her nearest drifting hand, Aiden clasped its lifeless form and wrapped it around his cock. "My turn," he whispered in her ear.

"Help me up." Her other hand reached out for assistance. Aiden obliged, and Sofia's hand tightened on his cock. Pushing him onto the step, she drifted into the water. With her face level with his manhood, she said in a coy voice, "My, you have a big cock, Aiden."

"All the better to fuck you with, my dear." He reclined back onto his elbows awaiting his reward.

Needing no further encouragement, she began licking his thick shaft. Long lazy strokes she lavished from the base to the head, each time glancing up at him. Grinning like a kid who just got away with a prank, Aiden settled back watching the performance taking place in his groin. With her tongue, she circled the ridge, then dipped the tip into the eye of his cock. Aiden moaned and closed his eyes, so he could appreciate all Sofia had to offer. Underwater his balls lolled. Frustrated and full, they began to scrunch higher up into his body, desperate for release. Suddenly her mouth was on one, sucking at it. He looked down to find Sofia's red hair floating like seaweed on top of the water, her face below, his ball being sucked to breaking point. She had his entire sack in her mouth. Whatever she was doing sent him mad, and he began tugging at his cock.

Abruptly, she came up for air, a triumphant smile on her face. "Now the other one." She took a deep breath and submerged to tease Aiden's other ball.

A deep, satisfied groan escaped his mouth and he lay back, giving her his body. Within moments, she surfaced, straddled him on the step and engulfed his cock. Over and over she sucked deep and hard, as if trying to extract some deadly poison while an exhilarating tension built in his body. Her mouth worked overtime, deep throating his cock down past a normal gag reflex. Aiden had never throat-fucked a woman this deeply before, and he lost all control. Exploding, he squirted a thick wad of cum down Sofia's throat but still she continued in her torment of him. Pulsing and purging, his cock rid Aiden of his stress, frustrations, and worries. Only when his penis lolled limply in her mouth, did she release it from her command.

"Do you like tennis, Aiden?" Sofia reclined beside him, a wicked smile teasing her lips.

He propped himself on one elbow and studied this woman who'd just given him the best head job of his life. A magnificently sculptured beauty, Sofia possessed hidden talents and assuredly, secrets.

"Yes, I don't mind tennis." His hand ventured to her mons.

"Good. Well, that means we're one set all." Her hand reciprocated and caressed his cock. "Want to try for another set?"

Remembering their earlier conversation, he said, "Absolutely."

"Good man. But I warn you, this set is much harder and requires real stamina." She arched her inked eyebrow and rose to her feet. Still sitting, Aiden looked up at her statuesque frame at the same time she straddled him. She opened her snatch for his indulgence. "More of this for you." She lowered herself onto his tongue which he eagerly slithered into her slick slit once more. With the taste of her on his lips and his cock ready for a second set, he followed Sofia out of the pool and towelled off. Every move she made was calculated for his pleasure. The way she angled her body and touched herself was a slow-moving exhibition of debauchery. "Now that you're dry, leave the towel. Come with me." She grabbed his swinging cock and led him towards the house. "Welcome to my lair." She released his straining cock and flourished an invitation into the mansion.

When he stepped inside, Aiden gave a long whistle. "Impressive. What business did you say your husband was in?"

"I didn't." She wagged her tail for Aiden to follow.

Across polar white plush carpet he trailed, admiring the style in which she lived. Oversized artworks decorated the walls in an entertainment room that could easily fit a hundred people. Multiple white couches and tub chairs were strategically positioned in conversation corners and alcoves, waiting for someone to use them. Though Vogue beautiful, Aiden thought the whole place felt sterile, unlived in, like so many other homes he'd seen on his morning walk. Down a long pale marbled corridor and through grand double doors, he followed Sofia into a master bedroom. An enormous circular bed dressed in white satin sheets and strewn with pillows sat pride of place in the room. Gossamer curtains draped the closed French doors behind which Aiden glimpsed the pool courtyard. Lamps and low-level lighting gave the room a feminine, subdued glow.

"There's champagne in the bucket." Sofia pointed to the sideboard on the far wall. "Why don't you pour us a glass and I'll freshen up."

"Okay." He sauntered across the room to do bar duties. He smiled and nodded approval at the Cristal champagne and at Sofia's well-executed plan to get him back to her boudoir tonight. *She's bloody crafty*, he thought. But she provided the perfect distraction from Carla. Anything to get his mind off her helped. With glasses in hand, he ambled to the bed and placed one on the antique bedside table. Sipping from the other, he wandered to the opposite side of the bed, drinking in his surroundings as easily as the champagne. Deciding to get comfortable, he stacked some pillows then sprawled out on the bed. Based on her performance so far, Aiden suspected he was in for a real treat when Sofia returned. He needed to fuck her and by the way his cock was behaving, it was going to be a long, hard night.

He'd nearly finished his glass of champagne when the door opened. There she stood, or Aiden suspected it was Sofia. He swallowed hard and tried not to look shocked. Clad in black everything with a cat-o'-nine-tails in her hand, she towered like a spectre in the doorway. Aiden's eyes blinked open wide while his mind assessed the challenge before him. Four-inch stiletto-heeled thigh-high gleaming black boots encased Sofia's bare, quivering legs and culminated in a row of sharp studs encircling her thighs. Strung high on her hips, a thin leather thong, cut so deeply into her slit it disappeared from view, eaten up by her insatiable vag'. Her bare breasts thrust through the holes in the rubber corset with nipple clamps ferociously biting into them. A studded dog collar encircled her neck and a full-face mask allowing only vision, covered her face. Silken, red hair erupted from the crown of her head like shimmering fireworks, barely softening the threatening dominatrix. The sound of the slapping whip in her hand made it perfectly clear who was about to be punished.

Aiden swallowed hard. *Fuck!* Without a word, she dropped to her knees like a cat and crawled over the lush, white carpet towards the bed. Aiden sat bolt upright, a reluctant witness to the unnerving spectacle on the floor. The vanishing thong separated into two pieces over her beautifully rounded arse cheeks, leaving her anus free for the sizeable butt plug jammed into it. Aiden bit his lip and inched back a little further. Sofia rounded the bed and with exaggerated predatory movements, slinked on top to join him. Her sea-green eyes sparkled manically from behind the mask, and Aiden suspected she was high on something because of her dilated pupils. *Drugs*, he thought. *That's the business her ex-husband was in. Now it made more sense.* She smooched up to him like a cat seeking affection and purred.

He refused.

Her glazed eyes scolded him with vicious contempt.

Aiden pursed his lips in apology to which she threw herself back on the bed, throwing her legs wide and growled. Thrusting her finger into her snatch, she wrestled the strip of leather from her folds. She locked Aiden with an insolent gaze and nodded for him to begin. He declined. Thwarted and furious, she shot him a death stare and hissed behind the mask. In one deft movement, Sofia took matters into her own hands and jammed the whip handle savagely inside herself. She began pumping and howling in such a frenzy Aiden thought she'd rent a hole internally.

Aiden's cock was out of there. "Sorry, Sofia. I was wrong. Game, set and match to you." Aiden was off the bed and striding out the door before she even noticed. "No way in

God's earth I'm going to fuck a female version of Hannibal Lecter. That chick's too fucking weird for me." Tearing down the hallway, through the ice palace of a living room and out the French doors, Aiden ran like a fifty-metre champion sprinter. Outside, he gathered up his clothes beside the pool and scrambled into them, chastising himself for not listening to his previous intuition about Sofia having secrets.

Unlike Lot's wife, Aiden didn't look back as he left the property and hurried to the safety of Casa de los ángeles. *No fuckin' angels next door at Sofia's, that's for sure,* he thought. *She's one sick, twisted demon.* With hard strides and a frightened dick, Aiden marched into the shelter of the villa.

Under a steaming shower, he rubbed Sofia's smell from his body and hair and vehemently spat the taste of her from his mouth. He then repeated the process twice over, until his skin glowed as if washed in lye soap. Finally satisfied he was rid of her, he turned off the taps. With a deep sigh, he watched the water swirl down the drain and with it he washed away the entire night as a distant and distasteful memory.

CHAPTER EIGHT

CARLA RAISED HER SUNGLASSES and lifted her eyes up towards his towering shadow. "Hi, Aiden, where have you been?" Taking the opportunity to improve her topless tan, Carla had been lying around the pool most of the day and had browned to a deep chocolate tint with only a thong mark left from her tiny bikini bottoms.

Bare bodied except for a pair of floral board shorts, Aiden plonked down on another lounge beside her, clasping his hands behind his head.

"I decided to go for a surf early this morning, so I took off before you two got up. It was a brilliant day down at El Palmar. Huge sets — so I got stuck in."

He looked as happy as a clam. With his shaggy blond streaked hair stiffened from the salt and wind, his scruffy beard glistening with sand and his muscular limbs twitching from the strenuous exercise, he looked truly relaxed. Carla nodded. She understood the satisfaction that came from working out by doing something you loved. Aiden's contented smile infected her expression and like a pair of lizards they basked, faces uplifted to the sun. Together, they enjoyed a few moments, grinning and saying nothing. "Where's Rafe?" Aiden said, interrupting the companionable silence.

"Oh, he decided to go for a ride. He got so antsy. I couldn't stand it any longer. He took off around lunchtime. I expect him to be back by dinner. Who knows?" She shrugged. Her patience was wearing thin with Rafael. She'd hoped a break away with some fresh company would do them both the world of good. Being someone new and easy-going, Aiden seemed the perfect choice. But even after the near-drowning and Rafe's promises to be a better man, he'd reverted to being egotistical, distracted, and on edge. Nothing was working out the way she'd hoped. She was so tired of worrying about Rafael and what was the matter with him. Shooing the repetitive, disheartening thoughts from her mind, she felt certain he never worried about her and her feelings. If he was off bike riding, who cares. It gave her a chance to relax, do what she wanted and enjoy some quiet time.

"How did last night go with Sofia?" Carla asked with a hint of naughtiness in her voice. She'd waited all day to ask Aiden this question. By the way Sofia had openly propositioned him last night during dinner, Carla felt sure hot sex would have ensued in the luxury mansion next door. Although keen for an answer, there was a secret part of her that hoped her assumption was wrong.

"You don't want to know. She is one messed–up woman." Aiden shuddered and shook his head.

"Why? What happened?" Carla propped herself up, curious to know more.

"Not too much happened and that's the way I'm keeping it. Seriously. There are some strange people in the world when it comes to how they like their sex."

Recalling the unsavoury sex she and Rafe had fallen into lately, Carla nodded in agreement and reclined back on the lounge.

"So, what are we going to do until Rafe gets back?" she asked. For the first time, Carla noticed Aiden glance in her direction. A sly smile twitched his lips, making her feel beautiful. When she reciprocated, he looked away.

"Why don't we hit the showers and decide then." Leaping to his feet, he offered his hand to help her, keeping his eyes firmly on Carla's face.

She accepted his hand, stood up and met his gaze. "Good idea." After she wrapped a sarong around herself, they wandered indoors, and she struggled to keep her thoughts from going where they didn't belong. To Aiden's body.

~ ♥ ~

By the time Carla strolled back into the living room, she felt brand new. A soapy shower, shampooed hair, and all-over moisturizer worked wonders for her feminine morale, as did a deep, rich suntan. With a brightly coloured, floor-length silk caftan floating around her perfumed body and her wet hair coiled high on her head, she realized how much she'd needed a holiday and how at last, she felt like she was having one.

Aiden was already sprawled on the couch. Like a tantalizing, new toy, he stretched out commandeering the space. His tanned legs extended from ragged-edged denim shorts slung so low on his hips, Carla felt sure they'd slip off the moment he stood up. The short-sleeve white cotton shirt he wore was unbuttoned, so his torso, with its polished chest, defined musculature and cut abs, lay on display like a tight, rippling human washboard. Clean-shaven, his strong jawline was even more defined, and his mop of unruly blond hair lay drying naturally around his face. Reading a book, he'd not noticed her hushed arrival, so she paused watching him. He seemed so at peace in his own body, in who he was as a man. *A magnificent, masculine man with no ego? A modest man. Could there be such a thing?*

As if sensing her presence, he lifted his eyes. They glimmered as blue as the summer sky outside, and a boyish grin lit up his face. "So what? Are you just going to stand there staring at me?"

"No, of course not." Carla moved closer, and as Aiden threw his legs off the sofa to make room for her, she nestled into the other corner, curling her legs underneath her. She inhaled the crisp, woody scent of his aftershave, holding its refreshing perfume in her lungs for a moment. Exhaling, she cocked her head at what he was reading.

He turned the small, shabby book in his hands. "It's a book of Spanish fables I found in my bedroom drawer. It's the only book in English around here, so I thought I'd have a read. I particularly like the story of the king in Granada who went looking for a wife with his magic mirror."

Carla's face brightened at the mention of the childhood story. "My mama used to read that to me when I was little." She cast her mind back to happy days with her mother and recited the story. "Although all the women in Granada wanted to be queen, none would look into the mirror. They'd been told if they had any blemishes in their characters, they would show up on their faces when they stared at their reflection."

"That's it. And the only woman to try was a shepherdess who didn't want to be queen but thought she'd lived a good life, protecting her sheep."

"When she looked in the mirror, her reflection had no blemishes and so the king chose her to be his wife." At the sweet memory, Carla felt her face animate with a childhood smile.

Aiden picked up the story. "And the kicker of the fable was the mirror wasn't magic at all. The king had set them up. He said if the other women had been as confident of their flawless characters as the shepherdess, they would've at least tried to look into the mirror, but they were too afraid. His little test proved to him the shepherdess was the best of all and deserved to be queen."

"I loved that story when I was little. Mama used to say if I grew up with no blemishes to my character, one day my king would find me." A hint of disappointment crept into Carla's voice. "Anyway, they're just silly children's stories to keep women oppressed. To think some man will come along and save us. Hah! What a lot of shit."

"Yeah, well maybe you're right. But it's still got a good message . . ." Aiden placed the book on the coffee table and leaned back on the couch. He paused and held her gaze. "Since we're talking about your mother, what's with the purple pouch you needed to get from your father's place before we left? You said it was a special time in Granada. Something to do with your Romani roots?"

Carla remained still. No one outside of the family knew. No one outside of the family ever knew. For generations, the Romani gypsies from who she descended never discussed their traditions.

"I'm sorry, Aiden. I can't tell you. We're sworn to secrecy." She longed to confide in him, but her respect for her mother, her heritage and herself prevented disclosure.

"Does Rafe know?" A flicker of more than idle curiosity flashed in his eyes.

"Oh, yes. He comes from the same descendant line. He knows."

Aiden cocked his head at her, and she watched the probing lawyer step from behind the rough-and-tumble beach boy. "So, what can you tell me?"

She considered a moment. "There's a large family tree that goes back to the most famous flamenco dancer of all time, Carmen Amaya, the Queen of the Gypsies. Although flamenco grew out of Andalusia, it was Carmen Amaya who brought it to the world. She was known for the greatest *duende*, the greatest emotion when she danced. She was extraordinarily talented and broke all conventions of dance at the beginning of the twentieth century. She was wild and powerful. A free spirit in love with the dance and the dance loved her."

"Sounds like someone else I know," he injected, shooting her a gleaming smile.

"Carmen had three sisters and two brothers who had children of their own. My mother was one of these children. She was named Isabella Amaya before she married Papa. Theresa and Marco's father, Domingo, who is my uncle, was born of another of Carmen's siblings. There is Aunt Lucette and Aunt Chantelle, who live in Paris. They were daughters of another of Carmen's siblings. Then there is Rafael's father, Sancho Flores. He's born from yet another of Carmen's siblings."

Aiden blinked at her. "Sorry, I'm a visual kind of guy. I need a piece of paper to map all this out." He made to find some.

Carla reached out and touched his leg in a request to stay. "It's not necessary really. Think of it as three lines of people." She held her hands up and drew in the air. "The top line is Carmen and her siblings. The next line under them is my mother Isabella, Uncle Domingo, Aunt Lucette, Aunt Chantelle and Rafe's father, my Uncle Sancho." She glanced at Aiden, who nodded that he was keeping up with her. "Good. Then under this line, there is a third line, and that includes my four brothers and me, Theresa and Marco, Philippe in Paris who is Aunt Chantelle's son and of course

Rafael. Plus, there's a few more, but telling you about them would only confuse you." She giggled when Aiden rolled his eyes.

"Okay, now that I've got that clear, sort of, what has all this to do with whatever is going on in Granada you can't tell me about?"

"All I can say is my Great Aunt Carmen, who's no longer with us, bless her soul" — Carla made the sign of the cross on her chest — "possessed certain Romani gypsy gifts. Some of her descendants have also inherited these gifts and . . ." She bit her bottom lip.

Aiden's eyes twinkled as his legal mind pieced together a possible outcome. "And, now it's your time to see if you too have inherited these gifts? And the purple pouch is somehow connected to all this?" His showmanship in posing the questions was impressive. She wanted to applaud but remained impassive. While his questions hung between them, Aiden steepled his fingers at his lips obviously delighted with his skills of deduction.

"No. That's not right at all. But it's a good try, even for a corporate lawyer from Australia." Carla laughed and smacked his foot.

Aiden narrowed his eyes and gave her a steely stare. "I don't believe you. However, I'll respect your privacy on the matter. But . . ." — he raised his index finger to his nose — "the time will come when you will tell me."

"And why will I tell you?" She shot him a playful smirk.

The levity of the moment suddenly disappeared. "Because if you don't, I won't be able to protect you and keep my promise to your father."

THE BALMY AFTERNOON HAD come and gone with dusk swooping in to seal the deal. Cheeky clouds now scuttled across the night sky doing their best to play peek-a-boo with the moon. Rafael wanted the moon to lose, so he could remain secreted in the shadows. The only light he enjoyed at night was a spotlight on his face when he performed. Otherwise, he preferred the cloak of darkness to protect his identity. His internal struggle a few hours ago to return to Casa de los ángeles had been brutal. Since a young boy, his father had told him of his destiny with Carla. A destiny he never wanted or believed. He loved Carla, but he didn't want to marry her. *Papa was wrong.* Even with all the stalling he'd done up until now, he'd hoped Carla would've discarded him, like the worthless piece of crap he was. But no. She'd clung to him and their love with a grip so fierce, it would break a man in two. And it'd nearly broken him.

Papa was wrong.

Even marrying Leta hadn't released him from his father's rage or vision. It was never the men who had the gift. It was only the women. If only Aunt Isabella hadn't died when Carla was a young girl, things would be different. Instead of being betrothed to marry her, he'd be free to live his life the way God intended. Soon. Soon he'd be in Granada and there the truth would be revealed. The truth could be told.

Papa was wrong.

The dark alleyway crawled with figures, ducking in and out of doorways. Like him, they too danced with the moonlight, trying to escape its illumination. Dressed in black, smoking cigarettes, slinking along walls, society's misfits littered the narrow passage like homeless dogs. Rafael spied a languid couple and wandered over. He lifted the visor on his helmet and nodded, his dark eyes darting from one to the other. Like dripping filth, their eyes inched down his leather-suited body, resting momentarily on his heavy riding boots before returning to his helmeted face. An appreciative sneer lit the woman's countenance while the other held Rafael's challenging gaze. Without a word, the pair turned, and Rafael followed them into one of his darkest nights.

~ ♥ ~

"Where the hell is he?" Having asked this same question repeatedly over the past hour, Carla was at the end of her patience. She didn't expect Aiden to know where Rafael was, but her frustration, anger, and worry had now broken free of her self-control. Had she worn a *Fitbit*, she would know how many kilometres she'd walked this evening by endlessly pacing around the villa. Up and down the corridor, around the entertainment room, outside in the courtyard, around the pool. She'd even walked a few circuits of the driveway to and from the road, listening for the Ducati. But all to no avail. Rafael hadn't returned for dinner. And although Aiden had done his best to entice her to eat, she'd refused. Her appetite had disappeared, just like Rafe.

"Listen. I'm sure he's okay." Aiden's reassuring tone did little to assuage Carla's madness.

"Really?" Beyond caring, she spat her wrath at Aiden. "If Rafe is so fine then why hasn't he rung? Where is he that's so important, he can't be bothered ringing me to tell me he's safe?" She shrieked — a short, controlled screech. Digging her nails into the palms of her clenched fists, she jumped up and down on the spot. She wanted to lash out. Give Rafe a stinging slap across the face. That's what he deserved. She felt like she was going to explode. *How dare he? How dare he?*

"Carla." Determination rang in Aiden's voice, stopping her fit of outrage.

She cast a distressed look at him. "I'm sorry, Aiden. I shouldn't snap at you. It's just I don't know what to do. He doesn't pick up his phone. I'm sick with worry. Maybe he's had an accident. Or he's in the hospital?" She collapsed like a pile of litter on the floor, her silk caftan fluttering around her.

Joining her, Aiden crossed his legs like a Buddha and patted her knee. "What do you normally do if he takes off and doesn't come back for a few hours?"

"Dance," she said with a pout.

"What do you mean?"

"I dance. I choreograph something new for my flamenco spot. I take all my rage and pour it into the music and usually come up with something I can use in the show."

"Well, why don't you do that then? Don't mind me. I'll leave you alone if you like and you can dance it out." A disarming smile stretched across his face, and her anger began to melt. Aside from being ruggedly handsome with blue eyes that sparkled like chips of ice, Aiden possessed a sincere, generous nature. How could she possibly stay angry when he was doing everything he could to ease her pain?

"Would you like to learn?" she asked.

"What? To dance?" Aiden chuckled. "I'm good at sports, but when it comes to dancing, I've got two left feet." He declined her offer with a shrug.

"Nonsense. If you can balance on a surfboard, you can dance. Come on. I'll show you how to do some easy tango steps." Grabbing his hand, Carla sprang to her feet and heaved Aiden to his.

"Now first you have to hold me the correct way." Full of business, she grabbed his left hand in her right, lifting their elbows high and steady. She reefed his right hand behind her, placing it flat on her back, above her waist. "Now you must hold firm." Carla jiggled, showing him how to hold her tighter. "Remember, as the man, you must lead."

Shifting his weight from one foot to the other, Aiden looked adrift. Carla couldn't help but smile at his discomfort.

"How can I lead if I can't dance?"

Carla clucked her tongue. "Aiden, I'm sure you know how to have sex and be the man? *Si?*"

A big, fat grin brightened his face. "Absolutely."

"Well, tango is like having sex. Except instead of being horizontal, you're vertical. Here. I'll show you." Carla slithered her right leg in between Aiden's, the top of her thigh easing towards his crotch. "Now when we dance tango, we have to remain locked in this position, so we move as one."

"Carla, if I remain locked in this position, I won't be doing any dancing."

She giggled. "Why not?"

"First of all, I can't move, and second, I'd rather be doing the horizontal tango." A half-smile lurked on his face and his eyes twinkled with mischief.

"I see," Carla said in a soft, sultry voice. Tiny tingles raced from her toes, surging to her face in a hot flush. He'd not released his grip on her, nor the intense stare in which he'd trapped her. "Well, Aiden. That is tango. Tango is love. Tango is passion. You must love your partner. You must want to be passionate with your partner." The more she spoke, the slower her speech became. Gazing into his eyes, she recognized he had the requisite love and passion to dance tango. She moistened her lips, noticing how the slight movement with her tongue seemed to mesmerize him. "Let's proceed, shall we?" She tried to direct his attention back to tango.

Not breaking his stance or stare, Aiden said, "I'm ready."

"I'm going to step back on my right foot, and you step forwards on your left. Ready and step . . ." As Carla stepped back, Aiden obeyed with his left. Unsure of the power needed, he pushed too hard, and they stumbled. Quick as lightning, he crushed her in his arms lifting her up before they fell. He found his footing for them both though her feet dangled off the floor. His chest heaved, and she could feel his heart beating as fast as hers. With her arms wrapped around his neck, her face hovered at kissing distance and the yearning she'd disregarded since meeting him, resurfaced with a vengeance.

"Are you all right?" he asked, his masculine breath resting on her lips, making them ache.

"Yes. Thank you," she said, whispering her unspoken permission to be kissed.

"I told you I had two left feet." Aiden still held her firmly in his embrace, seemingly unaware of her weight and unwilling to let go.

Naked under her caftan, Carla felt her nipples harden against his bare chest. Glancing downwards, Aiden moaned. Suspending her in one arm, he slid his other hand to cup her buttocks, dragging her closer onto his body. His hot breath scorched Carla's neck, and she pushed against his cheek like an affectionate cat. With his face tucked into her neck, his breathing deepened like he was trying to suck the life from her. Big heaving breaths tied them together as they caught each other's tempo. Expertly, his supporting hand under her buttocks flexed and contracted, squeezing her arse and made Carla squirm with desire. Unable to stand the insistence of his hand any longer, she crawled onto him, wrapping her legs around his trunk. The thin silk of her caftan did little to conceal the wetness between her legs when her cleft opened onto his bare stomach. "Oh God, Carla," he groaned.

Wrapped like two desperate souls, they clung tight to each other — she like a frightened child reluctant to let go and he the championing hero to her rescue. "Carla."

She shook her head refusing to speak or break the moment. Instead, she ground her hips in seductive circles, tracing her wetness through the silk on his belly. Aiden shuddered. He stretched back and exhaled, releasing her slightly further down his body. Astride his hips, Carla hung suspended from his shoulders with the aid of his sheer strength. Splayed atop his low-slung shorts, she could feel his straining cock driving upwards through his underwear, seeking her out. Spurred on by her growing attraction to the big Australian and the unsatisfactory relationship with Rafael, she lifted her caftan, exposing her quivering snatch. Grinding her hips into him with the force of a tabby on heat, she rubbed her juices over his skin. The residue anger and frustration from Rafe's disappearance finally found an outlet. Rolling and contracting her hips, she clung onto Aiden's broad shoulders and whipped herself into a wanton frenzy, wiping her slickness over his stomach. "Oh God, Carla. If you keep doing that, I'm going to fuck you."

"That's the point, Aiden. I want you to fuck me." She wiggled down onto the head of Aiden's cock and dismounted. Facing off, neither of them moved. Not a sound could be heard above their ragged, heavy breathing. Everything came to a standstill.

Aiden pulled his shoulders back and locked her with a determined stare. "I'm not going to fuck you, Carla. Not like this. It isn't right."

Deflated, she blinked in amazement. "But, Aiden . . ."

Before she could finish, he stepped in and cupped her face in his hands. The power and gentleness of his touch quietened her distress instantly.

"But I will kiss you." Bending down, his mouth sought hers and she surrendered to his warm, wet caress, welcoming his tongue. As if lost but now found, their mouths possessed each other with deep, sensuous affection. She gave in to his passion, to be led in an exquisite dance of love, falling deeper and deeper into him. The more she yielded, the more Aiden freed her — like a magician releasing an apprentice from his spell. Pulling back, he traced her pulsing lips with his thumb. She whimpered, unhappy to be released from this magic. His blue eyes though glazed and dilated penetrated her carnal stupor. Cool and calm he said, "We have a problem, Carla."

She nodded dutifully unable to speak.

"It seems we both have feelings for each other. Not just lustful fantasies but deeper feelings."

She nodded.

"Taking everything into consideration, I think the best course of action is for us both to go to bed now."

Again, she nodded, though more vigorously, eager to get the lovemaking started.

"No. Not to have sex. Go to bed alone and see what tomorrow holds. Yes?" He reached out and held her chin, lifting her face.

Carla nodded in reluctant obedience. "Will you tuck me in?"

Aiden chuckled softly. "I'd love to tuck you in, but that's not going to happen tonight. Now off you go. I'm sure Rafe will be home soon. If he's not back in an hour, I'll call the police and the hospitals. Don't you worry about it. You get some sleep. Okay?"

"Thank you, Aiden." She stretched up and kissed him on both cheeks, lingering on the second for a final smell of his aftershave mingled with his masculine musk. "You really are a champion, aren't you?"

"Don't be silly. Now off to bed before I change my mind. Go."

Carla pouted, turned and drifted down to her bedroom.

~ ♥ ~

THERE WAS NO WAY in hell Aiden could contain himself any longer. Carla unravelled him. His emotions churned, his head spun, his heart rate jumped to about 160 beats per minute, and the excruciating ache in his groin needed attention. Standing sentinel for another hour had been a stroke of genius and it worked. Except now all he could smell was Carla's sexual lust wafting up from his stomach, making an enemy of his cock. Needing to bathe in case Rafe turned up, Aiden strode to his bedroom. He closed the door softly so as not to disturb Carla, who he hoped would stay put and not venture into his room. If she did, there'd be no going back this time. He had only one good intention per night, and he'd used that already. He slumped on the bed, head in hands. Now with his face inclined toward his stomach, her sweet smell enveloped him, seduced him. He breathed her in, unzipped his shorts and freed his groaning cock. Licking his finger, he swiped it across his belly and tasted her. As he suspected, she was sweet, clean and moreish. He took another taste and then another. Within moments, his lips and tongue were coated in her juice, and he lay back on the bed. Closing his eyes, he visualized his sweet Carla and her delicious wet snatch. Although he'd not seen her private beauty this evening, he pictured what it would look like. Tight, full lips stretched over an apple-shaped pelvic mound. A fully waxed mons with the neatest slit exposing nothing of the delights within. He rolled his tongue around in his mouth and licked his lips. Tugging slowly at his cock, he allowed the fantasy to satisfy him. Sweet Carla opening her fleshy folds for him, dripping for him, rubbing her clit, teasing him, grinding herself on his face, calling out his name. While his mouth watered, longing to taste her, to fuck her, he yanked his cock more savagely. Rigidity crawled through his body as he imagined Carla's smiling face looking at him. "I love you, Aiden. I love you." The sound of beating flesh echoed in his bedroom and he gasped for breath. And when a low growl escaped his throat, he ejaculated thick and fierce over his belly and chest. Relief. At last.

Aiden rested for a moment, enjoying the afterglow before he heaved a satisfied sigh and rose to clean up. The only disadvantage with wanking off tonight was that his pleasure had covered all of Carla's longing she'd left on his stomach. The scent of her yearning was gone. Standing at the basin sponging himself, he considered the delicate balance at play between the three of them. He'd not come to Spain to fall in love or ruin another couple's relationship. More trouble wasn't what he wanted or needed right now. But Carla had unexpectedly stolen his heart adding a whole new complexity to his life. Deciding on a cautious approach, he planned to not be left alone with Carla until they drove to Granada. *Maybe she'd even ride pillion with Rafael for that trip?* Regardless, keeping his distance would allow him to regroup and consider the most effective plan of action. Getting himself caught in a three-way love affair clouded everything. He needed time to think. But as he wandered back to the living room to wait for Rafe, a persistent thought from law school dogged him. *The best-laid plans of mice and men often go awry . . .*

AT ONCE ELATED AND disappointed, Carla jumped onto her bed and scrunched some pillows into her body. If Aiden hadn't been the gentleman and said no to her advances, they'd now be fucking themselves stupid. And that's exactly what she'd wanted and still wanted. Her once well-ordered, predictable and at times miserable life spun out of control. Instead, hope and happiness filled her heart. An enormous grin covered her face, and she rocked gleefully on the bed. She was in love — a young, giddy, unstoppable love that danced around her like joyous Spring sprites. Relishing the fever and optimism of brand-new passion, she closed her eyes and soaked up the bliss for a few moments. But like portends of doom, a dark thought steadily manifested on her periphery, creeping tenaciously towards her — Rafael. What was she going to do about Rafael? How could she possibly break off their relationship to be with Aiden without jeopardizing both their dance careers? Rafael would be unforgiving and furious. They'd worked too hard to get this far and to lose it all because she'd fallen in love with Aiden. The more she thought about the situation, the bigger the sacrifice became. Yet what if she decided to stay with Rafael? Give up loving Aiden to remain in an unsatisfactory personal relationship with Rafe just to preserve her professional status, financial security and save face was flawed decision making. Unsatisfied, she mused over both options and her initial exhilaration when entering her bedroom quickly disappeared.

She needed her mother. Mama would tell her what to do. Carla missed her mother so much and so often, but she never spoke to anyone about the emptiness left inside from her mother's death. Carla closed her eyes and crushed the pillows under her chin. *Mama. I miss you. Mama. I need you.* Isabella's soft-hearted smile, classically beautiful face with raven black hair and unusual grey eyes fluttered onto the screen in Carla's mind. Since her mother's death nearly twenty years ago, Carla had never forgotten her mother's loveliness and recalled it often to comfort her when life threatened to overwhelm.

"Now, Carla." Isabella's gentle voice echoed in Carla's head. She'd been hearing her mother's voice for many years, mainly with words of reassurance. That she could do this seemed perfectly natural to Carla and since she'd never discussed it with anyone else, she believed other people might also hear the dead. Although never receiving any clear instructions or answers to the many questions she'd asked, Carla had heard her mother's words of love and encouragement which sustained her, persuading her to never give up.

"It's time, Carla." Carla's eyelids snapped open, and she looked around the bedroom, convinced someone was there. Never had her mother's voice sounded so clear or loud. A slight chill prickled Carla's skin as a wisp of air brushed past her. *"The runes, Carla."* Insistent and crisp, Isabella's voice echoed in the room. Carla sprang to her feet and tried to dash from one corner on the bed to the other, searching. For what, she didn't know. Maybe the ghost of her dead mother. With

pillows still clutched to her chest, she leapt off the bed and retreating from the room, backed into the chest of drawers.

"*Mierda*," she swore and rubbed her Achilles, which collided with the foot of the bureau. The chest teetered awkwardly, and when the lower drawer slid open, her mother's plush purple pouch caught Carla's attention.

When she lifted it from its hiding place, an eerie chill tingled the back of her neck. Undeterred, she returned to sit cross-legged on the bed and stared at the pouch, velvety and warm in her hands. Her mother's fragrance wafted past her and unconsciously Carla turned in its direction, inhaling deeply. She upended the pouch and nine small flat river stones tumbled from their long hibernation onto the quilt. Inscribed on each grey stone was a different mark, signifying a specific meaning. Carla had never read the runes before, but as a young girl, she'd witnessed her mother give readings to friends and family. Mama had told her these were sacred Gypsy runes, passed down from generation to generation. Only those descendants from Carmen Amaya and before her had touched them. And only those with the gift could read them. Carla shivered with excitement and trepidation. She wasn't supposed to touch them until Granada, but her mother had just communicated differently. Scattered like precious gems, the runes called for her to begin. But how could she begin since she didn't even know if she had the gift?

Once more, Isabella's voice resonated in Carla's mind. "*Trust, mi querida.*"

Summoning up her courage, Carla gathered the stones in her hands. Smooth and slippery to the touch, they clinked together when she rolled them around and around. She separated each stone and rubbed it between her fingers and thumb, concentrating on its coolness and the symbol engraved on its side. After acquainting herself with each rune, she bundled them together, clasping them to her heart. *Help me, Mama. Show me.*

She shook the handful of small ancestral treasures then released them to spill on the bed. Only those whose markings landed upwards held the message. Looking down at the scattering of stones, Carla cast her memory back to her childhood years when her mother told her the meaning of each rune. As she concentrated on the four stones whose symbol remained face-up, Carla pieced together the message sprawling on her quilt. The sickle symbolized a breakup, a death, an ending, perhaps even tragic. She mused this might mean her relationship with Rafael was going to break up. The moving stone represented journeys. This seemed obvious since she was currently on holidays motoring around Andalusia. But she had a dim recollection the waves etched into the rune indicated something moving on, a constant flow. *Maybe it had something to do with the ocean, Aiden's surfing and Rafael's near drowning?*

A deep frown knitted her brow as she struggled with the interpretation. Shifting her attention, she studied the inspiration rune etched with birds. This one she remembered well from watching her mother. It always appeared as prophesy of new events — someone soon to be pregnant, a new project or idea about to manifest, and it always meant success and good luck. Her mother had foretold many new, unexpected family additions when this rune appeared in her readings. Although desperate to have a baby, Carla knew she wasn't pregnant. She was a fanatic with her birth control, and she felt certain the rune wasn't revealing a familial message.

The final rune staring back at her was the all-seeing eye. This rune her mother had spent much time explaining to Carla. It related to a person's third eye, their intuition, and its message was to pay attention to their gut instinct. On her death bed, Isabella had cautioned Carla to always listen to her intuition, to act on her inner urgings and not overthink things. Now casting her gaze over the four runes, Carla tried to listen to her intuition and not overthink the runes combined message — ending, flowing, beginning and feeling. All she came up with was a sense of peace and enveloping tiredness. *Not very helpful* she thought, considering her current situation with Rafael and Aiden. *Where were the answers? What was she to do?*

A long yawn escaped her mouth and unable to keep her eyelids open, she decided sleep was the best medicine for her emotional quandary. She scooped the stones up and dropped them one by one back into the pouch. Slipping off the bed, she drew the string tight and laid the pouch reverently back in the bottom drawer of the bureau. Pulling her caftan overhead, she was naked before she turned down the covers. Into the crisp, cool sheets she slipped without a thought to distract her. As her head snuggled into the feather pillow, she realized she'd left the light on, but before she could remedy its brightness, she was asleep.

CHAPTER NINE

AIDEN GRIMACED AT THE sound of Carla's piercing scream bouncing off the soaring cliffs and echoing in cavernous rock crevasses in the canyon. Though it ignited his protective instincts, tearing a little piece of his heart loose, he knew her panic would be short-lived. The shock would be over soon. He and Rafael stood on the rock ledge watching her spear into the water feet first, disappearing like an arrow into its murky depths. Aiden wanted to jump in after her, but he waited, holding his breath until she bobbed back to the surface, safe and sound.

"Your turn." With a taunting grin, Rafael clapped Aiden on his wet-suited shoulder and nodded towards the drop.

"Too right." Eager for the thrill, Aiden broached the lip of the ledge, folded his arms across his chest and leapt into the air, clearing the ledge easily. Within a few moments, he plummeted the ten metres into the black swimming hole, barrelling deep into its freezing waters. Resurfacing, he bobbed up spraying water from his mouth and stroked over to join Carla, who'd climbed onto a nearby rock.

"Are you enjoying yourself?" he asked, face beaming as he scaled up beside her.

"Yes, I guess so. That jump certainly got my adrenaline going." She readjusted the safety helmet on her head, tightened the strap and cinched the buckle. "Except this type of activity is so out of character for Rafael. That he booked a private canyoning excursion for us, cooked breakfast and organized us to be here, suited and kitted up, just astounds me." Carla's big, brown eyes blinked at Aiden. "It's all so weird." She turned her gaze up to Rafael on the opposite cliff. "And he's jumping into unknown water. I just don't get it." She shook her head as Rafael stepped to the launch position above them, closed his eyes readying himself and leapt.

"He's definitely a hard one to read is our Rafe." Aiden watched Rafael hurtle downwards into the water. "I didn't hear him come home last night so he must have pushed the Ducati down the drive. I'd gone to bed after getting nowhere with the police or the hospitals. Did you hear him at all?"

"Nothing. I was in a deep sleep."

"Did he say where he was?"

"No. And I didn't ask. Just seeing him smiling and fussing around this morning in the kitchen was enough for me. How do you say? Let sleeping dogs lie. I've not said anything."

In no time Rafe swam up to them, a big, boyish grin on his face. "Now we slide down the waterfalls and swim through the canyons. Let's go."

Rafael clambered out of the pool, got to his feet and followed their guide leader, Teo, an impressive young man with a no-nonsense attitude. Rigged with repelling gear jangling on their hip belts, sure-gripped canyoning boots, full wetsuits and harnesses, they set off. Wet and squelching, Rafael, Carla and Aiden trekked after Teo whose strong, sure-legged strides set the pace, stepping across uneven rocks.

The second support guide, Rosa brought up the rear. Capable, powerful and watchful, she wasn't a pretty woman but possessed masculine features and strong upper body strength which made her highly suitable for her work. Like obedient ducklings, they single-filed behind Teo as they scrambled across jagged boulders and squeezed through tight fissures. Aiden purposely followed Carla. If she stumbled, he'd be there to catch her.

On purpose, he'd not mentioned their intimate episode last night. Neither had she broached the subject. It seemed she wanted to let all the sleeping dogs lie, including their feelings for each other. Rafael's change of character today served to dampen last night's heated sexual exchange, giving him, and Carla it seemed, time to reassess the situation. Regardless, Aiden knew his feelings towards Carla hadn't changed. She still unravelled him, but it'd be up to her to make a move. He didn't want to be culpable in the break-up of her and Rafael.

With limited opportunities to converse due to the concentration needed to remain upright and unhurt, they marched gingerly over the rocky terrain. Enormous escarpments of sheared grey stone seemed to swallow them up as they ventured further and further into the unknown. Created over centuries by the force of the Guadalmina River, the canyons' impenetrability appeared absolute, except to Teo, who forged forwards. Coming to another cliff face, he stopped. "Now we'll rig up and repel down to the pool below. Rosa, help everyone with their ropes while I go down."

Rosa moved forwards to Rafael first. While Carla admired the scenery, Aiden watched Rosa help Rafe with his harness and ropes. Ashen-faced, Rafael allowed Rosa to sort his equipment. *He's faking all this*, Aiden thought. *He's terrified.* Although Aiden couldn't hear what Rosa was whispering to Rafael, he did notice the effect it had on him. A grim smile set on Rafael's face and he nodded his head unquestioningly, allowing her to man-handle him. Just before Aiden averted his eyes to allow Rosa privacy to motivate Rafael further, he froze. Rosa's hand slid over Rafael's crotch, squeezing hard while she hissed something into his ear. Wild mania shone in Rafael's eyes as his tongue skirted his lips. Snapping his head, Aiden looked for Carla. Luckily, she'd not seen any of this. Aiden dragged a hand over his mouth.

What the fuck is going on here? And who the fuck is Rosa?

"Come on, Rafe, let's go." Teo's command erupted from beneath the cliff, drawing everyone's attention to the pool below where he stood waiting. Reversing to the edge, Rafael trusted his weight to the ropes and began the slow, heart-racing repel down the cliff. His glazed eyes fixed on Rosa whose lips twisted into a taut grimace.

"Are you okay, Rafe?" Carla called to him, concern in her voice.

"Yes. Yes," came Rafael's unconvincing reply.

The wild excitement Aiden had seen in Rafael's eyes only moments before had been replaced by a fearful vacancy, but there was no turning back. The other thing Aiden noticed was

Teo had called him Rafe. Knowing only those Rafael accepted into his inner circle called him Rafe, Aiden realized Teo, Rosa and Rafe were well acquainted before today's excursion. With no time to contemplate this further, Aiden shifted his focus to safety matters. Having repelled many times before, he organized his own ropes and harness while watching Rosa prepare Carla.

"Here let me help you," he offered and checked Carla's rig, while Rosa stepped away with a sideways glance at Aiden. Concern flittered in his mind while his expert hands slipped over every clip and connection ensuring all was safe and secure. "Have you repelled before?"

"No," Carla said a little shaky.

"You'll be fine. It's easy. Just don't look down. I'll stand on the edge, and you just keep looking at me. Before you know it, your feet will touch the bottom. Now off you go." Without wasting a moment, Aiden walked to the edge with Carla and called out to Teo. "Carla's on her way."

Teo gave a shout and a thumbs-up and he began to take Carla's weight below.

Carla stared wide-eyed at Aiden, her lips pursed shut. With a determined nod, she began to inch backwards. As she lowered herself, Aiden's eyes locked onto hers. With firm reassurance, he said, "Keep looking at me, Carla. Ignore your sweaty hands, ignore how fast your heart is beating, ignore the fear in your gut. Repelling is just like tango." Aiden shot her a killer smile hoping she'd remember what she'd told him last night about tango. By the sparkle flickering in her eyes and her cautious smile, Aiden knew his comparison had hit the mark. "All you have to do is keep putting one foot after the other. It's about staying horizontal although you're going down a vertical cliff." She nodded in acknowledgment of his implied message. Leaning forwards, Aiden watched while her confidence grew and with quickening steps, she touched down. Sporting an enormous smile, she waved up at him.

Without a word, Aiden turned and repelled down the cliff in double-time as did Rosa after him.

Aiden hit the bottom, unclipped and turned to Carla and Rafael. "Well done you two. You'll be action heroes in no time."

"Once I got used to it, it was more fun than I thought. I'm sure, next time, I'd enjoy it more." Carla grinned from ear to ear.

"Yeah. I prefer this to the board riding. At least I'm tied in with ropes and can't drift off and drown," Rafael said, hooking his gear into his belt.

"Okay, everyone. Follow me," Teo called before striding off to the next adventure.

Soon they were sliding down mini waterfalls, slipping from one small pool to another until at last, they arrived at a massive swimming hole inside the gorge. Surrounded by rock carved from the river's ferocious journey over time, the group listed in the clear, pristine water.

Gently treading water, Carla gazed at the cavernous ceiling above. "This is amazing." Mauve, aubergine and claret hues etched spidery veins through the grey rock, tracing centuries of change — a vast sculpture of earth, travelling through time. And like pit-stops along the way, occasional sparkles of crystal glimmered when the light polished them on just the right angle. "They look like little stars twinkling in the sky." She pointed upwards.

"Yes. Nature at its best." Aiden floated on his back, admiring the spectacle above him.

Rafael swam over to join them. "I thought you'd like it, Ace. It shows you a different side to Andalusia. Only a handful of kilometres from the coast and this is what you get."

"How did you find out about this?" Aiden asked keeping his tone casual.

"Oh, I met Teo and Rosa last night in town. We got talking, and when they told me they were canyoning tour guides, I thought it'd be a good surprise. Particularly for you, Ace, since you love these types of action sports."

"I do. But I'm surprised you'd even think about doing this type of thing . . ." Aiden waited, curious for Rafael's response.

"Rosa convinced me that if I didn't start taking calculated risks, my life would simply slip through my fingers. I'd end up dying an unhappy man." Rafael cast a grateful glance at Teo and Rosa, who lingered on the edge of the conversation.

"Well I think Rosa's right," Carla said, loud enough for Rosa to hear. "It's good to see you happy, Rafe, and doing things you wouldn't normally do. It keeps the juices flowing."

Rosa and Teo nodded in agreement. "Yes, living life fully is the greatest action sport of all," Teo said, his dark eyes taking them all in. "Now let's swim through this part of the gorge. It's the most beautiful. There are lots of boulders underfoot so be careful." Setting off through the narrowing gorge, they fell in line, once more assuming their previous single file positions.

Look after my daughter, keep her safe and make sure you tell her the truth. You understand? Carla's father's words swam in Aiden's mind with each stroke he took. Keeping Carla safe was the easy part. Telling her the truth was proving more difficult. There was only one truth Aiden knew for certain. And that was how he felt about Carla and his conviction to protect her. Until he could work out what was going on, he decided to keep the incident he'd witnessed between Rosa and Rafael to himself.

~ ♥ ~

Wanting to sear the image into his memory for all time, Aiden stood spellbound. At the end of the corridor and dressed in a short, black skin-tight dress with deadly black patent silhouettes, Carla oozed sex appeal. Although not the voluptuous, buxom Spanish woman, her elegance and style outstripped the stereotype. With her black, glossy hair drifting in soft curls around her shoulders, smoky eye makeup, and red wine lips, she looked every bit the fashionista. She all but luminesced like a guiding star. Aiden's cock stirred in his jeans, restless to explore her warmth. But since that wasn't going to happen, he instead gave a slow, appreciative whistle as Carla tip-tapped up the corridor towards him.

"Wow," he said, feeling much like a cartoon character trying to reel in his lolling tongue.

"Thank you." The twinkle in her eyes telegraphed she found his inability to control his drooling, pleasing. "Rafe's nearly ready."

"Good. Let's wait outside where it's cooler." Since he couldn't lave Carla's body with his tongue, Aiden curled it back in where it belonged.

Under the moonlight and with Carla's perfume swirling around him, Aiden longed to take her in his arms. To crush her in an intimate embrace. Pledge his love for her, take her away and care for her. But unable to offer her any of this, he said, "So what do you think of Rosa and Teo?" He speared his fingers through his shaggy hair, flicking it from his collar. Since being on holiday, he'd allowed his hair to grow and enjoyed the freedom this rebellious act afforded him. Instead of the business hairstyle he'd arrived in Spain with, his hair now resembled an unruly mop of wild, flaxen wheat, its natural curl brushing his neck.

"They seem nice enough I guess." Carla fidgeted with a bougainvillea blossom. "What do you think?" She glanced over at him, a thoughtful expression on her face.

"I'm not sure. They both seem a little strange to me. She hardly says a word and Teo reminds me of a bloke I once knew in Australia. We call them dark horses."

"What does that mean?"

"They pretend to be someone they're not."

Before Carla spoke, Rafael joined them, helmet in hand. "Okay. I've locked up. You follow me. I know where the club is. We're meeting Teo and Rosa there." He strode to the bike, lashed on his helmet and started the engine.

Aiden helped Carla into the Ferrari, admiring her smooth tanned legs when she spun them into the passenger hub. He jumped in and started the car. "Well, I guess we'll find out more about Teo and Rosa tonight," he said with a wink to Carla. The thunder of the Ducati and Ferarri drowned out her response but did little to assuage his curiosity.

~ ♥ ~

For Rafael, today had been a good day — in fact, a great day. His whole body tingled with aliveness and freedom. The exhilaration of last night and canyoning today spurred him on, and he gunned the Ducati down a small stretch of road. Liberated was how he felt. Meeting Teo and Rosa had liberated him. He wanted to share this liberation with Carla and Ace. Carla — talented, beautiful, sensuous Carla. Shifting his weight, Rafael angled into the corners, lying his bike low into the camber. The Ducati thrummed under his body, matching the intensity in his groin. Every time he straightened the bike, he thought of Ace. Smart, reliable and strong. Ace was a thrill-seeker who also wanted to live life to the fullest, but Rafael suspected Ace wasn't seeking thrills the same way as him. He threw the Ducati into another chicane, swerving right, left and right, his mind going from Carla to Aiden with each manoeuvre. He was looking forward to tonight. Fun, he needed more fun.

When he came to the edge of town, he depressed the brakes and reduced speed. People stopped and stared at him as he cruised past. *The black horseman of the Apocalypse,* he thought, *that's who I am.* His insatiable appetite unleashed.

Rafael parked, dismounted and removed his helmet. Throwing his head back in one dramatic move, he shook out his thick black mane of hair and sensed passers-by appraising him, whispering of his magnificence. A broad self-satisfied grin graced his face as he strode to meet Carla and Ace.

~ ♥ ~

Escorted by two handsome men either side of her, Carla felt particularly pretty. Neither she nor Rafe reached for each other's hand which wasn't unusual. Sometimes he preferred not to hold hands in public and tonight was one such occasion. For the first time, Carla didn't take this as a sign of rejection but enjoyed not being conjoined to him. After last night with Aiden and the runes reading, being independent of any man's influence was exactly what Carla wanted — no, needed.

The club groaned with locals and holidaymakers alike. Much larger than Sevilla Flamenco, this place was a hybrid of a traditional flamenco *peñas* and a sexy modern nightclub. As usual, Rafael took the lead and weaved through the milling crowds to a reserved table in front of the stage. Teo and Rosa hadn't arrived. "What do you want to drink?" Rafe asked.

"Just a Corona." Aiden pulled out a chair for Carla.

"Me too," she said, sitting down. "Looks like they do shows as well." She nodded to the two dancers on the stage. Dressed in tight black and white striped G-string leotards, the two female dancers gyrated and pulsed seductively. With fleshy breasts thrusting from the low-cut necklines and well-rounded bottoms on display, the dancers played to the audience with gusto. Their attempt at a nautical theme seemed obvious by their lower legs covered in knee-high white socks atop red skyscraper stilettos, topped off with white sailor caps and red scarves knotted at their throats and waists. Both girls' buttocks bore brightly coloured tattoos of gigantic roses which stretched and contracted when they moved. Every now and then, the girls reversed to the audience and folded forwards, thrusting their cheeky flowers at the men seated closest to the stage's edge. The crowd went wild when they exposed their painted blossoms while the men in the front row salivated like Pavlov's dogs.

Carla glanced at Aiden, who sat grinning like a loon watching the girls strut their stuff. "You like?" she said, trying to control the slight jealousy in her voice.

"Oh yes. These girls are something." His eyes hadn't left the stage.

"Is this the dancing they do in Australia?"

"Pretty much." Aiden turned to Carla and his expression changed. "However, I'd much prefer to watch you dance flamenco." He winked at her, and she melted. She so hoped last night was not just a moment of raw passion for him either.

"Really?" She needed to be sure.

"Absolutely." The intensity in his voice seemed to confirm the truth as did the sincerity in his eyes.

Relief washed over her.

"Here you go . . ." Rafael set down the bottles and pulled in a chair next to Carla's. He raised his glass for a toast. "To us."

"To us," Carla and Aiden agreed, holding their bottles on high.

"Sorry we're late," Teo said, as he and Rosa dragged out chairs and sat down.

After polite "hellos," Carla left the conversation and pondered on Aiden's earlier question. *What did she think of Teo and Rosa?* Until now, they'd been their canyoning guides and she'd not given them much thought. But as they sat chatting animatedly to Rafe, like old pals, Carla began to wonder. *A dark horse* was what Aiden had said about Teo — someone who isn't who he appears to be. With his wide grin and fresh, open face, Teo seemed a likable sort of guy. Maybe a bit overbearing, but Carla thought that was a trait most Spanish men proudly owned. Casually dressed in jeans and a T-shirt, he was just an average type of guy. Whereas Rosa was most definitely not average. With her short, spiky hair tipped in purple, Rosa made a statement, as did her clothing. Her tight jeans strained to hold her burgeoning legs and a white cotton singlet stretched across her muscular torso which she topped with a tan suede vest. A rugged woman, Rosa was more butch than feminine. Carla was pleased she didn't sit next to her because she doubted she'd know what to talk about. Anyway, Rosa seemed far more comfortable talking to the men.

"I'LL GET THE NEXT round of drinks? Coronas all round?" Aiden stood and on everyone's acceptance made his way to the bar. He weaved through the throng and before heading to the bar, he took a detour to the toilets. Spying the neon sign, he made his way towards an outer wall of the club. Just as a waiter passed him, he stepped back and realized he'd bumped into someone.

"Sorry," he said, half turning to the person he'd knocked.

With the crowd at his back and Aiden blocking his escape forward, the man froze, an awkward expression on his face.

"Hey, you're the guy who was hanging around at El Palmar the other day."

Down casting his eyes, the man didn't respond.

"It is you. What the fuck are you doing, man? Why are you following us?" Heat flashed across Aiden's face as he stood opposite the stranger. His muscles twitched, readying for a showdown.

Again, the bloke said nothing.

"Listen, man, you need to talk to me quick smart, or I'm going to lose my patience. Who the fuck are you?" Aiden's voice rose just enough to alert the nearby crowd of something unpleasant about to happen. Their attention triggered the stranger into action.

"Please follow me, Aiden." He made a beeline to the men's room with Aiden hot on his heels. Inside the toilets, the stranger waited for the other men to leave then locked the door behind them. He turned to Aiden and offered his hand. "I'm Estéban Armando, the eldest of Carla's brothers. Papa sent me to watch out for Carla."

Aiden refused his handshake. "Prove it."

Fishing out his wallet, Estéban produced his driver's license which Aiden scrutinized closely. It confirmed the Spaniard's identity.

"But what the fuck are you doing? I told your father I'd look after her."

"I know, but Papa is very worried about her." He opened his hands in submission and shrugged. "I do what Papa tells me."

"But what is he so worried about that he has you tailing us wherever we go? I saw you down at the beach, and since you're here now, you've obviously been watching Carla all this time." Aiden gave a silent prayer of thanks for the fence of olive trees around the villa. If Estéban has been lurking around the villa, the last thing Aiden wanted was for him to report back to his father about the hot and sweaty interlude between Carla and him last night in the living room.

"Papa doesn't trust Rafael." The bitterness in Estéban's voice matched what Aiden had heard in Manolo's when he'd spoken of Rafael.

"Yeah, I figured that, but why?"

"He thinks he has secrets, and he wants to know what they are." A muscle in Estéban's jaw twitched.

"But what secrets does your father think Rafael's hiding?"

"He doesn't know. He just wants me to find out."

"God." Aiden smacked his brow. "You Spanish men with your overprotective natures. It's crazy shit. I get how you feel, but Carla is a grown woman. I'm sure she can look after herself, and I promised your father I'd keep an eye on her. He doesn't need you here as well." Aiden's patience was wearing thin with all this cloak and dagger stuff.

"Papa knows that. So, when she's been with you, I've been tailing Rafael."

This was good news to Aiden. At least Rafael has been the main target for surveillance and not him. "And?"

"When he went out on his bike last night, he went to a very bad part of town." A flicker of disgust edged Estéban's face.

"What part?"

"Where you pick up prostitutes and people with strange persuasions." His previous flicker of disgust grew to unconcealed, full-blown revulsion.

"And? What did you see?"

"Nothing. I saw him walk into the alley, but I lost him in the shadows."

"For goodness sake." Aiden's shoulders slumped in disappointment. "That's it? Listen, Estéban, I'm a lawyer. Unless you have evidence of wrongdoing, supposing something is going on, means nothing. There are any number of reasons Rafe walked through that part of town. Maybe he gets his jollies off looking at the women. I don't know. But I think your father needs to butt out. If Carla finds out you and he are playing detective, she'll have nothing to do with you ever again. Got it?"

Estéban nodded in reluctant agreement.

"I'll tell you what I'll do. I'll see if I can get to the bottom of this secret, whatever it is, and I'll make sure I let Manolo know. Okay? Give me his phone number and I'll call him the moment I find out anything."

With loud voices demanding to be let in, Aiden typed Manolo's number into his phone while Estéban unlocked the door. Lots of raised eyebrows and cock-sucking gestures intimated what the other men thought Aiden and Estéban had been doing to each other in the toilets. A fierce glare from Aiden stopped their sarcastic antics, and he pushed Estéban out the door in front of him.

Back in the club, Aiden said, "Now get out of here without being seen by Carla or Rafael. You're so bad at this tailing business, you're sure to be blown sooner rather than later. Tell your father I'm on the case." Aiden gave Estéban his business card to give to Manolo. "I'll let him know if I find out anything."

With a sharp nod of his head, Estéban snapped a turn and drifted into the crowd. Aiden could only hope the young man did as instructed. This holiday was turning into anything but relaxing. He'd left Australia to get away from intrigue and danger. Yet Aiden felt he'd landed smack bang in the middle of more. Ambling to the bar, he realized he could no longer sit back and wait this out. He needed to push Rafael to find out what was going on. *Who were Teo and Rosa? And what hold did they have over Rafe?*

Aiden returned juggling the beers. "Where's Carla?"

"You'll see," Teo said.

Aiden glanced over to Rafe for more information except he resembled a storm cloud. His expression telegraphed something of major proportions had taken place in his absence. Concern prickled his skin. "What's wrong? What happened, Rafe?"

"The manager recognized Carla and asked her to dance flamenco, and she accepted." Rafael sounded outraged. "She shouldn't be dancing without payment. It's not good for our careers." He swallowed a large mouthful of his fresh beer.

"I'm sure doing one little performance won't have a major impact. Maybe you should join her and do tango?" Aiden said, hoping to ease the tension.

Rafael simply glared his answer and returned stony-faced to the stage. Teo and Rosa shrugged and turned their attention likewise. For Aiden, it was a windfall. He longed to see Carla dance again, but he wondered what she'd wear since she had no costume. She couldn't possibly dance flamenco in that short dress. No sooner had the thought crossed his mind than an amplified voice filled the club.

"Ladies and gentlemen, we are proud to present our special surprise guest, the famous Miss Carla Armando."

Applause resounded as the recorded sound of a single acoustic guitar filled the venue. A hush fell, and Carla strode onto the small stage. She still wore her short black dress and killer high heels but around her body she'd tied a red fringed shawl which fell like a gypsy skirt, fluttering at her knees. Coiled high on her head, her glossy hair was pinned with an assortment of red and black roses. In her hand, she held closed a massive white fan and her face beamed with elation. Aiden's heart filled with admiration, and he leaned back ready for the entertainment.

With her opening pose, Carla commanded everyone's attention and the room held its breath. Delicate and powerful, she remained still with one hand ruching up a small section of the shawl and the other clasping the fan by her side. The moment the flamenco guitarist brought his instrument to life, Carla lifted and twirled one arm overhead and then the other. Snap! She opened the fan, and the magic began. With each deliberate and calculated step, she danced across the stage never faltering. Her lithe body with its amazing arched back and flexible waist moved like a snake being charmed. Instead of a surly expression, her demeanour was one of sheer joy and pleasure. Turning this way and that, lifting one shoulder and then the other, Carla seemed to dance at once for herself and for the audience. The fan became an extension of her body, and she crafted intricate continuous shapes with it, like an artist endlessly stroking her brush to create a masterpiece. The bright, happy melody had Aiden bobbing his head along with the music as he remained riveted on every move she performed. Smiling, he recalled how when they first met, he'd thought she was beautiful, dangerously so and how right he'd been. No grinding hips or half-naked body needed for Carla Armando to get the attention of everyone in the room. She was dance incarnate. When she slowed to take her final pose with the fan opened, suspended above her head, the applause and cheering boomed before she'd finished.

Aiden cast a quick sideways glance at Rafael. Though obviously still miffed at her agreeing to dance, he couldn't hide his respect for her talent and performance. Clapping loudly, he rose to his feet yelling, *"Olé"* as did Teo and Rosa. Aiden added to the enthusiastic applause with a couple of shrill whistles. Bursting with delight, Carla took her bows and left the stage. The music style sped forwards a few hundred years and the venue pulsed its modern persona once more.

Carla returned to the table within moments. Her tousled hair fell over her shoulders in big, bouncing waves and the flush on her face from dancing, added an enticing glow to her skin. All Aiden wanted to do was kiss her on a magnificent performance. Instead, he stood by politely. "That's was terrific, Carla."

"Muchas gracias, Aiden." She tilted her head and cast him a coy smile.

Rafael encircled her in his arms. *"Mi pequeña luciérnaga,* you were wonderful as always." He kissed her on both cheeks and hugged her close. Aiden realized the love of dance and their professional partnership joined Rafael and Carla together in what seemed an unbreakable bond, despite the difficulties in their personal life.

"Really, Rafe? Are you sure it was all right? I felt in the middle eight I may have lost a step . . ."

"Nonsense. You were perfect." Rafael pulled out the chair for her and together they sat doing a quick post-mortem on her performance. Rosa returned a few minutes later with another round of drinks which were quickly consumed while Carla accepted more congratulations on her performance.

"It's time we all danced." Teo grabbed Rosa and hauled her towards the dance floor.

Rafael rose to his feet and offered Carla his hand. "Come dance with me."

"But what about, Aiden?" she said, with a steady glance in his direction.

"Hey, don't worry about me. As I said yesterday, I'm not big on dancing. You two go and show everyone how it's done." He waved them away and busied himself with a slug of beer.

After they disappeared into the pulsating crowd, Aiden stood and wandered around to watch unobtrusively. Rafael and Carla joined Teo and Rosa and the four of them cut loose. Edging closer to their position on the floor, Aiden grooved alone trying to fit in. But his eyes never left the interplay between Rafael, Rosa, and Teo. Subtle and calculated, the exchange of looks was unmistakable. These three had some connection and the covert display of sexuality between them whenever Carla turned her back on them, irritated him. Either they'd shared some sort of intimacy or were on the brink of doing so. Regardless, Aiden decided it was time to call it quits for the night.

Back at the table on their return, Aiden said, "I'm buggered from all that canyoning today so I'm off home. Are you coming with me, Carla?"

A look of surprise flitted briefly across her face. "Ah, yes. Sure."

Not allowing for further conversation, Aiden turned to Teo and Rosa. "Okay then. Nice to meet you both and thanks for a great canyoning adventure today. It was terrific." He grabbed Teo's hand and pumped it a little too hard. Catching the younger man's attempt not to wince, Aiden squeezed tighter. "You take care and don't go getting into any trouble." A flash of his champion smile sealed his meaning.

Not bothering to be any more polite, he nodded at Rosa and stepped back allowing Carla to pass. She embraced Teo and Rosa, giving them a kiss on each cheek to say farewell.

"Okay, Rafe. Let's go. Time to hit the road." Aiden forced Rafe's decision to stay or leave now with Carla and him.

Obvious indignation and suspicion flickered on Rafael's face at being placed in this position. Aiden waited for him to consider, regroup and then acquiesce. "Yes. It was great meeting you both. Next time we come to the coast, maybe we can catch up." Reaching out he shook Teo's hand and kissed Rosa, grinned awkwardly and exited the club with Aiden and Carla.

On the walk along the busy pavement, Aiden prattled on trying to fill the awkward energy left from their unexpected departure. "Teo and Rosa seem nice enough. Good idea coming out and partying for a while, Rafe. Thanks for the entire day. It was great."

Rafael grabbed Carla's hand in what Aiden suspected was a show of one-up-man-ship. "I'm pleased you enjoyed it, Ace. Nothing like doing something you've always wanted to do with people who know how to do it."

"Absolutely." With a tight grin, Aiden gritted his teeth. Tonight, he knew how Carla's father must feel. Something was off with Rafael. And in this game of cat and mouse, Aiden fiercely disliked being the one kept on the run.

CHAPTER TEN

DISTANT YET INSISTENT KNOCKING jolted Aiden awake. He squinted to see the time on his phone. 6:00 A.M. *God, who's banging on the door at this hour?* He dragged on some shorts and struggled into a T-shirt. Whoever was on the other side of the front door was damn annoying.

The knocking started again. "All right, all right," Aiden called, increasing his pace along the corridor. On opening the door, he faced a swarthy man with a crop of slick, black-dyed hair and wrap-around, reflective sunglasses. The man's lips drew a thin, grim line on his face, then split open to speak rapidly in Spanish.

Aiden held up his hands in mock defence. "Sorry, I only speak English."

"Okay," the stranger replied, changing to thickly accented English. "My name is Franco Costello. My wife, or should I say, my ex-wife, Sofia is your neighbour. May I come in?" At the mention of Sofia's name, Aiden's senses snapped to full alert, and he scrutinized the man guardedly. Half a head shorter than him, Franco epitomized an old-style gangster. Pin-striped business suit, hands the size of hams, polished patent shoes you could eat off and a voice rumbling with authority. *Who wears a business suit at six o'clock in the morning in May on the Costa Del Sol?*

"Sure. Sure. Come in." Aiden stepped aside to allow him entry. As Franco strolled past, Aiden caught a whiff of an expensive aftershave and noticed the tailor-made quality of the visitor's suit.

"Where are the Capellos?" A hint of curious concern tinged Franco's voice as he removed his sunglasses and scanned the villa.

"Who?"

"The Capellos, they own this house. And who are you?" Stashing his glasses in his jacket pocket, Franco eyed Aiden with obvious suspicion.

"I'm Aiden, and the Capellos are doing a house swap in Australia. I'm here for another couple of days. Then they'll be back." Aiden offered the guest his hand.

Franco cocked a brow at Aiden's paw hanging in mid-air. Reluctantly, he shook it. He then extracted a white, crisply pressed handkerchief from his suit lapel pocket and wiped his tainted appendage. "Sorry. I have an aversion to germs," he explained.

Funny, I have an aversion to rude bastards, thought Aiden. "How may I help you, Mr Costello?" Aiden didn't venture further into the villa, so the men faced off in the foyer.

"I came down to meet with Sofia, but she's not at home, and she's not answering her phone. I wonder if you've seen her?" Although Franco's tone sounded casual, Aiden sensed there was nothing casual in the inquiry.

"Yes, we met the other night. She came over for dinner with me and my friends. But we haven't seen her since. Sorry." Aiden worked his best lawyer face, hoping Franco didn't see through his veil of nonchalance. The last thing Aiden needed was some irate ex-husband hunting him down because of his crazy ex-wife's sexual perversions.

"May I come in?" Not waiting for permission, Franco stepped around him and headed to the living room.

"Sure. Why not?" Aiden followed behind, battling to control his frustration at Franco's rudeness. "Would you like a coffee?"

"No thanks."

Well, I bloody well do. "Take a seat if you like." Aiden tried to be as polite as possible considering the tricky situation. He detoured to the kitchen, put on the jug and readied his mug.

"Thank you. I'll stand." Franco paused. "As I said, I can't locate Sofia anywhere. Did she say anything to you or your friends as to what she was doing over the next few days?"

"No. We had dinner, and she went home. She didn't mention anything." With his back to his guest, Aiden divulged only the salient facts. The air thickened with Franco's subtle, yet undeniable interrogation and Aiden tried not to squirm.

"Perhaps I can speak with your friends. Maybe they can help?"

Fuck, this guy's persistent. Aiden turned and eyeballed him with a firm, friendly gaze. "Listen, Mr Costello. They're asleep, and I don't want to wake them. If you give me your card, I'll give you a call if they know anything more. But I'm sure they haven't seen Sofia either." By now Aiden's hands were wrapped tightly around his coffee mug and with each sip, he forced himself to remain in control.

Another flick of the handkerchief and Franco dusted off a kitchen stool. Sliding across it, he reminded Aiden of a bullfrog — beady, penetrating eyes, an insincere grin and a neck so choked by an expensive silk tie, his head looked ready to explode. Perched on the stool, Franco continued in an oily voice, "I'm not sure if you know this, Aiden, but there are some sinister places and people here on the coast."

"So I've heard, sir." Another sip and his stomach rolled.

"My ex-wife sometimes finds herself in compromising situations." Franco lifted his eyebrows high on his forehead, emphasizing his obvious meaning.

You're fucking telling me. "Mr Costello, I don't know anything about your ex-wife. I'm sorry I can't help you."

"Very well." Since Franco seemed satisfied with the conversation, he made to leave. An old Frank Sinatra melody rang from his phone, diverting his attention. He opened it and read the message. Changing his mind, he slid back onto the stool. "So where are you from, Aiden?"

"Australia." Aiden's heart rate broke into a gallop, and it wasn't from the coffee.

"And what do you do in Australia? As a profession I mean?"

"I work as a stockbroker." With his intuition clanging every bell in his head, Aiden lied. He needed to get this guy out of the villa.

"Stockbroking is a very interesting game. I dabble in stocks as well, Aiden. Buy, sell, buy, sell. I find the riskier ones are the most dangerous, don't you?"

Fuck. Who is this dude? "I agree. Safe is better than sorry." His coffee mug now empty, Aiden placed his prop on the bench as calmly as possible. "Well, I do hope you find Sofia soon, Mr Costello." Aiden motioned his caller to the door.

"I'm sure she'll turn up under someone, somewhere. Don't you?" Franco's tone had turned downright sinister.

"I couldn't rightly say, sir." Aiden jammed his fingernails into his sweaty palms, rerouting his fear. "Did you want to leave your card in case she turns up?"

"Oh, I don't think she'll be turning up anytime soon." Franco Costello snarled a gummy, wide-mouthed grin at Aiden.

Fuck, what's happened to her? Aiden opened the door. "Well, you can count on me, sir. I'm discretion itself." He tried for one of his champion smiles and failed.

On his way out, Franco propped suddenly. Turning back towards Aiden, he invaded his personal space in one stealthy step and locked him with a steely stare. "I am counting on you . . . Mr Bishop. I'm counting on you to leave here with your friends today and remain incommunicado while my brother-in-law's trial takes place in Australia. You remember him, don't you? Mr Coco, the Italian businessman — your evidence against him aided the authorities in his arrest?"

Aiden swallowed hard trying to suppress the panic hurtling up from his stomach at the speed of light.

"And if you don't do as I say, Mr Bishop, Sofia's body will turn up in a shockingly brutalized condition."

He's fucking killed her! Aiden swallowed harder still, imagining the horrors this man had subjected her to before she finally died.

Franco flaunted an arrogant smirk. "If you recall, your fingerprints are in her house, and the recording of your bedroom fiasco is in my safe. I've been secretly recording Sofia's lewd improprieties for some time now. How fortuitous for us, that the young lawyer we couldn't turn in Australia, ended up next door to my sick, twisted Sofia and couldn't keep his cock in his pants." A bone-chilling, evil chortle echoed from his throat. "They say fact is stranger than fiction. And in this case, it's certainly true. Good day, Mr Bishop. Enjoy the remainder of your holiday." With a horrific leer, he pulled his sunglasses from his pocket, placed them on his ugly face and swaggered up the driveway, like the toad he was. Aiden stuck his head out the door and spotted the black town car parked at the end of the driveway with three gorillas in suits waiting for their boss. Aiden pressed the front door closed and leaned against it, exhaling an almighty breath.

Fuck! Fuck! Fuck! I'm about to be set up for Sofia's murder. Fuck!

~ ♥ ~

BY THE TIME CARLA and Rafael got up, Aiden had packed, cleaned out the fridge and done a quick tidy up of the villa. A lame smile graced his lips when he greeted them. "Morning guys. Sorry about this but the owners are returning this evening, so we need to leave today."

"Oh, that's a pity," Carla said. "I was hoping to darken my tan just that little bit more." She perched on the stool awaiting the coffee Aiden was brewing.

Rafael twisted his mouth and frowned. "Pity. Can't be helped I guess."

"Anyway, it's a beautiful day to be on the road. We'll have breakfast, finish housekeeping and once you're packed, we'll head off if that's okay with you?"

"Sure," Carla said, unperturbed by the change of plans.

"Listen. I need some money, so I'll pop into town and grab some now before we go. Carla, will you get my things together for me?" Rafael stood to leave.

"Sure. Okay." Confusion furrowed her brow. "But you won't be long, will you?"

"No. I'll be back in no time." Rafael's promise trailed behind him as he left the kitchen. Within minutes he was dressed and out the door. Outside, the Ducati thundered to life and disappeared up the driveway.

~ ♥ ~

THINKING HE STILL HAD another couple of days left, Rafael was determined to make the most of this last liaison. Over the past twenty minutes, both he and Teo had relentlessly pummelled Rosa's gaping cleft and willing anus with their fingers, tongues, and teeth until she lay dazed and exhausted. Endlessly climaxing, her juice now covered them like a liquid shroud and the bed was damp and sticky. Deep heaving breaths escaped the three of them and a manic frenzy gleamed in their eyes.

Sprawled on the bed, Rosa pulled open her inflamed labia once more and begged, "More. Give me more."

"You're such a greedy little bitch," Teo chided in a demonic whisper. Reaching under the pillow, he found his mark and inserted an enormous vibrator into her, stretching her wider and wider. Purposefully, he worked the massive plastic dildo deep into her. In and out, in and out. When she winced, he rubbed more lube on her and rotated his sexual weapon, drilling deeper. She opened her muscular legs wide as her lips curled back in agonized pleasure.

Mesmerized, Rafael lay beside her, tugging his cock with vicious strokes. "Take it. Take it," he snarled as she squirmed onto the monstrosity, eating it up with her maw.

"Rafe," Teo commanded like an army sergeant. "Come here." Eager to please, Rafe crawled over to the side of the bed as instructed. In a deep growl Teo said, "While Rosa sucks the life out of this, you can suck the life out of me." He thrust his engorged cock at Rafael, who opened his mouth and devoured it frantically. Every time Teo inserted the dildo further into Rosa, he thrust his cock deeper down Rafe's throat. Sounds of slurping, gagging and slapping flesh filled the darkened room while the smell of debauchery stimulated their senses.

While Rosa succumbed to being fucked by the gigantic dildo, Rafael kept pace with the rhythm, watching her wanton performance from the corner of his eye while he sucked ferociously on Teo's demanding cock. Fast and faster the tempo became. With the dildo hammering at Rosa and Teo face fucking Rafe so hard he repeatedly gagged, they couldn't get enough of the depravity, secreted away in the dingy room. On and on, like desperate predators they tore at each other until they exploded, howling in delight.

Pulling the dildo out of her, Teo commanded, "Roll over, bitch." Rosa obeyed without question. On all fours, she wiggled her arse in the air. Juice trickled from her loosened snatch as she fingered her clit.

"Aren't you pleased you met us, Rafe?" Teo's voice dripped with wicked malevolence as he stroked Rafe's cock back to life.

"Oh yes. Oh yes." Rafe's head spun in ecstasy. "I've waited all my life to find you two." He leaned back on his haunches while Teo stroked and sucked Rafael's cock to another raging erection.

"And aren't you pleased I introduced you to *Viagra*? Look how your beautiful long cock responds to my touch." His teeth nipped the head of Rafael's cock hard. Twirling his tongue around its smooth shaft, Teo licked at it like a lollipop, over and over again. Rafael could do nothing but moan while his body quivered in submission.

"What about me?" Rosa's impatience at being left out was evident in her tone.

Releasing Rafael's cock, Teo locked his eyes on him. "Fuck her, Rafe. Fuck her 'til she bleeds."

Rafael sprang at the command and scrambled behind her. His raging cock bobbed eager to be unleashed. Grabbing hold of Rosa's tits, Rafael plunged his cock deep within her, making her shriek.

"And now me." Accompanying his decree, Teo slapped lube on Rafael's arse and speared his cock into his anus. Rafael faltered and groaned in delight. With Teo wedged to the hilt in his arse and he in Rosa's cunt, Rafael gyrated and rolled. All that was missing was someone under them to suck his balls. *Maybe next time?*

Teo fisted Rafe's long black hair, like a rider with a horse's mane. He leaned down and whispered in Rafe's ear, "I will ride you both until you whinny for mercy." For Rafael, the sensation and intimidation shattered his senses into exquisite shards of carnal passions. Mindless, he lurched into Rosa while keeping his arse high enough for Teo's youthful cock to remain jammed inside. Wet, slippery snatch enclosed Rafael's tormented penis as a hot, pulsing cock buried itself deep into his arse, demanding more. He was in bliss. Every orifice of his body salivated. His skin prickled with scorching licks of erotic fire. At once, he wanted to laugh hysterically and sob from relief. Fucking and being fucked, fucking and being fucked. At last his voracious sexual appetite could be satiated. As Teo wrenched Rafael's hair setting the pace, Rafe tugged and dug his fingers into Rosa's tits telegraphing the tempo. Harder, harder and harder — Teo drove them on relentlessly. Yet no one surrendered. Driver and team rode like their lives depended on it.

AIDEN DECIDED HE NEEDED to confide in Carla about Franco Costello's early morning visit. Putting her at risk wasn't Aiden's intention, and she deserved to know what was happening. At least then she could make an informed decision as to part ways or continue travelling together. "Carla, I need to tell you something." He motioned for her to sit beside him on the couch. "You know when we met, I told you I came to Spain to lay low for a while because of a court case in Australia."

Carla nodded, and he noticed a flicker of concern dash across her face.

"Well, it seems the guy my evidence helped arrest, Mr Coco, has a brother-in-law here in Spain."

"Really?" This time, the concern settled into her expression.

"Yes. His name is Franco Costello it seems. And to make matters worse, he's our next-door neighbour, Sofia's, ex-husband."

Carla's hand shot to cover her mouth. "How do you know?"

"He paid me a visit this morning at six o'clock." Aiden shook his head in disbelief at how any of this was happening.

"What? Here? At Casa de los ángeles?" Her brow knitted.

"I'm afraid so. The angels certainly haven't helped us on this one." He tried for a brave smile, but it proved a lame attempt.

"Oh God, Aiden. What happened? Are you all right?" Carla clasped both his hands and her warmth calmed him a little.

Not wanting to go into details, he rushed the narrative. "If you recall, I didn't want to tell you the details of the night I went over to Sofia's place because she was one strange woman. Well, Mr Costello informed me this morning he has a recording from that night in his safe and reminded me my fingerprints are all over the house."

"So? What business is it of his? They're divorced."

"From what he said, Sofia's dead. He's going to frame me for her murder if I don't leave here now and I must stay uncontactable while his brother-in-law is on trial in Australia."

Carla sat speechless for a moment. "*Mierda!* You think he killed her?"

"There's little doubt of that in my mind. He's one mean mother fucker and from what Sofia implied, he's made his money illegally, probably from drugs. All I know is I believe him, and I can't take the risk of something happening to you because of my stupidity."

"But why do you think it's because of your stupidity?"

"If I hadn't been so hell-bent on having sex with Sofia in order to get my mind off you, I would never have gone over to her place, and all this wouldn't be happening." Realizing he'd said too much, Aiden bit his lip. "I'm sorry, Carla, I shouldn't have said that."

Compassion replaced the concern on her face. "Aiden, these men are criminals. It's not your fault. They will do whatever it takes to protect themselves — even kill their ex-wives." Carla shuddered at their cruelty. "What are you going to do?"

"I have no choice. I need to get out of here and make sure you and Rafe are safe. Either we can continue to Granada as planned or you two can go your separate ways?" For Aiden, the pause felt interminable. Losing Carla now would be the final blow to an already untenable situation. He watched her consider the options, her eyes cast upwards in thought.

"I'll be back," she said and patted his hand. He heard her trot down the corridor and return a few moments later. "Okay, Aiden. Now it's my turn." She placed the purple pouch on the coffee table in front of them. "When we spoke about Granada, I couldn't tell you certain things because of my Romani gypsy heritage and, you said the time will come when I will tell you. Do you remember?" She cocked her eyebrow.

"Yes. I remember. I said because if you don't tell me, I won't be able to protect you and keep my promise to your father."

Carla's face split with a beaming smile. "I think now is the time. Not because you won't be able to protect me, but because you're the one needing protection."

He shook his head. "I've no idea what you're on about."

Picking up the pouch Carla explained, "These are Mama's sacred Gypsy runes. They've been handed down over generations to the women in the Amaya line. At Granada, my aunts will gather and together, we will do readings to see if I possess the gift, like them and like Mama." Carla sounded wistful and a little sad at the mention of her mother. Aiden supposed it must be hard not having her mother with her at Granada at such an important time. "The other night after we danced tango . . ." Her lips twitched in a devilish smile. "Afterward, when you sent me to my room, I heard Mama telling me it was time to do a reading with the runes. I didn't have to wait until Granada."

"You hear your dead mother speaking to you?" Aiden blinked in disbelief.

"Oh yes. I've heard her for the past twenty years."

"Okay . . . Continue." Not needing any more distractions, Aiden side-stepped the hearing-dead-people conversation. He had enough going on in his life at present.

"So, I did a reading for myself, and although I didn't understand it totally, I think I got the basic meaning. So now, since you're in a situation where you need some help, I thought I'd do the same for you." Looking confident and pleased with herself, Carla dipped her hand into the bag and recovered the nine runes. Each one she delivered singularly to the tabletop with quiet reverence. "Now, you must pick up all the runes in your hands, hold them to your heart and expect an answer to whatever issue you want clarity on. When you feel you're ready, you circulate the runes in your hands then release them to fall onto the table."

Brimming with unconcealed affection, Aiden admired Carla's enthusiasm and child-like trust in nine little stones. Who was he to be cynical and discuss how far-fetched it all seemed to his legal, logical mind? "Okay, Carla. I'll give it a go." Collecting the stones, he rolled and turned them before holding them to his chest. Mimicking Carla, he closed his eyes and waited a few seconds. Strangely, he relaxed for the first time that day. Tiredness surged through his mind and body. He needed a holiday. God, he was on holiday. Blinking his eyes open, he shook the stones like a gambler at the roulette wheel and tossed the runes onto the table. They clattered to a standstill. The nine stones spread before them, five of which showed their Gypsy symbols.

"Wow, that's a lot of messages," Carla said obviously surprised. "I'll start with the ones I know the best." She reached for the runes and held each one in her hand as she proceeded. "You actually got the same three as I did. The sickle which means something is coming to an end."

"I hope all this shit is coming to an end," he interjected.

Carla frowned at his interruption. "You also have the waves, which means journeys, a moving on. Whatever is coming to an end, you will move through. Then there is the all-seeing eye, your intuition. You mentioned intuition is something you have as a snake in the Eastern zodiac. Well, here it is again. You must listen to your gut feelings." She gave him a serious look. In fact, it reminded him of a look his mother gave him whenever she demanded his concentration. "Now here are three extra runes you threw. Goodness, you have the sun, the moon, and the stars. How strange?"

Aiden tilted his head but didn't dare speak. He liked having Carla's attention solely on him, even if it all seemed like hocus-pocus.

"The sun signifies male energy, prosperity, wealth and happiness. Something good is going to happen." She lifted her head and smiled. "The moon means the feminine energy, something is clouding your vision, you have to use your feminine intuition before you make decisions. And the stars mean hopes, wishes fulfilled but only if you have clear vision. I guess until you clear your vision, these hopes and wishes will remain unattainable."

While Carla fixated on the runes, pushing them around the table, Aiden exhaled long and slow. "Thanks, Carla. I'm not sure what all this means except my all-seeing eye, my intuition is telling me we need to go. The sun is shining, that's the male energy saying time to get on the road and my hope, that's the stars, is that we get to Granada safely before they come out tonight. What do think?"

"Aiden, you're such a lawyer." She lifted her hand and brushed his wayward hair from his brow. Her tender touch sent little shock waves through his body.

He caught her hand before it fell. "And there's a secret part of me wishing for an ending, one which we can move through together to new beginnings." On impulse, he turned her hand over and kissed her palm. She didn't withdraw or flinch. Instead, she cast him a glorious smile and nodded. From a distance, the Ducati roared Rafe's imminent arrival. Carla collected the runes, returned them to the pouch and retreated to get her handbag. Aiden sprang to his feet and opened the door before Rafe walked in. With luggage over his shoulder, Aiden said, "Did you get what you wanted in town, Rafe?"

"Absolutely," he replied, a gigantic smile slashing his face. Aiden flinched at Rafe's cheeky use of his favourite affirmation. He felt sure Rafe was using the word just to needle him. When Rafael reached down to collect his bag, Aiden's gut twisted. On closer inspection, Aiden was sure Rafe's hair was damp. *No showers at the bank*, he mused. *What have you been up to Rafe, my man?*

With long, determined strides Aiden couldn't wait to be in his prancing horse speeding away from the Costa del Sol and towards Granada.

CHAPTER ELEVEN

CARLA HAD TO AGREE. It was a sensational day to be driving — more so, in a red convertible Ferrari. With the roof down, the scorching heat from the sun was tempered by the wind rushing over their faces. Pushing the built-up speed limit, they cruised down the palm tree-lined streets out of town and onto the A-92. Unleashing the Ducati Rafael took off, as did Aiden hot on his heels. With the rolling hills pressing in around the highway, Carla stretched back and relaxed. Prepared for the drive, she'd subdued her hair under a securely tied scarf and sun visor. Enjoying the role of celebrity passenger, she even wore red sunglasses and lipstick to match her red and white sundress. Pretty as a picture is how she felt, which was surprising considering the deteriorating situation with Rafael. Since that night of rough sex nearly a week ago, he'd not propositioned her at all. Firstly, she thought it was because of his drowning scare, and he was evaluating his promise of becoming a better man for her. But that didn't last long. His unpredictable moodiness had returned. Like a roller coaster, Rafe's emotional peaks and troughs had escalated steadily.

Shadows from the hills snatched the warmth of the sun from the highway and she shivered for those few seconds. Rubbing her arms, she wished for the road to curve back into the light again, to feel the sun's warmth. She glanced across to Aiden concentrating on the road and realized he could be her sun. Had Rafe become no more than a shadow of the past? One she must now move on from. *But how?*

"I'm pleased Rafe knows where we're going," called Aiden over the whine of the engine. "I'm not looking forward to driving this baby around busy city streets trying to find a park."

"The hotel we've booked has parking. It's a tight squeeze to get there, but I'm sure you'll handle it." She flashed him a sunny smile. Aiden shot her one back.

"I'm pleased I told you about Franco," he said simply, returning his focus to the road.

"Me too. I dislike secrets," she said with intensity, her mind casting to Rafe's secretive behaviour of late.

"And I'm pleased you decided to continue travelling together, despite the mess I've made of things." Aiden glanced across at her.

Carla reached over and patted his thigh. "It's okay, Aiden. As I said, none of this is your fault. Mama used to say everything happens for a reason, so I'm sure something good will come out of this."

"That's one of the things I most like about you, Carla. You always look for the best in people and life."

"Yes. But maybe I'm too trusting and patient with some people." Again, she thought of Rafael. "Anyway, in Granada, I'm sure all will become clear. I'm pleased you'll be with me to meet my extended family."

"Me too. If they're anything like you, I know I'll like them very much."

The repetitive hum of the tyres on the bitumen silenced further conversation. Alert, Aiden returned to the command of his red horse, while Carla closed her eyes. Contented and calmed by the sun's warmth, she drifted into that wonderful place a passenger retreats to when they have absolute trust in the driver.

"Trust, mi querida." Isabella's voice whispered in her ear once more. *"Trust."*

ALONE FOR THE PAST couple of hours, Rafael took full advantage of the ride. With only his thoughts as pillion, he contemplated the destiny of his life as he rode towards Granada. The place he prayed would be his salvation. But a familiar recurring thought haunted him. His father. He hated his father on so many levels, but mostly because of the violence and the sex. The cruelty in killing the pigs, their shrieking, the rivers of blood — images, sounds and smells seared into his memory for all time. The horror Sancho had forced Rafael to be part of as a young boy, spread like an evil cancer eating away at his soul. Dancing had been his only escape. When he danced, the urges stopped. When he danced, he was in control. When he danced, he forgot. He forgot about the slaughter. He forgot about seeing his father's maniacal sneer and raging erection during the carnage. He forgot how his father masturbated after killing the pigs and made his son do the same. When he danced, he forgot. But now he could no longer forget. Now Rafael had finally succumbed to the hideousness of his past. The one thing he vowed to never let happen, had. He'd become his father. The urges he'd tried so long to ignore had consumed him and found an outlet with Teo and Rosa. The sins of the father had now perpetrated themselves on the son. How much longer could he keep up this charade with Carla? Keeping this unspeakable secret was not only unfair on her but him as well.

In Granada, things had to change. He needed to change. In Granada, his destiny lay, but it had to be a truthful destiny, one of his choosing not as a residual condition of his vile past.

Slowly, his thoughts cleared, his jaw unclenched and his grip on the bike loosened. Glittery sunlight streamed into his helmet as if for the first time today, brightening his disposition. Like Carla, he was sick and tired of his dark moods. He longed to live in the light, not in the dark. The highway snaked before him, beckoning him to an optimistic future. Perhaps it was possible. The delightful tune of "Granada" and the promise in its lyrics, crept from his soul and pervaded his thoughts. He began to hum the melody and a slither of hope sparked in his heart. Perhaps he'd fall under the spell of Granada and be touched by the blush of the Sierra Nevada? Beauty and stars would entrance him and weave their magic. And while a thousand guitars played, romance and love would once more live in his heart. Perhaps it wasn't too late for Carla and him? Rafe inhaled deeply, and a sanguine smile lifted his expression. Infused with courage, he opened up the Ducati and raced to a better future.

~ ♥ ~

CARLA WOKE WHEN THEY entered the city limits, and although a regular visitor to Granada, her visit this time was special. One she'd looked forward to for many years. This time, she'd meet her aunts again and see if she too had the gift. "We're here, Aiden."

In front of them, Rafe swung the Ducati up a steep, narrow street, backed it into a narrow bay and dismounted. With a wave of his arm, he motioned Aiden to follow.

"On your left is the Hotel de Los Páramos, and there's our parking spot. Beside Rafe." Carla pointed to an angle park on the cobblestoned street, directly opposite the hotel door. "Only guests at the hotel can normally park in this street," she said. Standing kerbside, a dapper middle-aged man wearing *Pince-nez* glasses waved. With an effusive grin, Carla waved back.

He scurried over to her door. "Miss Armando. So good to see you again." Dressed in a black and red livery coat over flawlessly pressed black trousers, the cartoonesque little man sported a thin layer of greased-back black hair which glistened brighter than his black patent shoes. He bowed and scraped, personifying old-world charm and service.

"*Muchas gracias,* Victor." She accepted his assistance to alight the car. "Victor, this is our friend, Aiden Bishop. He's a lawyer from Australia, holidaying in Spain for a while. Victor Moreno is the manager of the hotel."

"Welcome, Mr Bishop, to Hotel de Los Páramos. I hope you enjoy your stay." Victor flourished his arm towards the historic three-story building across the street. Like so many of the impressive buildings Aiden had seen in Spain, Hotel de Los Páramos swelled from the ground with the striking grandeur of long-ago architecture. While Victor helped remove the luggage from the trunk, he continued his welcome spiel. "This fifteenth-century building dates back to the time of the Moors, which by the way, I'm descended from." Pride in his lineage jutted his chin higher. "We have lovingly restored and modernized the hotel but have also retained its 500-year-old charm. There are only fourteen rooms so you will receive five-star service at all times." Because he refused to allow his guests to carry their own bags, Victor struggled with the luggage as he led the way. They followed him through an enormous antiquated front door and walked over to the reception. From nowhere, a young grovelling porter arrived to manhandle their bags to their rooms.

"Mr Bishop, I've taken the liberty of giving you a room overlooking the street so you can keep your eye on your precious Ferrari." By the twinkle in Victor's eye, he thought he'd made an excellent decision in allocating this room.

Aiden accepted his room key. "Thank you, Victor. *Muchas gracias.* That was very thoughtful of you."

Victor all but puffed his chest at the compliment.

"And for you, Miss Armando and Mr Flores, your usual deluxe room with the best view of Alhambra." Victor handed them a key each.

"*Muchas gracias,* Victor," Rafael said. "It was fortunate you were able to bring our reservations forward a couple of extra days on such short notice."

"For you and Miss Armando, I will work magic. Now, if you will follow me?" Another flourish of his hand indicated the way.

Following Victor's brisk waddle, they entered the hotel's interior. Carla gave Aiden a few more facts along the way. "Hotel de Los Páramos is not that different to your hotel in Seville. Except this hotel is a couple of centuries older. But both have similar designs with the rooms running off an open, indoor courtyard."

Overhead balcony balustrades, worn terracotta flagstones, Moroccan tiles and taupe coloured stucco walls, encircled the central courtyard and fountain, creating a cloister of peace. Aiden nodded. "Yeah. It's an oasis of calm, same as Casa del Jardín. Once inside, the madness of the world is left behind. I like it." *And I most definitely need it*, he thought. They walked up three flights of stone stairs and along the Moroccan carpet runner laid on the narrow internal balcony which overlooked the courtyard below.

Victor stopped at a room and flourished his arm. "Miss Armando, Mr Flores."

"Thank you, Victor. Where's Aiden's room?" Rafe asked.

"Directly opposite, sir." Victor nodded for Aiden to follow him to the other side of the balcony.

"See you when you unpack and freshen up. Knock on my door when it suits," Aiden said and followed Victor.

~ ♥ ~

WITH A QUICK SURVEY of his room, Aiden walked to the far side and opened the windows. Just as Victor had promised, there was the Ferrari, directly below. If anyone tried to steal her, Aiden would hear the alarm from here. Comfortable in this knowledge, he unpacked. The room was one of the hotel's standards, featuring a double bed with a semi-circular, gold velvet upholstered counterpane flanked by dark timber bedside tables. He threw himself on the bed for the obligatory bounce test. *Just right,* he thought grinning agreeably. Not only was the crisp, white linen top quality, but it was also monogrammed — HLP. *Nice touch.*

Taking his wet pack into the bathroom, he discovered more surprises. Modern floor to ceiling tiles, a sizeable shower, and an illuminated shaving mirror. He had one of those back home and had missed it ever since arriving in Spain. At last, he'd get a really close shave the way he liked it. Plenty of fluffy towels also monogrammed, were folded awaiting his use. In a contented mood, he set up his toiletries and returned to unpack his clothes.

Within the hour, he shaved, showered and changed into a pair of blue jeans and a pink polo shirt. He squelched some product through his hair and scrunched. Unsure as to how much longer he could tolerate it falling into his eyes, he speared his fingers through its unruliness and frowned. Although he did like that Carla felt obliged to brush it away for him. That alone was reason to keep growing it.

Dressed and ready for action, he ambled to the window and leaned on the edge looking out at Granada. From reading the room's compendium, the hotel was situated in Albaicin, the old Moorish quarter of the city. He was within walking distance of the town centre and the region's biggest tourist attraction, the Alhambra. Both places he intended to visit. He stared out at the picturesque scene of steep, winding streets squirming through this part of town. It was getting later, and as the smell of nearby tapas cafes wafted up to him, he realized he hadn't eaten anything all day after Franco Costello barged into his life this morning. Aiden swore. He knew he couldn't keep running from these bastards. And he loathed the thought of allowing them to get away with their murders, threats, and corruption. He'd need to take a stand, but his timing had to be impeccable. And he needed Carla, but again it was all about the timing.

~ ♥ ~

WITH RENEWED HOPE, RAFAEL stretched his hand towards her. "Come, Carla. See Alhambra. Remember how many happy times we've spent in this room, looking at her ancient beauty?" Towelling dry her hair, Carla strolled over beside Rafael on their balcony. The amber glow of hundreds of lights danced up the majestic red stone walls of the old sultans' palace.

"Oh, Rafe, it's beautiful, isn't it?" She paused in her grooming and stood beside him, drinking in the man-made magnificence sprawling across the mountain. Located in the foothills of the Sierra Nevada, the citadel's huge compound had for centuries been the crowning glory of Granada.

"And it's one of your favourite places, I know. With its history and legend of long-ago princesses, noble knights and hidden treasures, Alhambra is filled with romance. That your mother was named after Queen Isabella, the first Spanish queen of the Alhambra, adds special meaning for you too." He placed a gentle kiss on the top of her head.

"Yes, Rafe. Alhambra holds a special place in my heart."

"Remember how we used to come here and make love with the balcony doors open, wishing upon the magic of Alhambra?" Rafe gazed down at her, and his heart melted at the sweet memory. *How have I let my life get so off track?* he thought.

"Yes, I remember, Rafe. They were happy times together."

Hearing a hint of disappointment in Carla's voice, Rafe hurried on. "I'm going to set up a meeting with Leta over the next few days so we can finalize the divorce." He hoped this piece of good news would heal the deepening rift he'd created between Carla and himself over the past few months. His getting a divorce may be the panacea to their relationship woes and hopefully, defeat his papa's wicked legacy.

A long pause ensued. Finally, Carla said, "Okay, Rafe. But this is my time, and I want to meet with my aunts first. After that, we'll meet with Leta. Okay?"

Looking down into her soft, brown eyes, Rafael agreed to her request. "Of course, *mi pequeña luciérnaga,* whatever makes you happy." Squeezing her to his side, he breathed in her fresh, soapy scent and smiled wistfully. He sent a silent prayer up to Alhambra to be free of the haunting of his father's demons and find peace in his soul so he could love Carla as she deserved.

THIS TIME, THE KNOCK at the door was one Aiden had been expecting. "Hey, guys. I'm ready and starving." He joined Rafael and Carla on the internal balcony, closing the door behind him.

"It's not far, Ace. About a fifteen-minute walk. We're going to the club in Sacromonte where Carla and I will be dancing when the current performers go on holidays. They do great food."

"Terrific." Aiden picked up the pace.

"Slow down a little, please. I have shorter legs than you," Carla said. "I don't want to do an ankle keeping up with you two." Although dressed in casual jeans and low-heeled boots, Carla was doing a quick shuffle beside them.

"Sorry." Aiden slipped back a notch to allow Carla to set the pace.

"Don't worry, Aiden. They'll look after us as soon as we arrive," Rafael said, "you won't be hungry for long."

~ ♥ ~

TWO HOURS LATER AND with a big sheepish grin, Aiden gave Rafael a thumbs-up. "You were right, Rafe. That food was fantastic, and this sangria is hitting the mark." Pumped with the stress from the past few days, Aiden had plied a few too many sangrias into his belly. Despite the goat's cheese, beef, chicken, potatoes, and vegetables he'd devoured, the sangria was working its magic, and Aiden had a glow on. Propped up next to Carla with Rafael on her other side, they sat at a table against one wall of the El Ritmo de Flamenco.

"This place is great," Aiden called out loud and clapped along with the flamenco dancer currently performing. "I love how these clubs are caves carved out of the rock. So cool." His eyes scanned the white-washed stone walls lit with electric candle sconces. With his head lolling a little from side to side, he enjoyed how the tension had finally left his neck.

Carla reached up to him and whispered, "Aiden, you must be quiet. They're dancing."

With an exaggerated 'oops' plastering his expression, Aiden put his finger to his mouth and whispered an exaggerated, "Shhhh." He returned his attention to the stage, and although he did his best to contain his enthusiasm at the end, he whistled loudly and pounded his feet on the wooden floor. Catching a waiter's eye, he nodded for another jug of sangria.

"Don't you think you've had enough?" Carla shot him a reproachful look.

"Listen we all need to relax a little. Things have been a bit strange of late. Don't you agree, Rafe?" Aiden squinted at him and smirked.

"In what way do you mean strange?" Tension and suspicion crackled in his voice.

After pouring them all another glass of sangria, Aiden continued, "You know what I mean. What with your near-drowning accident, then going off at all hours on the Ducati and not telling anyone where you were. And what about those two canyoning guides — Teo and Rosa. Don't you think they were a weird pair?" When Aiden lurched forwards rocking the table, Carla reached out to steady her glass. But neither Aiden nor Rafael moved.

"Not really," Rafael said. "Maybe they seemed weird to you because they're country people, they come across different. I found them to be friendly and polite." After a conclusive nod signifying that the conversation was over, Rafael picked up his glass and slurped a good slug of sangria.

With a cheeky lop-sided grin, Aiden leaned across the table. "I think Rosa had the hots for you, Rafe. She certainly wanted to get into your climbing gear at the canyon." He gave a conspiratorial wink at Rafael and turned to Carla, giving her a knowing nod. "She wanted our Rafe. I'm telling you. And it wasn't for orienteering practice either." Aiden drank down his glass of sangria in one swallow, slammed it to the table and refilled.

Carla grabbed Aiden's shirt sleeve and pulled. "Aiden, enough," she hissed into his ear. "We have to work here, and I don't want you embarrassing us."

"Okey-dokey," he slurred. "Here have some more." Before Carla could protest, he topped her glass. "So, where did you get off to on the Ducati? You sure you don't have a mistress stashed somewhere on the coast?" A naughty chuckle sprang from Aiden's mouth. He was most pleased with his cleverness.

"Aiden!" It was Carla who drew attention to their table this time.

In a slurred whisper, Aiden persisted, "Come on, Rafe. What were you up to, man?"

There was no mistaking Rafael's discomfort and barely concealed contempt for Aiden. "I don't know what you're playing at, Ace, but it's none of your business what I do. I think you've had a little too much sangria. Let's forget about this conversation and we'll go back to being three friends on holiday. Okay?" By the time Rafael had finished speaking, he'd calmed down visibly.

"Okey-dokey," Aiden said. "Now when are you two going to dance the tango?"

Both Carla and Rafael snickered. She patted Aiden's arm and said, "Not tonight, Aiden. We're not dancing tonight."

Aiden pouted. "That's a pity. I love it when you dance the tango." He bent down and rubbed his nose against Carla's before she could retreat. "And if you were sitting next to me, I'd give you an Eskimo kiss too, Rafe. But since you're not, I'll come over." Aiden staggered upright and lost his balance slightly. He lumbered and grasped for the wall.

"Right. Time to go." Rafe jumped up and wrapped his arm around Aiden's waist. "Come on. The fresh air will do you good." With Carla clutching Aiden's other arm over her shoulder, the three amigos departed the club as elegantly and quietly as possible.

~ ♥ ~

AIDEN GRABBED HER HAND. "Don't go."

Caught in his grip, Carla's skin tingled, and she wanted nothing more than to crawl into bed with this tantalizing man. She and Rafael had rolled Aiden safely back to the hotel where they partly undressed him and tucked him in bed. With Rafael already retired back to their room, Carla folded Aiden's clothes before leaving. "Aiden, you must get some sleep. I can't stay." She placed his wayward hand under the covers.

"But I want you to stay, Carla." Hearing the soft plea in his voice, she delayed.

"I can't. I'm with Rafael, and you're drunk." She bent down to kiss his forehead. Once more Aiden clutched her hand. The speed and accuracy with which he did so, caught her attention. Frowning, she stared down into his sparkling blue, undazed eyes and watched a wicked grin crease his face. "You're not drunk at all," she said, amused at how well he'd acted.

"Not in the least." He beamed, obviously happy with his performance.

"So, what was all that about at the club?" She pulled her hand free of his grip and tilted her head.

"Carla, I need to know what's going on with Rafe and so do you. Aside from the promise I made to your father, you're about to make some serious decisions here in Granada, and I want you to have all the information before you do."

She frowned recalling the incident at El Ritmo de Flamenco. "At the club, you mentioned how Rosa had the hots for Rafe. And did he have a mistress on the coast. Why did you say that?"

"I wanted to see how he'd react. It was giving me a baseline of Rafe's responses."

"What's a baseline? What are you getting at?" Carla had the distinct impression Aiden wasn't telling her everything.

"I'm not sure yet. But from Rafe's reaction, I touched a nerve."

She paused; her lips tight with emotion. "I'm so confused, but I agree with you. Rafe has secrets. What they are I don't have a clue. But since we've arrived here in Granada, he's being the man I fell in love with. More than that, he wants to set up a meeting with Leta as soon as possible so he can finalize the divorce." She collapsed on the side of his bed. Her whole body deflated like a leaking balloon.

Aiden propped on an elbow. "And what did you say?"

"I told him not to make any plans in meeting Leta until I've met with my aunts." Hot tears seared the back of her eyes. She was tired. "Everything seems such a mess." She rubbed the heels of her hands on her eyebrows, wishing things were different, clearer.

Aiden leaned forwards. "Look. You've bought us a little time. Don't worry about anything. I'll keep digging and see if I can't find out the truth. Remember what your mother used to say, everything happens for a reason. Once you meet your aunts, I'm sure everything will work out. By the way, when do you meet them?

"On the new moon."

"When's that?"

"Next Sunday." She wished it was sooner.

"We have a week from tomorrow. Plenty of time." Aiden sounded pleased.

Carla lowered her eyes and fidgeted with the bed covers. "It may be plenty of time for you but for me it's too much time."

"I don't understand?"

"What if Rafael wants to make love with me? It's been well over a week since we've had sex and the last time we did, it was so . . ." She shuddered. The thought of giving herself sexually to her unpredictable fiancé scared her. Water pooled in her eyes and trickled down her cheeks. No longer stopping their flow, Carla allowed her tears and fears to be released.

Aiden wrapped his big, strong arms around her, and she buried her face into his shoulder. For a few extended moments, she surrendered to the safety Aiden offered, before gathering her defences. Sniffling, she raised her head and smiled. "I'm sorry. I'll be fine."

Holding her at arm's length, he said, "I know you will. You're one helluva woman, Carla Armando. And if you need anything, I'm right here."

She giggled. "Oh God, Aiden. You remind me of that wretched fable about the protective king, the magic mirror and the shepherdess who became his queen."

"Some of us fellas just can't help it." He chuckled. "Personally, I like independent, feisty women who can look after themselves. But at the same time, I don't mind a little of that white knight stuff as well."

Brushing a curl from his forehead, Carla rose. "Well, Aiden. Thank you for your offer. I'll see you tomorrow no doubt."

"Absolutely." The brilliance of his smile lightened her spirits and she left his room, closing the door softly behind her.

CHAPTER TWELVE

GROGGY FROM THE SANGRIA-INDUCED sleep, Aiden struggled awake to the sound of someone pounding on his door. *No, that was yesterday,* he reminded himself. *Can't be today.*

"Ace, wake up." Rafael's frantic voice sliced into Aiden's twilight state while the banging got louder. "Ace, Ace, wake up."

Realizing it wasn't a dream, Aiden sprang upright in bed. Still in darkness, his hotel room possessed an eerie, neon glow from the streetlights outside. Everything looked alien to him until he remembered where he was. *Granada. I'm in Granada.* Grabbing his phone, he swiped it on. *Five o'clock.* He shook his head free of his brief sleep's residue.

"I'm coming. I'm coming." He dashed to the door in his underwear and when he opened it, Rafael barged into the room. "Ace, you've got to drive Carla back to Seville. I can't take her on the Ducati because I didn't bring a spare helmet." Ashen-faced, Rafe looked desperate.

"Why? What's happened?" Aiden hauled his hair off his forehead.

"Manolo, her papa has had a heart attack. He's in the hospital, and he's asking for her. Can you take her, please?" When Rafael gripped Aiden's shoulders, he sensed Rafe's panic transfer into his body. "They're not sure if he's going to pull through."

Aiden flung his clothes on. "Sure. Sure. I can drive her there. Is she ready?"

"She's just throwing some things in a bag. You get some stuff together too in case you have to stay a night or two. I'll ride down shortly once I let Victor know." Rafael snapped a turn and dashed back to their room.

In the bathroom, Aiden brushed his teeth then threw his toiletries into his wet pack which he jammed into a knapsack with some clothes. Closing his door behind him, he strode to

Carla and Rafael's room, and when he entered, Carla stumbled from the bathroom. With red, puffy eyes and nose, she'd obviously been crying. She bent to collect her overnight bag, and Aiden noticed her delicate hand shook like a falling leaf.

"*Mi pequeña luciérnaga,* let me." Rafael scooped the bag onto his shoulder and wrapped his arm around her waist.

Floundering from the room, Carla looked at Aiden. "*Muchas gracias,* Aiden. *Muchas gracias.*" Aiden stared at her and thought she'd shatter in a strong wind.

As they hurried down the stairs, Rafael said, "Are you all right to drive, Aiden, after all that sangria?"

Carla glanced up at Aiden with a knowing look.

"Sure. Sure. I didn't drink that much really. It just went to my head. I'm fine." He shot a furtive smile at Carla, who nodded.

Outside, Aiden jumped in and started the Ferrari while Rafael helped Carla settle and seat belt. "I'll only be an hour or so behind you, *mi pequeña luciérnaga.*" Leaning in, he kissed her on the cheek and closed the door.

Aiden slammed the car into reverse, then turned to Carla. "Do you know the quickest way to get me out of here?" He slipped into gear.

"Absolutely." She gave him a brave smile and pointed the way. Flooring the Ferrari, Aiden launched them to Seville.

OUTSIDE MANOLO'S HOSPITAL ROOM, Aiden chatted in hushed tones with Carla's four brothers. José and Gerado looked badly shaken by their father's situation. Not venturing far from each other's side, they stood shoulder to shoulder like tin soldiers. Contributing little to the conversation, they simply nodded and listened. Their twinship seemed to anchor them. Aiden suspected as long as the other was close by, they'd survive the shock. Alone, they'd drown in emotional meltdown.

Having given up all pretence of being straight, strong and mature, Raúl openly sobbed and blew his nose. Handfuls of crumpled tissues filled his sweater pockets as he rotated clean for dirty. "What happens if Papa dies? What are we going to do? What will happen to me?" With each question, his voice became more shrill, and his big, brown eyes widened.

"Raúl, pull yourself together," Estéban said in a stern tone. Like the rock of the family, Estéban remained solid and unmoving. "Papa's not going to die. He's strong. He'll be all right."

Retreating from Estéban's reprimand, Raúl backed into Aiden, who placed his hands sympathetically on his shoulders and squeezed. "I'm sure Manolo will recover, Raúl. Don't get yourself worked up."

Resting a shaky, delicate hand on Aiden's, Raúl turned and mouthed a silent "thank-you" to him. Passive and uncertain, José, Gerado, and Raúl awaited their eldest brother's further instructions.

Aiden assessed the dimly lit ward and concluded that the hospital standards in Seville didn't compare favourably with Australia. The concrete walls needed a fresh lick of paint, and a good dose of bleach would remove the grunge along the edge where the linoleum floor met the walls. With only a handful of aluminium chairs, other visitors would have to stand if the five of them decided to sit rather than hover in a solemn circle. As for support staff, they all seemed to be on a break. For everyone's sake, he hoped the medical attention was of a higher quality than the operational infrastructure.

Estéban eyed his brothers. "Since we've got to wait until Carla has spoken to Papa and the doctor, why don't you three go get something to eat while Aiden and I wait here."

When they disappeared around a corner on their mission to find food, Estéban motioned Aiden into a chair.

"Is Rafael coming?" Estéban's voice was tight and blunt.

"Yes. He's riding down after us. He shouldn't be long." Aiden checked his watch and calculated Rafael would arrive within the next thirty minutes.

"Then we don't have much time. I don't want you to be angry, but I didn't do as you asked me in the club on the

Coast." Estéban's jaw set as he stared unapologetically at Aiden.

Aiden tilted his head. "What do you mean?"

"Instead of leaving right away, I waited around and watched you, Carla and Rafael leave the club. Then I waited for the other two you were with to leave, and I followed them."

"You what? God, Estéban. Those other two jokers are no good, I'm sure of it. You could've wound up in serious trouble." Aiden shook his head in disbelief at the risk Estéban had taken.

"You're right, Aiden. They're no good." Estéban snarled.

"Why? What did you find out?" Aiden leaned closer, eager for evidence.

"They went to the same area of town that Rafael was in the night before when I tailed him."

"And?"

"I hung back in the shadows of the alley for a while, just watching. Some man came up to me and offered to have sex with me. I made out I wanted a man and a woman, and he pointed to the two from the club. I walked up to them and told them I wanted a man and a woman."

"And?"

"They told me if I like fucking and being fucked, really rough, they could help me out." Disgust dripped from Estéban's face, but he was obviously pleased with his detective work.

"Shit. Are you sure they were the two we were with?'

"They told me their names were Teo and Rosa . . ."

"That's them all right. So, what were they? Prostitutes?"

"Yes. Very expensive, but from what they said, they were worth the money." Clearly appalled at their perversions, Estéban folded his arms across his chest and leaned back. "Papa was right. Rafael is a faggot and is just using our Carla for his own purposes."

"Hang on a minute. Did you tell this to Manolo when you came back?" Aiden shuddered waiting for the answer.

"Of course, I did. That's what Papa sent me for." Righteous indignation stirred in Estéban's voice.

"God, Estéban. No wonder Manolo had a heart attack." Aiden sprang to his feet, and the chair skittered away. "You could have at least told me first. We could've worked out a game plan. Poor Manolo. The shock's nearly killed him. What the fuck am I going to tell Carla?

Estéban jumped to his feet. "The truth. Tell her the truth. That's what you promised Papa you'd do."

"Hold on a minute. I can't just go blurting this out. Carla's in there with her father who may or may not survive. This isn't the time to be telling Carla her fiancé is one fucked-up, twisted mother fucker. Timing, Estéban, timing!" Aiden slapped the back of his hand into his other palm three times, like a judge's gavel. He pivoted and paced the corridor in long, ferocious strides, his mind spinning with too much information. Soon, Rafael would be here and by the look of Estéban, if he came within swinging distance of Rafael, he'd floor him. *No contest there.* Having spent the last thirty minutes at her father's bedside, Carla would emerge in no fit state to receive any more bad news. The doctor would also shortly advise the medical options and Manolo's likelihood of recovery. And Aiden was now on a wing and a prayer. He couldn't tell Carla about Rafael. Currently, it was all hearsay, although pretty damning hearsay. He needed unequivocal evidence. A confession. From Rafael in front of Carla. *But how?*

The door to Manolo's room opened just as the three brothers returned from the canteen. With the doctor by her side, Carla looked rattled but composed. Determined chin jutting high, she walked over to stand next to Estéban. Raúl crept in on her other side and wrapped his arm around her waist. In that instance, Aiden realized how much of a mother Carla had been to him and in fact, to all her brothers when Isabella died. Her strength and duty of care was admirable.

She wrapped her arms around her eldest and youngest brother. "Doctor Rivero has something to tell us." Looking like a long streak of bacon, the doctor stepped forwards.

Holding his clipboard in one hand and his stethoscope in the other, he appeared too young to have passed medical school, let alone be a cardiac specialist.

"Everyone I have some good and some bad news. Your papa has suffered a severe heart attack. He's lucky to be alive." Aiden shot Estéban an irate glare while the other brothers mumbled and gasped. "He has a clot and needs to undergo heart surgery as soon as possible. This is a routine operation. We'll insert three stents into his heart to assist with the blood flow so the clot can move freely around his heart. He'll remain in hospital for a few days or so, but he should make a full recovery."

"Will he be able to still do everything when he comes home?" Gerado asked, controlling the waver in his voice.

"Usually, patients can return to their previous life as long as they're careful and take the prescribed medication."

"What caused the clot?" José asked, also trying to manage his emotions.

"We don't know but as I said, this the good news. Now if you'll excuse me, we have to prepare your father for the operation." With a sharp nod of his elongated head, Doctor Rivero turned an about-face and marched down the corridor.

Manolo's five offspring began speaking in rapid Spanish while Aiden stood on the periphery. Carla held out her hand, beckoning him into the family circle. She held onto him, drawing him closer. "*Muchas gracias,* Aiden. Thank you for bringing me here so quickly to be with Papa." Her brothers chimed their appreciation, particularly Raúl whose doting admiration reminded Aiden of a loyal lap dog.

"It was nothing. That's what a Ferrari is for." His self-deprecating humour and tentative chuckle broke the tension, giving them permission to smile.

Another voice rumbled in the hall. "Carla, Carla, how is he?" Helmet in hand, Rafael's elegant figure strode toward them.

Blocking Estéban with a sharp snap of his arm, Aiden said to Carla, "You stay with your brothers. I'll tell Rafe what's happened." Not waiting for a reply, Aiden lurched from the group. Arms outstretched, he met Rafael halfway, preventing him from going further. "Rafe, Manolo will be fine. They're prepping him now for surgery. Maybe we should give Carla and her brothers some time to be alone as a family."

"But I want to be with Carla," Rafael protested, trying to dodge Aiden's muscular frame.

"Listen you've had a big ride and so have I. Let's go and grab something to eat. Calm our nerves a bit. Then, we'll come back. I really think Carla wants to spend some time with her brothers."

Rafael looked past Aiden's shoulder. "Okay. You're probably right." He did an about-face and fell into step with Aiden to the canteen.

~ ♥ ~

As the day wore on Carla's world turned to quicksand. Everything she'd come to depend on seemed to be sucked into a bottomless pit and with it, her confidence, sanity, and ability to think clearly. Although surrounded by her four loving brothers, she felt utterly alone. Despite the silent war she and Papa had engaged in over the past couple of years, she never lost faith in the family bond. But now with Papa's major health scare, she realized nothing mattered more to her than the Armando men. Papa, Estéban, Gerado, José and Raúl set the tempo in her life. Coupled with her cooling feelings for Rafael, this truth struck an even louder chord in her soul.

"How are you doing?" Aiden's warm voice drifted down to her as she slumped in the chair.

She gazed up at him, dazed and timid. "Not so bad. Doctor Rivera said the operation went well. Papa is in recovery, so we just have to wait. Where's Rafe?"

Aiden squatted in front of her. "I convinced him to go home and wait for my call. I'm not sure his being here is such a good idea with Estéban. You know he feels the same way about Rafe as your father."

Carla glanced over at her brother and nodded. "Yes. He and Papa really dislike Rafe, so maybe it's best he's not here. There's nothing he can do anyway."

Aiden clasped her hands in his, staring down at her delicate fingers. "I'm so sorry this has happened. You've been going through a tough time as it is." Lifting his head, his eyes glistened like sunlight on the sea. She wanted to dive into them and swim away. "If you need anything, anything at all. I'm here." Lowering his head, he pressed a soft kiss to her hand.

Misty-eyed, she said, "*Muchas gracias. Muchas gracias.*" Finally, Carla's tears burst forth, and she wrapped her arms around his neck desperate for comfort and assurance. Her brothers rushed over, and while Aiden consoled her in his embrace, they stood sentinel.

Leaving her brothers in Manolo's hospital room, Carla walked into the corridor towards Aiden. Even through the drama of today, she couldn't help but notice how handsome he was. Balancing gracefully with one foot propped behind him on the wall, he looked at once relaxed yet ready to spring into action. Like a finely tuned coil, Aiden never seemed to be inert. His hands dug deep into his jeans' pockets, pulling them down to expose a slither of burnished abs under his T-shirt. The muscles of his upper torso though hunched and loose, triggered a memory of happier times when Carla found herself enveloped by their impressive strength. A juxtaposition of action man and intelligent advocate, Aiden and his ongoing presence at the hospital gave her strength.

"How is he?" Aiden stepped forwards to meet her.

"He's groggy but fine. The doctor's satisfied with his recovery and says we should all go home. By the time we come back in the morning, Papa will be awake and talking." For the first time since she awoke this morning, Carla felt a flicker of a smile grace her lips.

"That's great news." Aiden's face opened into a cheerful expression.

"I'm going to go back to the flat with the boys tonight." She was disappointed she couldn't offer Aiden somewhere to sleep at home.

"Good idea. I've called Casa del Jardín and got a room there, so don't worry about me. Do you need a lift home?"

"No. It's fine. We're going to stay a little longer. You go now and get some rest. I'll call Rafe and tell him what's happening."

"Okay. Call me tomorrow?"

"Of course." She fixed him with a steady gaze and wished. Wished it could be different.

He lifted his hand to rest his thumb gently against her chin. "I promise everything is going to work out fine." Impudent curls of sun-streaked hair flopped forwards covering his eyes.

Reaching up, Carla grinned at their cheekiness and brushed his hair back where it belonged. "I believe you, Aiden," she whispered.

Lowering closer to her face, he said, "*Que duermas bien, mi amor.* Sleep well, my love." Surprised by Aiden's Spanish, Carla was about to ask where he'd learnt the phrase, but his lips pressed her question closed. Respectful and tender, his gentle kiss lingered and Carla's panic from the day passed. Stepping back, Aiden set his shoulders, nodded and winked. He turned, and she watched him stride away down the empty hospital corridor, around the corner and out of sight. It was an image she'd never forget.

CHAPTER THIRTEEN

OVER THE PAST THREE days, Aiden had held vigil with Carla and her brothers. Visiting the hospital, checking to see if they needed anything and making up excuses as to why Rafael should leave the family alone for a little while longer, Aiden had tried his best to pacify everyone and minimize the risk of further upsets. Until today, he'd not visited Manolo but, on his insistence, Aiden found himself seated next to Carla at her father's bedside. The brothers had retired and left them alone on Manolo's request.

Propped up in his hospital bed, Manolo said, "Carla, you must go back to Granada. I'll be okay. My boys will look after me." Carla opened her mouth for a rebuttal, but he cut her off. "I'm going home tomorrow, and Doctor Rivera is very happy with me. You must stop worrying. After all, I have Raúl, who can fuss over me like a woman." A lurking half-smile and a cheeky twinkle in his eye caught their attention. Tilting her head, Carla reciprocated with a tentative smile. Her father continued, "I know my youngest son is gay. I've known for some time, but I'm a stubborn man. No. That is wrong. I was a stubborn man. Now, the only thing that matters is my family being together, and if Raúl is gay, it doesn't matter. He is my son, and I love him."

Squealing, Carla leapt from her chair and lavished her father's face with kisses. "Oh, Papa, oh, Papa," she cried. "I love you. I love you."

Manolo beamed while his daughter squeezed him in a tight hug. "Sit. Sit. I can't take too much excitement yet."

Wiping away tears of joy Carla perched on the chair, obviously thrilled with her father's new attitude toward Raúl.

Manolo shifted his attention to Aiden. "Thank you for looking after my daughter and bringing her to me so quickly. I was right when I first met you. You are a good man and one to be trusted." He extended his strong, baker's hand towards

Aiden, who grabbed it in a solid shake. "Now, Carla, leave us alone for a minute. Go tell your brothers the good news about Raúl."

"Yes, Papa." Carla kissed her father once more and all but skipped from the room.

"Help me with these pillows please, Aiden."

Aiden reached behind him and restacked the pillows, so Manolo sat more upright.

"Thank you. Sit. Sit" He motioned Aiden to return to his chair. "Now Estéban tells me he has told you everything he knows about Rafe's night-time excursions. Is this correct?"

"Yes, Mr Armando." *Here it comes*, he thought.

"Good. And he tells me you won't tell Carla yet because you need more evidence. Is that correct?"

"Yes, Mr Armando." Aiden's heart rate increased at the thought of having a disagreement with a man who just had three stents implanted in his own heart. But he was committed to not telling Carla anything at this point of time. A thin film of perspiration coated his palms.

"I think that's a good idea," Manolo said in a decisive voice.

Aiden's audible sigh of relief made the older man smile. He continued, "I'm pleased you're a man who has my daughter's best interests at heart. One person suffering a heart attack because of the news of Rafael's perversions is enough in this family."

"From what I understand, sir, Rafael had a terrible childhood on the farm with his father. So maybe that has something to do with—"

Manolo's hand flew into the air, stopping Aiden. "I don't care about Rafael and his family. I care about my daughter and mine. She must not marry Rafael. Once she knows the truth, she will break off their relationship. Then we will be a family once more." With a curt nod, Manolo's decree became absolute.

"I agree, sir. Once she knows I'm sure she won't want to go further with their relationship. However, for you not to lose your daughter or appear to be meddling in her life, she needs to find out for herself. Not by hearsay."

"And how do you plan on doing this?"

"I'm not sure yet, sir. But with everything that's happened and this ceremony in Granada with the aunts and Isabella's runes—"

Manolo fixed Aiden with an unwavering stare. "She told you?" A sharp edge of friction sliced between them.

"Sort of. Not everything of course." Uncomfortable he'd perhaps said too much, Aiden waited for Manolo's response.

"Interesting that my Carla would tell you . . ." Manolo's eyes shifted to the window out of which he stared for a few moments. A sudden peacefulness settled into the room and he said, "Very well, Aiden. You seem to know what you're doing. I've trusted you this far with my daughter's welfare, so I will continue to do so. Take her to Granada and hopefully there, the truth will reveal itself. Then she will know."

"Yes, sir. I'll look after her and bring her back safely to you." Aiden stood to depart.

With lightning quick reflexes, Manolo's hand darted to catch Aiden's wrist. "I'm not sure who brought you to us, but I am pleased you're here. Now go. I need to rest."

"Of course. Goodbye, sir."

Manolo's eyes were already shut, and a contented smile graced his mouth before Aiden turned to leave.

HAVING INSTIGATED A CARE schedule for her father to be maintained by her brothers, Carla satisfied her concerns enough to leave. She also drew strength from the fact her father was walking around the flat unassisted, giving instructions to everyone. That was a very good sign of recovery for Manolo.

"I'll see you soon, Papa." She kissed him on both cheeks.

"Go, Carla. Go and be your mama's daughter. I am very proud of you, and I love you dearly." Tears pooled in the old man eyes as he hugged her close. For Carla, receiving her father's blessing and approval healed a deep wound in her heart, and she wept into his neck.

"I love you too, Papa. I'll be back soon." She turned to Raúl, dressed in his signature silk gown and scuffs, standing beside their father. "You're the primary caregiver now, little brother. I'm counting on you to look after Papa until you have to come to Granada for the shows next week." She squeezed her youngest brother in a big hug and kissed him.

"I'll look after everything."

The self-assured tone in his voice sounded strange. She'd not heard him speak with such authority before and particularly not in Papa's presence. Carla realized her father's love and acceptance also impacted Raúl in a significant way. Funnily enough, he was now more of a man than ever.

By early Thursday evening, Carla was seated once more next to Aiden in the Ferrari, heading back to Granada. As they zipped up the highway, the sky entertained them with a magnificent costume change of burnt sunset oranges to luminescent evening blues. Finally relaxed, she stretched back in her seat.

"I can't thank you enough, Aiden, for all you've done over these past days. Not only looking after me and my family, but also with Rafe. Without you acting as a go-between, I'm sure there would've been an altercation at the hospital between Rafe and Estéban. They've never liked each other." She cast Aiden an appreciate smile.

"Did Manolo say anything about Rafe not visiting him?" Aiden asked.

"No. He didn't mention him at all. I didn't bring it up either. I'm just pleased I was able to talk Rafe into coming back to Granada yesterday." But what was she going to do now? Despite the upheaval caused by her father's heart attack, the situation between her and Rafael remained the same. Nothing had been resolved. Her feelings for him seemed even more distant now that she'd only seen him periodically over the past days.

"When do your aunts arrive?"

"They actually arrive tomorrow for the ceremony on Sunday." The thought of being with these amazing women replaced Carla's anxiety about Rafael. Somewhere lay the answer to her current dilemma, and her aunts would help her find it.

"Where are they staying? At Hotel de Los Páramos with us?"

"Oh no. They're staying in the Amaya house at the foothills of Alhambra. It's been in the family for many, many years. We're having dinner with them there tomorrow night at six o'clock."

"Well, I'm sure you'll have a wonderful night."

"But you're invited as well, Aiden. Men are allowed to come tomorrow night, and I want them to meet you. Please join us," Carla pleaded, leaning toward him.

"Is Rafe going?"

"Oh yes. He wants to see his aunts again too. It'll be such a fun night, drinking, good food, dancing. You must come." She shot him a sunny smile.

"If I won't be intruding, I'd love to meet these aunts of yours. They sound like a coven of witches with their hocus-pocus."

Carla gave his shoulder a playful punch. "Don't be silly. They're much better than witches. They're descended from Carmen Amaya, the Queen of the Gypsies. Their magic is much stronger than witches."

AT HOTEL DE LOS PÁRAMOS, another glorious Andalusian day dappled through the fern-covered pergola of the outdoor breakfast room. The softness of the greenery broke the harsh lines of the stone floors and walls, and colour-matched the mosaic tiles on the filigree circular tables. Unlit Moroccan lamps lay in wait of dusk when they'd come to life, adding a romantic atmosphere to this private sanctuary. Having found a quiet corner and a table to himself, Aiden leisurely breakfasted.

"*Buenos días, señor.*" Victor bowed at Aiden's side; his hands clasped.

"*Buenos días,* Victor," Aiden said, happy for some company.

He flicked out Aiden's crumpled napkin. "How is Mr Armando in Seville? I trust he is feeling better?"

"He's recovering well, thank you, Victor."

He folded the napkin and laid it on Aiden's side plate. "And Miss Armando? What a terrible shock. How is she?"

"Carla is much better knowing her father is recovering well." Aiden sipped his freshly squeezed orange juice and nodded his approval at the manager. "This is great orange juice, Victor. It's like a super-hero juice. I've never tasted oranges this orangey before."

Victor smiled humbly. "Thank you, sir. We do our best. Remember, if there's anything I can do for you, please do not hesitate to ask." He bowed once more and continued his morning rounds of guest ministrations.

Aiden finished his power-packed glass of juice just as Carla and Rafael appeared. "Good morning you two. How did you sleep?"

"Really well, thank you, Ace." Rafael pulled out the chair for Carla.

"Me too. By the time I unpacked and had a shower I crashed. I didn't realize Papa's hospitalization had taken such a toll. But better now."

While Rafael and Carla ate breakfast, Aiden ordered and sipped another juice. "I thought I'd do the touristy thing today and go to Alhambra. Do you want to join me?"

"Not me," Carla said. "I think I'll rest and get more sleep."

"What about you, Rafe? Care for the tour?"

"No thanks, Ace. I'm going to stay with Carla. She needs my support, and I want to be here for her." When Rafael reached over and squeezed Carla's hand, Aiden noted her non-responsiveness to his considerate gesture and thought she would've preferred some alone time.

"Okey-dokey. I'll see you two later this afternoon then. Have a relaxing day." Pushing back his chair, Aiden rose and with map in hand, set off for the old sultan's palace.

~ ♥ ~

ASIDE FROM THE TOURISTS swarming everywhere like annoying insects, Aiden found himself captivated by the history and magic of Alhambra. The sheer scale of the complex overwhelmed. He began his solo excursion by consulting the tourist pamphlet and map, stopping to admire the points of interest along the way. Constructed by Muhammad I as his residence and court, a barracked citadel and a city within the city of Granada, Alhambra was secured by a fortress ring of red stone walls. Though it wasn't until Aiden began to walk its vast twenty-six-acre interior, he realized what an immense architectural achievement it was.

Within Alhambra's enormity were three smaller palaces, the Comares Palace, the Palace of the Lions, and the Partal Palace, each of which was built during the fourteenth century and linked by enchanting landscaped gardens, terraces, canal, and pools. Every detail in the complex had been exquisitely executed with mathematical precision. But by early afternoon, Aiden's tolerance for the crowds and the constant neck craning from viewing decorative vaulted ceilings, archways and windows had sorely diminished. He needed space. *That's what I miss most about Australia*, he thought. *Space.* Wandering out into one of the many gardens, the smell of orange blossoms greeted him. He ambled along the slender pathways under the broad Cyprus trees hoping to find a quiet spot to sit and regroup.

With the sun already past its noon point in the sky, early afternoon shadows moved to give respite from the scorching heat. Now all he needed was to find a seat under some shade where he could sit and think. Rounding a corner of a neatly clipped hedge and tucked back off the main foot thoroughfare, Aiden spied a vacant garden bench. It was tucked under a sprawling tree with the pinkest of flower blossoms. *Perfect*, he thought and strode determinedly towards it. Plonking down he sighed a deep contented breath. He stretched his tired legs in front of him crossing them at the ankles and clasped his hands behind his head. Staring into nothing, the beauty of the garden charmed him, and his eyelids began to droop. The distant noise of people faded, and the warmth of the sun soothed his weary body. Like Carla, he also was tired from these few days of stress in Seville. He decided to leave shortly and grab a siesta this afternoon before going out tonight. After all, he was on holiday.

"Do you mind if I sit down?" An elderly voice pulled Aiden from his reverie.

When he opened his eyes, he stared into a pair of piercing grey eyes and a face fanned in wrinkles. The old woman looked so frail she might snap in a strong gust of wind. Aiden figured she must have been in her eighties or perhaps older. With wiry, grey hair twirled on top her head in a loose bun, stuck through with chopsticks, she wore a flowing caftan and a fringed shawl draped over her thin shoulders.

"Of course. Please sit." Aiden stood and offered her a spot on the seat.

"You're most kind, young man." Even though the garden seat was short, she still chose to sit in the middle leaving little space for Aiden at either end. He had little choice but to sit close beside her or fall off the edge of the bench.

"Where are you from?" She eyed him with the inquisitiveness and directness reserved for only those who've lived a long time.

"I'm from Australia. My name's Aiden." He held out his hand in polite introduction.

"Nice to meet you, Aiden. I'm from Paris. My name is Lucette." When she wrapped his hand in both of hers, she didn't shake but held firm and closed her eyes. "*Mmm*, Aiden from Australia," she said trance-like. Her eyes snapped open, and her steel-grey stare drilled into him. He squirmed, and she released her grip.

Shifting her gaze to the garden surrounding them, Lucette said in a cheery voice, "Isn't Alhambra beautiful, Aiden? I used to come here quite often, but now I'm too old to travel much anymore. Did you know that all the designs in Alhambra are based on the circle and the square? Every design comes from those two geometric shapes only."

"No, I didn't. That's amazing." Aiden remembered the intricate patterns he'd seen on the ceilings, walls, and floors. To think they'd been designed from only two shapes seemed impossible.

"Yes. The geometry of Alhambra represents the divine aspect of the universe, nature, and man." She returned her gaze to him and her lips tipped in a shrewd smile. "Do you believe in the divine, Aiden?"

"I'm not sure, Lucette." *It was the oddest question to ask a stranger*, Aiden thought. *But then she seemed an odd, old duck.*

"'God alone is victor' is written everywhere on the walls of the palaces. Did you know that, Aiden?"

"No, I didn't know that either." He blinked feeling like a schoolboy disappointing his teacher.

"It seems there are a lot of things you don't know, Aiden." Normally such a remark would have stabbed his pride, but Lucette said it with such acuity tinged with kindness, he considered its truth.

"I still have much to learn and life to live," he said, nodding in agreement.

"What about love, Aiden? Do you know what love is?" Deliberately, Lucette swivelled on the seat, her craggy hands folded in her lap, her eyes bright as the sun.

"Now that's a question to ask a young man who's fallen madly in love with a woman he can't have." Aiden finally voiced aloud his feelings.

"And why can't you win her affections?" she asked, a twinkle in her eyes.

"I think I have won her affections, but she needs to break off the relationship she's currently in. I won't ask her to do that. It must be her decision alone." Surprisingly, Aiden found comfort in telling this wizened woman his emotional woes.

Lucette shuffled around to look at the garden while Aiden waited for her response.

"Aren't these pink blossoms *magnifique,* Aiden?" Her fingers fluttered overhead toward the flowers dripping from the tree sheltering them from the heat.

"Ah, yes." He wondered if the previous conversation had ended without her answer.

"Pick me some please." She batted her eyelashes at him in a coquettish manner.

Aiden sprang up and collected a small posy of flowers and handed them to her. "Here you go," he said, and he sat down.

"Love is like these flowers, Aiden. It will blossom into spectacular beauty only when it is nourished. Without nourishment, love will die. Do you understand?" She cast him a sly sideways glance then she sniffed the blooms.

"Sort of?" he said, trying to keep up.

"If this young woman isn't being nourished in the relationship she's in, she'll wither and die. In your opinion, is this happening?"

"Yes. Most definitely." He believed Carla was desperately unhappy and with what he now knew about Rafael's exploits, Aiden was convinced their relationship was doomed.

"Then you must nourish her. Tend to her garden so she may blossom once more. A good gardener knows he must never take leave of his responsibility. He never waits for the garden to tell him what it wants. He never allows another gardener to ruin the delicate blossoms." Lucette's lips curved upwards in an enigmatic smile.

"But I don't want to be responsible for breaking up their relationship."

"How can you possibly break up a relationship that is already unhappy, that is already unhealthy? You can't break up something that is already broken," she said with conviction. "But you can nourish the woman you love so it is easier for her to leave her unhappy relationship and choose you." Lucette reached over and patted Aiden's hand. Her gesture reminded him of someone, but he couldn't quite place who?

Aiden exhaled a deep sigh. "My life of late has been filled with unhealthy people and unhappy situations, because I stepped in and spoke up about the bad things going on. I guess I'm a little hesitant to do it again because this time, I might lose what I want most. I don't want to lose the love of my life."

"Aiden, you can only lose by not living with integrity, by not living with love. You obviously live with integrity, so now you must choose for love. You remind me of a young dancer, also from Australia, who stayed at my boarding house many years ago. She was frightened of loving a man, her director in fact. She didn't know he actually loved her just as much, perhaps more."

"And what happened?"

"I told the man to declare his love for her . . ."

"And?" By now, Aiden had lost all reservations with this strange French woman and hungered for her wisdom.

"He did and at her worst hour, he nourished her, and they started a new life together." Proud and regal she sat on the garden bench and cocked an eyebrow in his direction. "Isn't it time you nourished your young woman?"

Aiden blinked. "Yes. You're right. I can't keep waiting around for something to happen to shake her into making her choice. I have to do the shaking."

"*Exactement.*" Lucette wagged her index finger in agreement. "Now go. Hurry, Aiden, and tend to your garden. Nourish her."

"Thank you, Lucette. Thank you." He reached over and kissed her on both cheeks, and she giggled. The familiar sound of her laughter interrupted his gratitude. He pulled away and gave her a wary look. "Lucette, who are you really?"

"I am nothing more than the person you were supposed to meet today. I read you in my cards. Now go." Waving her frail hand at him, she shooed him away.

CHAPTER FOURTEEN

DISAPPOINTED AT NOT FINDING Carla on his return, Aiden waited out the afternoon in his room. Too pumped for an afternoon nap, he was dressed and downstairs at the appointed time to meet Carla and Rafael. Fingers of dark cerise streaked the sky as they left the hotel and walked along cobblestone streets to the foothills at the base of Alhambra.

"This way now," Carla said, veering from the pavement and onto a worn, dirt track, partly hidden by shrubbery.

"What? Through there?" Aiden looked ahead and saw nothing but dense forest.

"Yes. The track takes us up to the house. Come on." Resolute, Carla strode onwards, leaving Aiden to follow.

He glanced at Rafael, who flourished his hand and said, "After you."

Once more Aiden found himself in the middle . . . a place he was becoming increasingly uncomfortable with.

With the uneven path carving limited access through the encroaching forest, Aiden admired Carla's sure-footedness and spirit. She made a far superior guide to the odd couple of Teo and Rosa. Plus, her tight, denim-wrapped butt was far more enjoyable to look at. Grinning to himself, he enjoyed his clever internal musings. Suddenly, the path opened before them and was replaced by long, low donkey-steps which made the climb easier.

They walked upwards into the cool embrace of the shadowy forest while Carla gave a quick history lesson. "Although this is public land, the Amaya family has been permitted to keep their ancestral home, which was built here in the mid-1800s. As children, we were told many stories, true or otherwise of the magic and soothsaying skills of the Amaya Gypsies. It was the threat of a gypsy curse which scared the local authorities all those years ago, not to evict us from this land. The Amaya name has always possessed a mystical power.

Due to those long-held superstitions, we still own the Amaya property. I know it sounds unbelievable, but we've been virtually ignored and left to go about our business."

Traipsing up the final flight of stone steps, Aiden said, "Bizarre. But hey, I wouldn't want to risk a Gypsy curse either, if I believed in them. Who else from your family aside from your aunts is going to be here tonight?"

"Uncle Domingo, Marco, and Theresa will all be here. None of my brothers will come now because of Papa, which is a shame."

Aiden paired names with faces in his mind.

"Is your father coming, Rafael?" Carla asked, glancing back over her shoulder.

"I don't know. We don't talk much, so I'm not sure," he said with indifference.

Being an only child, Aiden wasn't used to big families or family resentments. Still, he wondered if a showdown between Rafael and his father might finally clear the air. When they crested the last few steps, the old stone and mortar house appeared. Topped with a slanting tin roof and bordered with a hand-made dry-stone wall, the Amaya house and property exuded a rustic, yet dilapidated charm. Sequestered back into the rock, the simple square abode was surrounded by olive trees and an assortment of thick aromatic shrubs like those Aiden had seen at Alhambra. The smell of burning firewood and cooking food filtered out to welcome them as they tramped towards the door. With only two small casement windows and a faded green-painted wooden door thrown open to the night, Aiden winced at how cramped it'd be inside. Definitely not large enough to shelter all the people Carla thought would attend the reunion. Thank goodness there was an external stone terrace where they could congregate when it got too stuffy inside. Like stepping back in time, the entire scene transported Aiden to a world he was unfamiliar with.

"*Hola. Hola.*" Carla rushed towards the open doorway.

Aiden delayed, allowing Rafael and Carla to enter and embrace their family. Hoping to slip inside unnoticed, he felt like an intruder crashing their family reunion. *Maybe this wasn't such a good idea,* he thought.

"Aiden. Aiden," Theresa cried as she raced over and threw herself onto him. Her fleshy breasts struck his chest squashing hard against him. He extricated her body from his with a gentle but firm push. "Hello, Theresa. Good to see you again." Out of the corner of his eye, he spied Domingo and Marco glaring at him from beside the open fireplace. The heat in their eyes matched the licking flames cooking whatever it was in the suspended pot about the fire.

No way was he going to allow Theresa to get anywhere near him tonight. Fortunately, the room was only sparsely furnished with a few pieces of handmade furniture, a woven floor rug, and some traditional handicrafts, so keeping space between them would be doable. "If you'll excuse me."

Peeved, she blinked and pouted at his cool welcome and hasty departure. Ignoring her response, he marched over and offered his hand to Domingo and Marco, who reluctantly shook it, but never smiled. *Good enough*, Aiden thought. Turning around he saw Rafael, sullen and quiet in the corner.

Aiden surmised the man with the booming voice and intimidating manner speaking with Carla must be Sancho, Rafael's pig-killing father. An imposing, wide-girthed man, he stood slightly shorter than Rafael. He was fashioned for manual labour whereas Rafael was finer, more elegant. Aiden suspected Rafe took after his mother. Like Domingo, Sancho possessed a beer barrel body, a no-nonsense attitude and an inflated opinion of himself. It was evident by Carla's body language she didn't much care for her Uncle Sancho and Aiden couldn't blame her. He'd taken an immediate dislike to the man without having met him. Brow-beaten, Rafael skulked in the corner, not speaking to anyone. Being in his father's presence, he was completely subjugated, his bravado and authority squashed. Sancho's brutality and god-knows-what-else had reeked such severe damage on his only son that Aiden felt sorry for him. Rafael had great talent and natural charisma. It was a shame his father hadn't shown him more love and kindness. Fixing Carla in his line of sight, he watched her excuse herself from Uncle Sancho and rush to a well-dressed, handsome woman standing furthest from the door.

"Aunt Chantelle," she squealed, wrapping her in a tight squeeze. Carla brightened like a happy child coming home to the welcoming embrace of her family. After more kissing and chatting, he followed Carla's gaze to the decrepit armchair in the back corner of the room and gasped. There, staring at him was Lucette. Even from this distance, her otherworldly grey eyes pierced his disciplined demeanour. Her half-smile acknowledged him, then she turned to Carla, who dropped to her knees hugging Lucette tightly. Shaking his head, Aiden remained on the side-lines, piecing the coincidences together. Casting back to when they were at Casa de los ángeles, Carla had told him the names of her aunts, but he'd not remembered them. Recalling people's names had never been his strong point. Now standing in the Amaya house watching Carla hug her aunt, the lady who introduced herself to him today at Alhambra, it all came flooding back to him. He closed his eyes and mapped it out in his mind. Aunt Chantelle and Aunt Lucette were sisters who lived in Paris, and they were the first cousins of Uncle Domingo and Uncle Sancho. Carla's dead mother, Isabella was the only first cousin missing. "And they all descended from the Amaya line. The same as Carmen Amaya, the Queen of the Gypsies," he whispered finally connecting the dots.

"That's correct, Aiden." By his side, Lucette smiled up at him in wry amusement.

He gazed down at her and flashed a cheeky grin. "Did you know who I was talking about today when we met at Alhambra and spoke about love?" He needed to know if this shrewd old woman had played him.

"Not at all. But it's clear you love my niece," she whispered and tapped his arm with her fan.

"Just because I'm here with Carla, doesn't mean I was speaking about her." But as the words fell from his mouth, he knew his attempt at subterfuge was pointless.

"Do not try to fool an old woman about love, Aiden. Anyone who has eyes can see how you feel about her."

"And Rafael? He's your nephew?" Aiden swallowed hard and frowned at the diminutive woman beside him who barely reached his shoulder.

"My dear, Rafael is terribly wounded. Sancho is a wicked man, and he has a lot to answer for. But that is not your concern. Your concern is to nourish my niece." She patted his hand and shuffled back to the group. Then he remembered. Lucette patted his hand the same as Carla did. He needed to pay more attention to these things.

Glasses filled with burgundy wine were offered, and Aiden accepted his as he joined the group. In a big, baritone voice, Sancho held court in the middle of the small room. "A toast. To my wonderful cousins, Chantelle and Lucette who came all the way from Paris."

"To family," Domingo chimed in, the timbre of his voice matching Sancho's.

"To family," the others cheered, and everyone drank.

With red wine tainting the corners of his mouth, Sancho continued, "To my son Rafael and his beautiful fiancé Carla. May they marry soon and have many babies." Standing next to each other, Rafael clutched Carla's hand and together they accepted the toast, although, to Aiden, their smiles looked disingenuous. Everyone swilled more wine except Lucette who trundled back to her armchair.

"Dinner is ready everyone so come over with your plates when you want. Domingo put on some music please." Chantelle tied on an apron and with a ladle in hand waited to serve. A home-cooked meal was what Aiden longed for and the aromatic, spicy smell wafting from the pot made his mouth water.

"Me first, Aunt Chantelle." Theresa stood with plate extended and Aiden hung back until she'd been served. Due to the open fire and body heat, the temperature inside the house steadily rose, and some people drifted outdoors to cool off. Flamenco music filtered from Domingo's phone and Aiden recognized a melody he'd heard at Sevilla Flamenco. He found himself humming along with it as Carla joined him.

"Aiden, come meet my aunts." Holding his free hand, Carla dragged him to the fireplace. "Aunt Chantelle, this is Aiden. He's a lawyer from Australia visiting Spain for a while."

Aiden offered his hand. "Pleased to meet you, Chantelle."

"And you, Aiden. Whereabouts in Australia do you come from?" she asked.

"The Gold Coast."

"Really? My son Philippe once loved a girl from the Gold Coast. He played the fool unfortunately and lost her. She was a lovely girl. Would you like something to eat yet?" She lifted the ladle from the pot bubbling in the fireplace. For a split instant, Aiden imagined her as a witch mixing her potion. *Pull yourself together, man.* She was far too beautiful and well-dressed for a witch. Shaking his head free of the image, he said, "No thank you, Chantelle. Not yet. I'll come back shortly."

With unconcealed excitement, Carla said, "Now I want you to meet my Aunt Lucette."

"I've already met Lucette," he said, his eyes twinkling with mischief.

"What now?" she asked.

"No. At Alhambra today. We sat on the same garden bench and got talking."

"Really? What did you talk about?"

"All sorts of things, life, love, gardens, the usual sort of stuff strangers talk about." A sly smile spread on his face.

Carla laughed. "You didn't. Did you?" Tilting her head, she regarded him trying to work out if he was joking or not.

"You go and ask her. Go on." With a slight shove, he pushed Carla to question her aunt. She dashed over to Lucette, who obviously confirmed Aiden's story with a wave and nod of her head. Carla hurried back to his side. "Well, that's very strange. She said the same as you. How peculiar the two of you met like that?"

Aiden shrugged. "Seems there's a lot of peculiar things happening to me of late. Let's get some fresh air and find Rafe."

~ ❤ ~

"Aunt Lucette, won't you talk to him for me? Please?" Rafael had waited until everyone was occupied either outside or eating before approaching his favourite aunt.

Feathering an affectionate stroke across his cheek, she said, "Of course I will, Rafael my sweet. Ask Sancho to come over and join us."

Rafael kissed her weathered hand and dashed off. Within a few moments, he returned with his father.

Lucette said, "Sit. Sit, Sancho. I think we should talk." Rafael and Sancho pulled up a couple of old milking stools. For Sancho, finding his balance proved difficult but eventually, they were settled. Propped in front of Lucette, they looked like they were awaiting an audience with the queen.

"Sancho, what I'm about to say may sound shocking, but promise me you'll listen and not raise your voice." She cocked an eyebrow at him and with authority, tapped her fan in the palm of her hand.

Rafael's father glanced and sneered at his son, already condemning him for whatever was to follow. "Yes, Lucette. I promise," he said begrudgingly.

"Very well." Lucette's voice remained calm and in control. "I know you think Rafael and Carla are destined to be married, but I'm not so sure."

"What do you mean?" He turned his wrath on his son. "What have you been saying?"

"Nothing, Papa." Rafael heard the pitiful panic in his voice and hated himself all the more. "But I've been telling you for ages I don't want to marry her. And I don't think she wants to marry me either anymore."

"Nonsense," he snapped. "You two have been destined to be married since you were small children. I know these things. It's not just the Amaya women who have the gift."

"Sancho you are wrong," Lucette said as simple fact. "You do not have the gift, and they are not destined to be married."

Heat raced up Sancho's neck. "What do you mean? What do you know?" Sancho leaned towards her, scowling in a menacing manner.

Ignoring his threat, Lucette continued, "Ever since Rafael was a small boy you have imposed your will upon him. I don't know what else you have done to him, but I know you should be ashamed of it." The intensity with which she glowered at Sancho sent a shudder through Rafael and Sancho recoiled as if smacked on the nose. "As Carla and Rafael grew up together and began dancing, you fantasized they would marry, be successful, be famous and have children. It was always about giving you more things for you to boast about."

"That's a lie. It's all lies." Folding his arms, he looked away.

"Look at me, Sancho. I do not lie. It is you who lies." Lucette slapped his knee with her fan, getting his attention. "If Isabella hadn't died, we wouldn't be having this conversation for she would've put a stop to this nonsense long ago. Since Chantelle and I live in Paris, you've been left to your own devices, manipulating your son and the rest of the family. It must stop now. You must release Rafael from this betrothal, or you'll lose him forever. He can no longer be your brutalized slave."

The small, wooden stool hurtled backwards halfway across the room with a shriek. Sancho rose like Poseidon from the ocean, lumbering over and bellowing down at Lucette. "How dare you speak to me like that!"

Rafael flew to his feet, defending Lucette against his father's rage. "Don't, Papa. Don't," he yelled.

Turning his fury on his son, Sancho hurled back his arm to strike him, but couldn't. Trapped, he spun around and snarled, deep and slow. "Let go of me."

Aiden's arm shook with every ounce of strength he had as he intercepted Sancho's attack. "I think you need to calm down, sir."

"Sancho, stop this right now." The demand came from Chantelle, who marched over from the fire to stand next to

Aiden. "Now I say!" Her voice rose higher and with it, the command to obey.

"Sancho, what's going on? This is a party." Uncertain as to what all the fuss was about, Domingo bustled in from outside. "Come outside and have a wine with me. Come on."

Stripping his arm from Aiden's hold, Sancho sneered at him. "How dare you interfere in family business. Get out of my way." Pushing past him, Sancho stalked outside with a litany of curses.

Carla hurried over to Rafael. "Are you all right, Rafe?"

"Leave me alone. I'm fine." Imitating his father, he pushed past Carla and glowered at Aiden. "Stay out of this," he growled. He stormed outside in search of his father. How dare Aiden save him from his father? He could look after himself. He'd show them he was a real man.

"You! Old man!" Rafael hollered at his father who was propped beside Domingo, leaning against the rock wall. Sancho glared at his impudent son and turned purple with rising rage. He reminded Rafael of the decomposing toads on the farm when they'd swell up before exploding. Striding over to him and with unconcealed hate in his voice, Rafael roared, "I'm through with putting up with your shit. You and your pigs, and the killing and the—"

Rafael's head snapped to one side. He heard his neck crack before he registered the pain. Screaming. He heard lots of shouting and screaming. He staggered, but he was okay. A little dazed, but okay. Slowly his hand rubbed his burning cheek. He remembered this sensation. His father had slapped him like this a thousand times before. Rafael's senses returned, and he blinked his eyes to regain focus. Domingo's arms locked Sancho motionless, but the loathing in his father's face still struck Rafael like a blow to the gut. Leaning closer, Rafael spat the words into his father's face. "And the sex. The sex you mother fucker. You've ruined me, you sick bastard." Dripping with abhorrence and contempt, Rafael's face contorted as he glared up and down at his father. "You pitiful bastard. You make me sick." He spat at Sancho's feet, snapped a turn and strode off.

The raised and concerned voices of his family followed his flight down the stairs until they were soon drowned out by the forest into which he fled. Rafe felt like his heart would explode. The fury he'd unleashed on his father did little to quell his own rage and pain. Decades of hot tears streamed down his face, burning deep into his soul. Great, heaving sobs burst from his throat, and he hurried deeper into the undergrowth. Sliding down a tree trunk, he dropped to his haunches, head in sweaty palms. He howled like a wounded animal, knowing not whether he'd live or die. His gut retched trying to expel the awful disgust for himself and his father. He choked and gagged. Nothing. Nothing but wretched wet tears and clear fluids came forth. The insidious, clotted bile of his past remained stubbornly entrenched in his body. Aunt Lucette had done her best. No matter how deserving, the outburst to his father had cemented a life-long rift in the family. He'd never be able to face any of them again. It was done now. No longer could he keep up this charade with Carla. He had to tell her the truth and let the chips fall where they may.

"AUNT LUCETTE, ARE YOU sure you're all right?" Carla helped her aunt sit in the rickety armchair having witnessed Rafael and Sancho's quarrel outside from the doorway.

"Yes. Yes. My dear. Chantelle and I are used to these silly men blowing off steam. Sancho has always been a bully. He doesn't frighten me. And poor Rafael has been so abused. I knew one day, he would turn. Today was that day." Lucette's wrinkled face broke into a compassionate smile and she patted Carla's hand. "So, enough about that. Are you ready for the new moon, Carla?"

"Well, I don't know what's happening on Sunday, so I can't be ready I guess." She tilted her head, hoping for more information.

"*Exactement.*" Lucette waved her fan in the air but didn't expand on the gypsy secret.

Carla looked towards the door. "Do you think I should follow Rafe? He was so upset." She knew Rafe's moods could swing out of control, but she'd never seen this level of rage in him before.

"No, my dear. He needs time to think about the future. Best to leave him alone. And don't go plying him with questions when you return this evening. Kindness. Rafe needs simple acts of kindness."

Tears welled in Carla's eyes and sobbing softly, she rested her head on Lucette's lap. "Oh, Aunt Lucette, what am I to do?"

"Dance my dear. Dance. Everything else will become apparent very soon." Lucette lifted Carla's face and her soft grey eyes comforted her.

"You know my mother had the same colour eyes as you, Aunt Lucette." Carla sniffed, gazing into the limitless love in her aunt's eyes.

"I know Carla. Isabella and I were very close. I miss her too. But she's here. You know that, don't you?"

"Oh yes. I know that. I talk to Mama a lot." She brightened a little at the thought of her mother.

"And does she answer you, my dear?" Lucette's fine eyebrows crept up her forehead.

"Of course. She always answers. It just that I'm not sure what she means . . ." Carla gazed off into the distance.

Lightly tapping her fan on her niece's forearm, Lucette called her back. "You will. Now dance for your old aunt. Please."

Carla so loved and respected her aunt, she couldn't deny Lucette's request. "Very well. A short dance I used to do for Mama when I was young. Just for you." She kissed her aunt on both cheeks and took her position.

~ ♥ ~

"So, where to from here?" Aiden walked beside Carla allowing her to set the pace on the way back to the hotel.

"Well, it's just around the next corner . . ."

"No, I don't mean the way back to the hotel. I mean with everything else?" Because Carla hadn't understood his inference, Aiden realized he'd opened a conversation in which he'd have to take the lead.

"Everything else?" she quizzed.

Scratching the back of his neck, he halted and turned to face her. "With you and Rafe . . . and me?"

Carla dropped her head giving Aiden the chance to admire how the lamplight reflected off her ebony hair. He reached out and stroked her slim shoulders, brushing the wayward locks behind them. She was diminutive, like Lucette. And like her aunt, she resonated with such a powerful presence, Aiden could barely resist her. Like a moth to a flame was how his mates used to describe how women reacted to Aiden. Now he knew its meaning. Here he was on the other side of the world, fluttering recklessly near to Carla's effervescent flame. The attraction, incontrovertible.

"Carla, I know you're unhappy. And I'm unhappy watching you be unhappy." She lifted her eyes, and he saw tears pooling in them. "I've seen too many tears in your eyes since I've met you. No woman as beautiful, talented and loving as you should be crying. You deserve to be happy. And I'd like to make you happy."

"Oh, Aiden. I am unhappy but more than that, I'm confused. In my heart, I don't believe Rafe and I will be married or even stay together. There are too many secrets and unanswered questions between us. And the love we shared is gone."

"So why not break it off? Let me show you how happy we can be together." He reached for her hands and caressed them tenderly with his thumbs.

"I'm waiting for a sign."

"What sort of sign? Here I am offering you all of me. What else are you waiting for?" His heart rate escalated, his breathing shallowed and his body prickled with the first signs of anxiety. Suddenly, Aiden realized loving Carla and the fear of her not loving him in return, far outweighed any fear he'd experienced repelling off cliffs, big wave surfing, jumping out of planes or any other action sport he'd tried to cram into his life.

She stretched up and cupped his face. "Give me two days. I need to do what I came here to do with my aunts firstly. But I have a feeling everything will work out. Don't you?"

Knowing that he had no other choice but to comply with her wishes, he shot her one of his champion smiles. "Absolutely."

CHAPTER FIFTEEN

Following Aunt Lucette's advice of simple acts of kindness, Carla didn't probe Rafael on her return to the hotel. With his feet propped on a chair and their room in darkness, she found him sitting in a corner, staring out into space. She touched his arm gently. "Come on, Rafe. Come to bed. You need to sleep. Here, let me help you." She assisted him to his feet and began peeling off his clothes. That he remained so unresponsive through the undressing concerned Carla. She'd never seen him so listless, so removed. She threw back the covers of the bed and guided him in. Like a sick patient, he slithered into the comfort of the luxurious bed, pensive and silent. Once changed into her pyjamas, Carla slipped in beside him. Lifeless, he lay absorbed in his own torment. She nestled in closer and cradled him under her arm. Stroking his hair, she hummed a sweet lullaby her mama sang to her when she was a little girl. The sweet melody hung in their room spinning memories of innocent childhoods. But as Carla sang, she mourned for Rafael. For it was only her with a childhood of innocence. Not poor Rafael. Sleep and its blessed respite carried her away into happier times, but how long Rafael lay there awake waiting for its relief, she never knew.

Now with the new day flooding their room in the golden glow of morning sunlight, Carla was determined to lighten Rafael's mood and make the best of things until the ceremony tomorrow night.

"Rafe, why don't we go horse riding today? You love riding? Being outdoors will do us all good." Purposely she kept her voice light and optimistic.

"Why not?" But he sounded unenthused, his tone distant.

"We could do a day ride from the Sierra Nevada National Park." She laced up her walking shoes and watched him on the balcony with his back to her, his hands gripping the railing, just staring up to Alhambra. "But if you don't want to go, we can do something else if you like," she added, hoping to find something to motivate him.

When he turned to face her, Carla felt a sharp pang in her heart. Her darling Rafe, the man she thought she'd marry, looked so forlorn, so beaten and so confused. The colourful man he used to be blurred into an abstract of monochromatic greys. Like a water painting ruined by too much liquid, Rafael's prior power dripped from him, puddling at his feet. She realized it wasn't just her who suffered from grief at the thought of their relationship ending. Obviously, he felt it too. Deeply. With long, graceful strides he walked over, kneeled at her feet and took her hands in his. "Carla, you know I have always loved you, don't you?"

"Yes, Rafe. I know." Her raw emotions began their now customary attack on her tear ducts. She swallowed hard, pushing them away.

"I've never meant to hurt you, and I know I have." His head dropped, his black mane of hair tickling her hands.

"Come on, Rafe. Let's not get maudlin. Let's enjoy today. Come on." She rose and dragged him up beside her. "You get dressed, and we'll have breakfast."

Putting on a brave face, he said, "We'll invite Ace. He's good company, and you can drive down with him. A ride on the Ducati will do me good."

Carla grabbed their coats from the closet. "Yes. I'm sure Aiden rides horses. He does everything else." She tried to giggle. It didn't work.

Rafael stepped behind her and wrapped his graceful arms around her waist. "Oh, Carla, I wish it could've all been different." His voice cracked with breaking emotion, and Carla felt sure Rafael heard her heart whimper.

Squeezing her eyes shut, she willed herself not to lose control. Together, she had to hold it together. What a terrible word to use since she and Rafael would no longer be together.

Not turning, she spoke to the gloom of the closet as she clutched his wrists. "Me too, Rafe. But everything happens for a reason. I have to believe that." She sighed a big, deep breath and gave up a silent prayer of thanks he couldn't see the tears streaking her cheeks.

~ ♥ ~

AIDEN WAS IN HIS element. Breathtaking scenery on a vast scale surrounded him. The rugged mountain ranges stretched like rolling swathes of purple-green fabric butting against the blue sky on their endless journey to the horizon. In the distance, soaring snow-covered peaks proved just how high the mountains of Sierra Nevada rose. *Vast, simply vast,* thought Aiden, breathing in nature's beauty. After a leisurely three-hour morning horse ride, they finally rested for lunch. Butt sore and thigh chaffed, they perched on a craggy outcrop overlooking the spectacular three-hundred-and-sixty-degree panorama. Awe-struck, he marvelled at the view while they chomped through their meagre lunch pack with little conversation. All too soon, the riding guide's call signalled it was time to hit the homeward trails.

"This place is amazing." Aiden stowed his lunch pack back into his saddle while keeping his eyes riveted on the surrounding landscape.

"Yes, it's pretty special," Rafael said, the dead tone of his voice indicating otherwise.

"Back home we'd call this God's own country." Aiden strapped the compulsory riding helmet onto his head, still impressed despite Rafe's gloom.

Carla gazed into the distance, smiling. "Sierra Nevada means snowy range in Spanish, but I prefer your phrase better."

Being called to mount, they hoisted onto their well-trained Andalusian Arabs, ready for the ride home. Like cowboys atop their steeds, they readied themselves, holding the reins.

"I love how these horses know every inch of these tracks. All we have to do is sit and watch the scenery go by," Aiden said, reclining in the saddle.

Taking a different route home, the horses navigated a narrow track of shale rock cutting its way through the side of a mountain. Although not a difficult track, Aiden thought if the horses got spooked and bolted, he'd been in for a hair-raising ride. Shale under hoof didn't make a good footfall. *We'd all end up like the man from Snowy River sliding down these shale ridges,* he thought. The mental imagery alerted his horse-riding senses, and he repositioned himself upright and ready, just in case.

Another couple of hours into the ride home, the guide hung back to join them. Conversing with Rafael, he nodded and pointed to an open space of grassland ahead. He rode off in that direction while Rafael reined in his horse.

Rafael turned to Aiden and Carla. "The guide says we can open the horses up a little if we want. They're used to it here. He's gone up ahead as the marker, and when the horses come to him, they know to slow down and stop. Who wants to give them a sprint?"

"Not me. I'm quite happy just plodding along," Carla said giving her dappled grey an affectionate pat on the neck.

The first rush of adrenaline hit Aiden's body. "I'm in. I'll follow you, Rafe."

"Remember, I grew up on a farm, Aiden. I've ridden plenty of horses." The sarcastic, yet cheeky challenge in Rafael's voice spurred Aiden on.

"Okay, farm boy. Let's see what you're made of." Aiden heeled his horse, and as Rafe kicked his in the guts, they took off. Rafael's black-maned, chestnut launched up the small knoll picking up speed. Close behind, Aiden leaned forwards into the gallop, lifting his weight to ride in the stirrups. The distance between them closed as they flew up through the grassland. With a quick glance backwards, Rafael scowled at his challenger. Readjusting his direction away from the riding guide who waited patiently on his mount, Rafael kicked his horse hard and galloped faster. Aiden's gut flipped. *What the fuck is he doing?* Aiden snapped his reins and urged his sixteen-hand white Arab to follow. Bolting past the riding guide, Aiden heard him yelling frantically. But he didn't look back. Upwards he drove his horse after Rafael. Lathered with sweat, the Arab obeyed, and Aiden knew he and Rafael were riding into dangerous territory, both on unleashed horsepower and into country they didn't know. *Fuck, the man from Snowy River.*

Cresting the hill, Aiden watched as Rafael's horse started a downhill slide. Digging deep, Aiden tore after them, praying the slope didn't end at a cliff to a gorge. The ground hurtled towards him when he reefed back on the reins, trying to control his horse, which he hoped, knew this landscape better than he did.

Sweat dripped in his eyes making it hard to see, but he dare not let go of the reins. At last, he was closing in and just as safety seemed to be in sight, he watched Rafael's horse skid and stumble. Rafael flew from the saddle, crashing hard to the ground. With an angry snort, his horse glared at him, then trotted away a few metres and finally halted. Hauling back hard on his reins, Aiden slowed his horse enough to jump off and help Rafael.

"What the fuck is wrong with you, Rafe?" Aiden hollered. "Are you trying to kill yourself or what?"

Slapping Aiden's help away, Rafael struggled to his feet. Dusting himself off, he stalked wildly in a circle. "I'm fucking sick of you sticking your nose in where it doesn't belong, Ace."

"What the fuck—" Aiden was through playing mister nice guy.

"You fucking heard me. You can't help yourself can you Mr. fucking action sports champion. Saving me in the ocean, saving me from my fucked-up father and now saving me from a bolting horse." With his hands clenched by his sides, nails biting into his palms, he screamed, "Fucking leave me alone. I don't need saving!"

"You mad son of a bitch. What is it do you need? Eh?" Aiden hurled himself at Rafe and wrestled him to the ground.

Dust, dirt, and sweat covered them as they rolled around, trying to find a handhold on the other. But Aiden's strength and power were too much for Rafe. "Answer me. What is it you fucking need then?" The force of the demand in Aiden's voice matched the strength with which he hauled Rafe to his feet, gripping his shoulders like a vice. Aiden shook him furiously. "I know what the fuck you, Teo and Rosa got up to, you sick mother fucker." With every word Aiden spat, he shook Rafe trying to extract a confession.

Rafe fought back, but his strength waned. He screamed in submission, flailing his arms and trying to break away.

"That's right. Squeal like the pigs your father killed." Aiden's voice thundered maniacally through the mountains, but he held firm.

"Aiden. Stop. Stop it!" Carla shrieked, standing no more than a few metres away. Her expression of shock and horror at Aiden's callous treatment of Rafe emasculated him and Aiden's rage withered instantly. Beside her, the riding guide lowered his head unsettled by the display. Aiden released Rafe, who dropped to the ground grovelling and crying.

Immediately, Aiden apologized, trying to calm Rafael, who scrambled away from his touch, terrified. Running over, Carla crouched beside him and in a gentle voice said, "Rafe, Rafe, are you all right?"

Coated in sweat, tears, and dirt, Rafael hauled himself to his knees. "I'm sorry, Carla. I'm so sorry. I can't do this any longer."

Livid, Carla snapped a flinty stare at Aiden, who shook his head and opened his hands in supplication. Regretting the violence of his actions, he remained silent and subdued.

"I've wanted to tell you the truth for a long time, but whenever I tried, I couldn't." Rafael dragged a grubby hand across his mouth and spat out specks of dirt and grass.

Carla removed her riding helmet. "Truth about what?"

"About everything. About me, my father and what I've turned into." Small sobs rippled up from Rafael's chest. Folding his legs underneath him, he dropped back onto the ground, defeated. He looked at Aiden. "How long have you known?"

"I had my suspicions at Costa del Sol. I knew something was off." Aiden knelt next to Rafael.

"Suspicions about what?" Carla's gaze flicked from one to the other.

Aiden looked at Rafe. It was up to him to tell her.

"Carla, I hate having to say this, but I have to. I've tried to hide it for too long. The physical, emotional and sexual abuse Papa inflicted on me for years when I was a boy has damaged me too much. I can't have a normal relationship with you. With anyone." Rafael hung his head in shame.

Aiden nodded. At last, his suspicions were vindicated. He knew Sancho was culpable in Rafael's behaviour. *The bastard!*

"Oh God, Rafael. What did he do to you?" Moist-eyed, Carla stroked Rafe's shoulder until he slowly lifted his gaze to her.

"Now is not the time. Maybe one day . . . But I can't suppress the sexual compulsions I've inherited from those terrible days on the farm. Forgive me, Carla." Whimpering softly, he grabbed her hand, caressed it with his cheek, then set it free. "Teo and Rosa were street prostitutes. I paid them to have sex with me. Rough, horrible, disgusting sex." He spoke the last words with bitter revulsion, then slumped motionless and silent. Aiden thought it was probably the posture Rafe had learnt as a battered child. Downtrodden and bullied, he waited for his beating.

Shocked, Carla said, "You were having rough, horrible, disgusting sex with Teo and Rosa?" She spun on Aiden. "And you knew this to be true?"

"No. I only suspected there was something going on. It wasn't my place to say anything to you. What if I was wrong? Rafe needed to tell you himself."

"Oh God, Rafe. I don't know what to say." With enormous effort, Carla rose to her feet and looked down on Rafael, whose face remained averted.

"I'm sorry, Carla. I'm a selfish, perverted coward." During the ensuing silence, Rafael regained some of his composure and rose awkwardly to stand facing her. "I didn't tell you because I didn't want to break up our relationship, personally or professionally. I'm nothing without you. You've been my world since I was a boy. You were all I thought about after those awful days and nights with Papa. The thought of losing you now was too much to bear."

Aiden rose to his feet and made the triangle complete.

A deep frown creased Carla's forehead. "So instead of telling me the truth, you kept me thinking we'd be married and live and dance happily ever after?" Carla's bristling indignation bared its teeth.

"I'm sorry, Carla."

"I'm sorry too, Rafael. But sorry isn't going to cut it." She snapped a turn and marched over to the riding guide. "Get me out of here."

"Ace, help me, please. Look after her. I know you're in love with her. Help her forget all this happened. Please?" Rafael grabbed Aiden's arms, shaking him, tears pooling in his eyes.

"Rafe, mate. I'll do whatever I can. She needs some time to calm down, be by herself and think. Come on, get back on your horse and we'll ride out of here together." Aiden walked Rafael to his horse and gave him a leg up. Once mounted, they fell in line behind the guide and Carla, giving them at least fifty metres leeway. On the slow ride back, Aiden's emotions were mixed. On one hand was his sympathy for Rafe and the horrors he must have endured at the hands of his father. On the other, Aiden felt guilty that because of Rafe's residual damage, he now had his chance with Carla. Rafe's nightmare had become Aiden's dream come true. And he couldn't get rid of the bittersweet taste it left in his mouth. He tried his best to shut out everything except the magnificent scenery because he knew that after they got back to Granada, new decisions were going to be made. Decisions that would change his life. Forever.

~ ♥ ~

AIDEN THANKED THE RIDING guide and dropped an extra fifty euro in his hand then joined Carla who waited next to the Ferrari, her face devoid of any expression. At his bike, Rafael stood gazing forlornly at her.

Aiden flicked the lock on the car. "See you back at the hotel, Rafe."

Rafe nodded at Aiden then called out, "Goodbye, Carla." He lashed on his helmet and jumped on the Ducati. Kicking dust and dirt behind him, he slewed up the driveway out of the riding school. When Aiden opened the door for Carla, it struck him. *Fuck!*

Hollering at Carla, Aiden raced to his door. "Buckle up and hang on." In no time, the Ferrari was screaming down the dirt road after the Ducati. Because of the dust churned up behind Rafael's bike, Aiden couldn't see the road and was driving blind.

"Aiden, what's wrong?" she yelled, pulling down hard on the seatbelt across her shoulder.

"Rafe." Fear rippled in Aiden's voice.

"What do you mean?"

"He said goodbye to you, Carla. Not see you at the hotel. He said good — fucking — bye." As the Ferrari slid around a hairpin turn trying to find traction on the dirt road, the dust from the Ducati no longer blocked Aiden's view. Instead, it fogged off to his left in an enormous cloud. With teeth clenched, Aiden slammed on the brakes. The Ferrari's tyres tried to grip, but it skidded over the loose dirt. While Aiden grappled to control the machine, the sound of an almighty crash and Carla screaming "Rafe" were the last things he heard before he leapt from the car.

CHAPTER SIXTEEN

CARLA ROCKED BACK AND forth, moaning. That her life had taken such a dramatic, unexpected turn, bewildered her. Her brain felt like a bowl of mush. Her thoughts were totally incongruent. Her fiancé lay broken in a hospital bed, and she'd not seen any of it coming. How could she be so stupid? She berated herself over and over for her insensitivity, her lack of insight. And to think tonight she would find out if she possessed the gypsy gift of sight. *Ha!* She no more had the gift of sight than pigs could fly. *God! Pigs! Poor Rafael.* Not caring, she cried openly into her hands. *When would all this be over?*

Beside her, Aiden waited, not speaking, not touching her. At least he had the sense not to tell her everything would be all right.

The door of Rafael's hospital room opened, and muffled footsteps approached. Wiping her face, Carla stood up, preparing for the news. "The surgery went well," the surgeon, Doctor Vela began. She was a middle-aged woman of statuesque deportment, who spoke with authority and compassion. "He has broken his left leg, fractured his right arm, has acute internal bruising and severe whiplash. He's lucky to be alive. Rafael has a long recovery in front of him, but I believe he'll make it."

Carla sobbed uncontrollably, and Aiden grabbed for her, halting her collapse to the floor.

"Thank you, Doctor Vela," he said as Carla folded into his arms.

"Take her home, young man. She needs to sleep. No one can see Rafael until he's conscious and is well enough for visitors. He's in good hands here." Through a haze of tears, Carla watched Doctor Vela's sensible shoes turn and walk quietly back into Rafe's room.

"Come on, Carla. It's nearly dawn. We both need some sleep. Let's go." With his arms cradling her shoulders, he directed her away from the nightmare.

~ ♥ ~

AIDEN CALLED VICTOR, TELLING him they were on their way. On his instructions, Victor had set up Aiden's room with food and beverages. Now as Carla huddled in a chair, wrapped in a blanket, Victor poured two hefty shots of Scotch, left the bottle on the table and departed with a silent bow.

"Drink this." Aiden handed her the glass. She sipped and screwed up her face. "I know you mightn't like it but just scull it back. Trust me, your nerves will thank you for it." Carla held her nose and obeyed. "Good. I know you're not hungry, but a few slices of the superhero oranges they grow around here will help get rid of the taste of Scotch." Reaching eagerly for the orange slices, Carla ate a couple and then cuddled deeper into the blanket. Aiden poured himself another Scotch and leaned back in his chair.

"Well, this is a fine mess we've all found ourselves in," he said. Carla scowled but didn't speak. "I've been trying to figure out what to do."

"And?" she said, sounding only mildly interested.

"I thought . . . what would I do if a client brought this type of situation to me? How would I instruct them to proceed?" Even though Carla looked so small, Aiden could still sense her inner strength clawing to the surface.

"And?" Carla sounded a little impatient, which Aiden took as a good sign.

"I'd tell them to consult someone far better at human relationships and life than me." With a tentative smile creasing his face, he locked Carla in his gaze. He breathed deeply and dived into his emotions. "Carla, I'm desperately in love with you. You know that by now. What I say about this whole mess is going to be prejudiced by my love for you. I can tell you I'm sorry, that I love you and want us to be together for all time, but none of that is going to mean anything to you at the moment. You need to go to the source you trust, who you've always trusted."

Carla frowned and shook her head. "And who would that be?"

"You, your mother and your aunts." He paused, waiting and watching for her response. In that instant, she stirred. *Perhaps with hope*, he thought. He forged on. "I've spoken to Lucette and Chantelle about everything. They're going to the hospital this morning, so you don't have to worry. Domingo, Marco, and Theresa — they'll all be there today. Lucette and Chantelle want you to get some sleep. Then this evening, you'll go with them as planned and do whatever it is you have to do."

"How can I possibly do anything with poor Rafe in the hospital?" Her reddened eyes tried unsuccessfully to secrete more tears.

"I'm not sure. But I do know you have to follow their advice."

Suddenly, anger replaced her distress. "What about Uncle Sancho?" she hissed.

"They've got it under control. They won't allow him anywhere near Rafe. I'm not sure what Lucette's got cooked up for him, but I wouldn't want to be in Sancho's shoes. I think I'm starting to believe in all this gypsy magic and curses." Aiden shuddered, remembering the icy chill that filled the silence on the phone when Lucette listened to Aiden's account and suspicions of what triggered Rafael's behaviour. "All you have to do now is sleep. At least rest."

Carla's shoulders slumped under the blanket. "All right. But I can't go back to our room. Really I can't."

"I figured as much. You sleep in my bed. I'll get Victor to bring in a roll-out cot. I'll sleep in that. Come on. Have a shower. Then we'll both get sleep." Aiden rose and walked over to lift Carla from her chair.

Shuffling toward the bathroom together, she said, "I don't know how to feel about anything or anyone anymore?"

He planted a tender kiss to the top of her head. "You will, *mi amor*. You will."

~ ♥ ~

"MY DEAR. COME TO me." With an expression of compassionate concern, Lucette extended her withered arms to Carla when she ran through the open door of the Amaya house. She was crying before the warmth of her aunt's embrace greeted her with much-needed comfort and reassurance. Aunt Chantelle fluttered behind, rubbing Carla's back and making sympathetic cooing sounds. "Sit. Carla. Sit." Carla and Lucette sat on opposite sides of the long, hand-carved table, while Chantelle moved to the fireplace. Flames blazed under an old kettle bringing it to the boil.

"Would you like some tea, Carla?" Aunt Chantelle gingerly picked it from its hook, her hand wrapped in a thick oven mitt.

"Yes please," she said, feeling the love of family encircle her. While Chantelle busied herself with tea brewing and cup placement, Lucette began.

"My dear, we saw Rafael today. His body is badly broken, but it will mend. He was in good spirits, all things considered. What pains him the most is his remorse over how he's treated you. But I told him not to worry. You are strong. He now has to think about healing himself." The wisdom in Aunt Lucette's words buoyed Carla's spirits.

"And what did he say?"

Chantelle placed cups of herbal tea in front of each of them and sat down next to her sister. "He's determined to heal, to be a better man and start a new life." Carla smiled wistfully. Somewhere inside, she knew Rafael would no longer be imperilled. Finally telling the truth had liberated him. He was strong too and would rebuild his life. A sense of closure consoled Carla rather than depressed her.

Aunt Lucette patted her hand. "He will mend, and we will help him. Chantelle and I will stay until Rafael is well enough to go home and his mother, Mariana can get here to look after him. Only when we think he has exorcised his demons, will we return to Paris."

Carla jumped up and ran around the table to embrace her aunts. "Oh, Aunt Lucette, Aunt Chantelle, you're wonderful. Thank you. Thank you." Laughing they accepted her appreciation and affection with modest acknowledgments.

"Sit. Sit." Aunt Lucette once more waved her bony hand. "Rafael is no longer your responsibility. You have loved him well and done your duty. Now we'll look after our nephew until he can find a way to forgive and move on from his tragic past."

"And Uncle Sancho, what's going to happen to him?" Carla did nothing to conceal her hate for Rafael's father.

"Not for you to worry about at the present. The family will sort him out. But rest assured, he won't go anywhere near Rafael again." Lucette narrowed her eyes with a determined scowl.

"Before Rafe's accident, Mariana had already started divorce proceedings against Sancho. She'll live with Rafael while he heals and until the divorce is final." Chantelle looked pleased with the expected unhappy outcome for Sancho.

"Thank you." Carla clasped her aunts' hands across the table. The circle was complete, and Carla breathed freedom.

"So, tonight is about you." Aunt Chantelle nailed Carla in her blue-eyed gaze and winked, sending a shiver of excitement and anticipation through Carla's body.

"Did you bring Isabella's runes?" Aunt Lucette asked in a matter-of-fact tone.

"Yes. I have them here in my bag."

"Very good. Drink your tea and we will go." Aunt Chantelle collected her own cup and saucer.

"Go where?" Carla asked sipping the last of her tea.

"Why, up to Alhambra, of course," Aunt Lucette said as if all was plainly obvious.

Carla shot each of the ladies an inquiring glance. "But we can't get into Alhambra. It's closed for the night."

"It may be closed to other people, but not to the Amaya gypsies." Lucette rose straight as an arrow, pulling her shawl around her shoulders. Chantelle stood beside her looking regal in her well-cut slacks, blouse, and jacket. "It is time, Carla,"

Aunt Lucette decreed. "Bring the runes and we'll see if you have the gift."

Lucette scooped up her tarot cards from the table and shoved them into a deep pocket in her skirt. Chantelle collected a little wicker basket which for all intents, looked like a picnic hamper with its brightly coloured cloth covering its contents. But Carla wasn't deceived. She'd lay bets on there being no food or drinks in that quaint, little basket.

They lowered their heads and filed through a low doorway into the solitary bedroom at the back of the house. Two well-worn single beds covered in vibrant, hand-crocheted quilts barely fitted in the room. Squeezed between them and resting on the stone wall wobbled a broken-down old wardrobe. As they went, Carla realized Aunt Lucette no longer shuffled. In fact, her walk was downright sprightly.

Aunt Lucette's been pretending she's weak and can barely walk, thought Carla, a grin spreading across her face. *Cheeky, old devil.* Stopping at the wardrobe, Lucette cocked her feathery eyebrow and stared at Carla. A wicked smile graced her lips, then she grasped the handle and tugged open the wardrobe door. What Carla saw made her gasp. "It's a tunnel."

"Yes. It took the Amaya gypsies many long years to dig out this tunnel up to Alhambra. Some of the stone removed over this time built the outside terrace and stairs up to this house," Lucette said with pride, giving Chantelle and Carla a torch each. Chantelle led the way through the wardrobe and Carla eagerly followed. Shuffling forwards they waited until Lucette joined them, closing the door behind her.

"Follow me." Aunt Lucette took the lead.

Carla walked in the middle of the single file, shining her torch on the rock walls, floor, and ceiling. Fascinated by the manual effort the tunnel would have taken, she studied the precision of its construction, marvelling at the resourcefulness required. With each step into the coolness of the mountain, she felt the passageway's slight incline heading further up toward Alhambra. "But why? Why did they build it?" she asked.

"The Amaya gypsies are descended from the Moors. When Alhambra was first built, they lived there within its walls, within its protection. But when the sultan was expelled, they too had to leave. They came down the hill, built what is now our insignificant Amaya stone house and tunnelled back to where they belonged."

"Goodness. I certainly come from determined, ingenious stock, don't I?" Carla was amazed at the tenacity of her forebears.

"Indeed, you do my dear. And tonight, we're going to find out if the Amaya gypsy gift runs with the same intensity in your veins." Aunt Lucette's pace quickened as the incline elevated a little more.

Another ten minutes and Lucette halted. In front of her, an old timber door stood shut like it'd hadn't been opened for centuries. Seeing Carla's look of uncertainty, she said, "Don't worry, my dear. It may look like it won't open, but . . ." Using only limited strength, Lucette pushed the door outwards. Blocking its full swing, tendril vines and thick brush held fast. Chantelle stepped forwards, and from her basket, extracted a small machete which made light work of the resistant flora. "Come. Come." Aunt Lucette wiggled through the doorway and into one of Alhambra's magnificent gardens.

"You did a good job the other day, Lucette." Chantelle stowed her machete and propped the door slightly ajar behind them.

Carla shot her a quizzical look, and Aunt Lucette explained, "Last Friday, when I met Aiden here, I came to pull the bushes back from the door so we could get out tonight."

"Goodness. You two are a crafty pair." Carla shook her head. "But if that door's been there for centuries, why hasn't it been discovered?"

"Gypsy magic, Carla. Gypsy magic," Aunt Lucette spoke in a conspiratorial voice and then snapped off her torch.

"And the growing powers of nature," Aunt Chantelle added in a pragmatic whisper, switching off her torch. Carla did likewise. With no moon in the night sky, inky blackness engulfed them. They paused, waiting for their eyes to adjust.

"This way." Lucette carefully stepped forwards and followed a gravel garden path. The sporadic sound of crunching underfoot amplified in the silence, while the exotic perfumes from the plants wafted stronger. Lonely leaves brushed their arms as they passed, and the muddy tang of impending rain tasted on their tongues. Being enveloped in the darkest of lunar nights, Carla experienced the magical awakening of her physical senses. Without light to see by, she had to rely on her other senses — sound, smell, taste and touch.

"And intuition, Carla," Aunt Lucette said, as if reading Carla's mind. After a while, the subtlety of the night shrouded Carla and a sense of coming home imbued her. She wished her mother could be with her tonight but on a deep level, she felt her presence walking beside her, guiding her forwards. Rounding a bend, Lucette slowed and pointing into the near distance, she said, "There. The Partal Palace." Aunt Lucette led the way across one tiled terrace down to another, while Carla blurred her vision trying to see clearer. The outline of a building formed slowly, but her concentration remained on her steps, ensuring she didn't stumble and fall. Following her aunt, she skirted a large central serenity pool and when they neared the building, Carla's focus finally sharpened.

"The Partal Place or the Portico Palace is the site of the oldest palace in Alhambra built at the beginning of the fourteenth century. See on the left, protruding above the roof is the Damas Tower." Aunt Lucette pointed her finger into the night. "And if you look up, Carla, you'll see the five archways which frame the portico. Five is the number of creative manifestation incorporating the five elements of earth, fire, water, air, and ether. The five archways align us with the mindful connection to the forces of nature, supporting us with the freedom to pursue purposeful joy and bliss. This way, my dear."

They stepped onto the tiled terrace and under the portico's protection. A few metres further, Aunt Lucette turned left into the rectangular shell of the building and with

Chantelle, headed in a beeline towards the centre of the space, leaving Carla nearby.

After uncovering her basket, Chantelle removed a collection of paraphernalia and laid it on the ground. Lucette sorted the items and strategically placed and lit candles.

With the candlelight flickering an ambient glow which complemented the building's red stone walls, Carla admired the intricate design of the arches. Her musings on the complexity of Alhambra's architecture led her to reflect on the complexity of all that had happened in her life recently. That she was trespassing on this sacred, historical site in some ways didn't feel out of place considering the strangeness of the events leading to this very moment. Once all was ready, Lucette and Chantelle positioned themselves on the cold stone floor and called to Carla.

"Come, my dear. Take the third position of the triangle we form." Aunt Lucette indicated the vacant corner of her shawl which she'd placed on the ground. Carla obeyed and slipped into the designated place. In the centre of the shawl, an old tapestry square, no bigger than a handkerchief lay stretched. Carla couldn't make out its meaning, but the shapes printed on it seemed to move endlessly in a continuous pattern. Scattered around them candles shimmered, and incense burned.

AUNT LUCETTE FLOURISHED HER hand in front of Carla. "Isabella's runes?"

"Now quieten your mind, Carla. Sit and listen." Aunt Lucette closed her eyes, and Chantelle began to chant a soft, almost dissonant, melody.

Carla closed her eyes and allowed herself to be transported back to a more mystical time and place where she surrendered to the sounds and sensations within and around her. Any lingering tension fled her body, and her heart slowed down as if readying itself for sleep. The encroaching coolness of looming rain stroked Carla's skin and instead of feeling uneasy being in this eerie setting, she settled peacefully.

"Now, my dear," Aunt Lucette began. "The runes."

Carla plucked each stone from the pouch and confessed, "I know I shouldn't have, but I did use the runes before now." She winced, hoping she'd not disappointed her aunts.

"And when was this?" Aunt Lucette asked, her voice serene.

"When I was in Costa del Sol. I heard Mama tell me I didn't have to wait for Granada. I threw them for me and on another occasion for Aiden."

"And?" Aunt Lucette cocked a brow in her customary non-judgmental expression.

"Well, we actually got the same three runes, and Aiden also got an extra three." By now, the sacred runes lay on the shawl, shining in the candlelight.

"And what were the three you got in common?"

"We both pulled the sickle, the waves and the eye."

"And what do you feel is the message?"

Carla paused. Aunt Chantelle, who'd not vocalized a word since they'd entered the garden except to chant, sat avidly watching her as did Aunt Lucette. "Well, for both of us there is an ending, a parting of ways of the life we knew before. This isn't a bad thing, for the waves indicate this ending will take us on a journey forward and if we both trust our intuition and honour our instincts, we'll succeed." Carla knew she'd not interpreted the runes this succinctly back on the coast. But as she listened to her recitation, she realized her understanding of the runes had grown with no mental effort on her part. Carla glanced at her aunts, who nodded, their expressions both astonished and pleased.

"Excellent, Carla. And what of the extra three Aiden threw?" Tinged with a higher note of anticipation, Aunt Lucette's voice rose.

Feeling more confident and allowing herself to tune in rather than think, Carla said, "Strangely enough Aiden also pulled the three celestial runes of the sun, the moon, and the stars. He must stand in his masculine energy against those forces which threaten to control him. Once he does this, he can then express the depth of his love, his feminine energy to those he cares about most and only then can his dreams be fulfilled and the future he desires most, will reveal itself."

Carla's hand covered her mouth. Feeling like someone else just spoke using her voice, she blinked wide-eyed at her aunts. Tingles raced up and down her spine. She wanted to spring to her feet and dance to release the energy coursing through her body.

Aunt Lucette reached over and patted her hand. "Excellent, my dear. Now throw the runes and ask them for the message for tonight."

Carla collected the sacred stones into her hands, clasped them to her heart and breathed deeply. Closing her eyes, she silently asked for their guidance. No sooner had she asked the question than her hands opened, and her mama's runes scattered onto Aunt Lucette's embroidered shawl. Three pairs of eyes surveyed the symbols turned face up.

Carla scanned the runes and began. "Of the six symbols, five are repeated from the two previous readings. Again, there's the ending of the past and the all-seeing eye of intuition. Like Aiden, I too have been given the message of the celestial runes of the sun, the moon and the stars. Standing firmly in my masculine energy, tempering it with my feminine energy and finding my wishes fulfilled, is clearly visible. My reading tonight is amplified by an extra rune — the symbol of the grains. I'm about to reap what I sow. Whether good or bad, my harvest is upon me. Because the moonstone is present in this spread, there may also be legal implications. But only time will tell." Lifting her gaze from the runes, Carla's lips curved into a knowing smile. A certainty of everything happening for a reason flooded through her. No longer seeing her recent past as a series of miserable events she'd endured, she intuited it was no more than a succession of challenges, shaping a future of her choosing.

Lucette and Chantelle remained silent, smiling proudly at their young niece. Mimicking their smile, Carla collected the runes feeling great affection for the slippery stones and placed them back into their pouch.

Picking up her tarot cards which had stayed stacked beside her, Aunt Lucette shuffled them with expertise. She placed them face down and cut the deck, turning a card over to reveal the oracle. In front of fields of wheat, the image of a flaxen-haired woman, robed in yellow garments stretched out her arms to the women in the circle. "The goddess of the harvest, of fertility, of earth. She signifies a time of growth, of plenty, of a sound relationship, even marriage, and children. She's the ultimate archetype of a well-ordered life of mother love and empathy, care and nurture." While Aunt Lucette spoke of the card's meaning tears streamed down Carla's face. Everywhere around her she felt love, her mother's love, her father's love, her brother's love, Aiden's love, her love for the life she was about to start and for the children she knew she'd one day bear.

"Carla, my dear. Isabella passed the sacred Amaya runes onto you in the hope you also had the gift. You have now proven you do. Even through the recent turmoil you've experienced, you've interpreted life's messages accurately, which the runes have mirrored back to you. The sacred Amaya runes indeed belong to you. And the goddess of harvest card from my tarot deck confirms your destiny. You must not impede the flow of your life, of your growth or your love any longer. You know what you must do?" Aunt Lucette's eyes gleamed in the candlelight awaiting Carla's understanding.

"*Si,* Aunt Lucette. I know." Solemnly, Carla stood and helped her aunts to their feet. Together they repacked Chantelle's basket in blissful silence. Before leaving, Carla took her aunts' hands and said, "I don't know how to thank you enough for everything — for believing in me and for supporting me, through everything." She kissed them both, not wanting the magic of the moment to end. "Aunt Chantelle, you've not said one word?"

"There was only one thing I needed to say, but it wasn't necessary."

"And what was that?" Carla asked.

"Trust, *mi querida.* Trust. "

Carla gasped. "That's what Mama said to me in Costa del Sol."

"And that's what I was to say if you faltered at any time. But you didn't." Aunt Chantelle wrapped her arms around Carla's waist giving her a tight squeeze.

"If Isabella were alive, she'd be so proud of you. You've taken her place in the circle now. Come, it is time for us to go." Aunt Lucette pivoted and led the way back through the enchanted gardens of Alhambra.

"Yes. There's much for me to arrange," Carla said as she fell peacefully in line with her new life.

CHAPTER SEVENTEEN

RAFAEL AND PAIN WERE old friends. Sancho had introduced them at an early age. They'd grown up together, playing around in the pig shed and in unseen, untouchable places. Even when Rafael fled pain to be a dancer, he'd found his old pal waiting for him after rehearsals and performance. Then two days ago, he leapt out from behind a tree, surprising Rafael and snatching his treasured Ducati from his grip. Now as a new day dawned in Granada and lying prone in a hospital bed with his agonizing life-long companion, Rafael found it little consequence. The morphine drip eased most of the relentlessness of his physical pain for which he was grateful. But what mattered most was he was alive and free. Free of the haunting secrets which had plagued his existence. At last, he was free of his father's contact, lies, and control. In fact, in Rafael's mind, his father had morphed into nothing more than an evil character in a memory the morphine helped to erase. No longer papa, he simply was Sancho — some beast with a six-lettered name, waning from Rafael's life for all time.

Perhaps one day, Rafael could forgive, but not today — maybe not ever. He prayed Carla's willingness to forgive proved better than his. An unappetizing breakfast came and went as the clock ticked towards an unappetizing lunch. Just as Rafael chose sleep instead of more morphine, a knock pulled him back from his slumbering escape. The door cracked open, and a familiar voice called his name. "Rafe, may I come in?"

My God, she was still gorgeous. Regardless of the lies and heartbreak he'd put her through, Carla Armando could still stop his heart. Walking towards him in her low-slung blue jeans and figure-hugging apricot T-shirt, her thick, black hair drifting past her shoulders, she reminded him of happier times when they'd made love, laughed and danced in each other's arms. Her dark chocolate doe eyes opened wide. "How are you, Rafe?"

"I'm so sorry, Carla. I never meant for any of this . . ."

"Shhh." She placed her delicate finger to his lips. "You've said all the apologies necessary. How do you feel?"

"My body hurts, but the morphine helps. My heart hurts, but now you're here, I feel better. My head hurts, but that's my fault because I should've got help a long time ago." He reached out to find her hand resting beside his on the bed. Doubly happy, he smiled when she squeezed back.

"Rafe, we need to talk."

"No, Carla, I need to talk. You need to listen. Sit beside me for a little." She levered lightly onto the bed, and he stopped himself from wincing when her slight weight changed the balance of his suspended leg. "Regardless of everything and forgive me for saying this, Carla, but you are still the most beautiful woman I've ever seen." He noticed a faint blush rise to her cheeks as she lowered her head and smiled. "*Mi pequeña luciérnaga.*" At the mention of his pet name for her, her eyes pooled. So did his. He watched her swallow her emotion like him. How he longed to crush her to him but fortunately his injuries prevented such impetuous actions. But they didn't stop his heart from breaking.

"Carla, I've loved you since I was a young boy, and I love you still. But I'm not the one for you. You and I both know this to be true no matter how hard we fight it or want it to be otherwise." He paused and she nodded in agreement. A little more of his heart broke away with her silent acceptance. "So, my love, I will free you of our engagement. We are no longer affianced. You are free to love another."

"Oh, Rafael." Carla's voice wavered. "I'm sorry all this has happened to you and that you could never confide in me so together we could've worked this out." She kissed his hand, smearing his skin in a trail of wet tears.

Although her loving expression of loss and compassion washed away some of his pain, the dull thud of another fragment of his heart tearing away intensified his grief. He pulled himself from the brink of changing his mind. "So, this is what will happen. I'm going to recover, get strong and make a new life for myself. I need to come to terms with my past, get stronger in the present and plan a new future."

"But what about dancing, Rafe? You must return to dancing?" The anxiety in her voice encouraged him to return as her partner.

"Perhaps. But I must heal first. Dance second." With determination, he held firm and mapped out his new life.

Rafael caught her in his penetrating gaze and lowered his voice. "Ace has loved you from the moment he set eyes on you. I always suspected you two were somehow destined to be together. If you recall, I even asked you at El Palmar how you felt about him?" With a disarming smile, he waited for Carla's response.

"I remember," she whispered.

"And?"

"I didn't want us to end, Rafe. I loved you so much, for so long. But you kept pushing me away. The secrets and moodiness . . . you never let me in. Then when Aiden turned up, he reminded me of what I was really looking for in a relationship." She cast her eyes downwards, and Rafael admired her thick eyelashes even though they glistened with tears.

He lifted her chin. "Then you must go and be with him. Give him all the love you tried to give me. Ace will know how to love you back. I didn't. I was too damaged, too ashamed. He's a man who deserves the love of a wonderful woman like you."

"Rafe, Aiden is outside and would like to speak with you. Is that okay?"

"Of course. Tell him to come in."

Carla walked to the door and returned with Aiden beside her.

"Rafe, how are you doing mate?" Aiden took Rafe's hand and shook it firmly but carefully.

"I'm doing much better thanks to you and Carla coming and visiting me. I wasn't sure if either of you would have anything to do with me again after all the grief I've put you through."

"Don't be stupid, man. You lived a tough life. Nobody should go through what you did. We understand. That's what friends are for. Right?" Smiling down at him, Aiden looked every bit the gallant, young hero. Rafael breathed a sigh of relief knowing Carla would be well looked after, and the three of them had a chance of a future friendship.

"Right." Rafael reached for their hands and clasped Carla's in Aiden's. "Now I know you two love each other, and I want you to make the most of it. Do your best to make it work. You have my blessing." Before either Carla or Aiden could respond Rafael continued, directing his instruction to Carla, "You have a show to do tonight. You better get a move on as from now on, you'll be dancing solo for some time Carla Armando." With a pout, she nodded like the dutiful partner. "And Ace, you better be at every show she performs to make sure no other foreign or local interloper tries to steal her away from you. No point coming back crying to me you lost her. Okay?" Rafael winked at Aiden, who reciprocated likewise. "Now go. Both of you. I need some sleep." He waved his hand in his usual directorial manner.

"We'll pop in tomorrow," Carla said, her voice positive and hopeful.

"No." Rafael's tone turned stern and absolute. He looked at Aiden, a silent but grave plea in his eyes. Man to man, Ace must know how hard this was for him to keep up a brave face while he watched the woman he loved walk away in the arms of another man.

Aiden placed his hands on Carla's shoulders. "I think Rafe needs a few days of rest. No visitors for a while. Is that right, Rafe?"

"Yes, Ace. I need rest now. Maybe come and see me at the end of the week. Maybe next Sunday." Rafael nodded a silent thanks to Ace, who responded in kind. Despite everything, he felt fortunate Carla was starting a new life with Ace. "Now go."

Choking back emotion, Carla said, "See you then, Rafe." She turned quickly and hurried from the room, her soft sobs scurrying behind her.

Rafael reached out his hand into which Aiden thrust his. "Thanks, Ace. Look after her for me please." The lump in Rafe's throat caught him off guard, and he choked on his final words.

"Of course, I will. I know she means the world to you, and me. I promise I'll keep her safe."

"And always tell her the truth . . ."

"Absolutely." As Aiden bent down, embracing him in a brotherly bear hug, Rafael's heart finally cleaved open, weeping.

~ ♥ ~

VICTOR ANSWERED THE PHONE and then nodded at Aiden. "Sorry. I'll be back in a moment." After he exited, Aiden scanned the hotel manager's office, which was precise and neat, just like its owner. Containing only a desk, two visitor chairs and a wall of discreet filing cabinets, the uncluttered office revealed nothing of the type of business conducted within its four walls. Victor returned shortly after and strode through the door followed by another dapper gentleman.

"Aiden, this is my cousin, Detective Paredes. I'm sure he'll be able to assist you with what you told me." With a nod and a bow, Victor retreated, leaving the two men to their business.

Aiden thrust his hand towards the detective. "Good to meet you, Detective Paredes. Thank you for making the time to see me today."

"Not a problem, Aiden. Victor informed me of your situation. Why don't we sit and see what can be done?" Taking the lead, the detective pulled out a chair and motioned Aiden to sit in the other next to him. "Based on the names you told Victor, I did some checking, and it seems Franco Costello is your ex-client, Dario Coco's brother-in-law. Very unfortunate for you to travel all this way to get away from the threat in Australia only to arrive next door to Costello's house on the Costa del Sol and bang his wife?"

Aiden realized Detective Paredes might look the part of the dapper gentleman, but he would not go lightly on a young, corporate lawyer from Australia, who acted the fool.

Nodding in resigned agreement, Aiden said, "Bloody unlucky."

"And may I venture, reckless?" He paused and Aiden respectfully nodded again. "Anyway, moving on. Until now, no one has reported Sofia missing which means A" — he pulled on his index finger — "she wasn't well-liked if no one has bothered reporting her disappearance or B" — he pulled on his middle finger — "they think she's off spending her divorce settlement on holidays somewhere, which by the way, could be the case. So, all we can do is begin preliminary investigations based on your suspicions of Franco killing her in order to keep you quiet. Trust me. Franco Costello has been on our radar for some time, so this will add more fuel to the fire we've been lighting underneath him. I'll get the forensics boys down to the mansion and dust for prints knowing that yours will be there. This will at least corroborate your part of the story."

Exhaling, Aiden slumped feeling a weight lift. "Thank you, Detective Paredes."

"In the meantime, I suggest you continue keeping a low profile. We'll get on about our business of seeing if we can find the ex-Mrs. Costello, dead or alive, and of gathering enough evidence to arrest and charge Costello for her murder if that's how it ends up. All I ask is that you let me know your whereabouts at all times so we can keep in contact on the progress of the case, if there is one." The detective rose.

"Of course. You have my full cooperation whenever you need it. I can't thank you enough for coming and seeing me." Standing, Aiden offered his hand in farewell.

Losing the officious tone, Paredes said, "Victor tells me you've been enjoying your stay in Granada despite the accident of Rafael Flores?"

Aiden wondered what the detective was alluding to. "Ah, yes. It's a beautiful region. I'll probably be here for at least another week I think."

"Yes, yes. I understand Carla Armando is dancing at El Ritmo de Flamenco for at least another week also?" The detective's eyebrows skipped up his forehead. There was no mistaking his inference.

Aiden smiled. "That's correct, Detective Paredes. And while she's here, I will be also."

"That's very good news. I'll be sure to tell Manolo Armando that his daughter is still in safe hands then." The detective slapped Aiden on the shoulder, turned and left the office before Aiden had a chance to speak.

Shaking his head, Aiden slowly collected his jacket from the chair. *They're all bloody related, I'm sure of it.* Sporting a champion smile, he went to organize the next item of business with Victor.

~ ♥ ~

BY THE TIME AIDEN arrived at the El Ritmo de Flamenco, the band was breaking for an early dinner. Carla had spent the afternoon rehearsing with them, restructuring the show's choreography and choosing a couple of new solos to replace the tango for which she no longer had a partner.

"Aiden," a high-pitched, effeminate voice trilled from across the room. Raúl raced over, throwing his arms around Aiden's neck. "Oh my God. So much has happened since you left Seville. I can't believe it." While Raúl prattled on about Rafael's accident, his wicked father, their aunts and Carla having the gift of sight, Aiden nodded his head indulgently. Settling into a corner table tucked to one side in front of the stage, he sucked on a Corona answering Raúl's endless questions.

Once he finished with 'Granada gossip,' as Raúl referred to their conversation, Aiden asked, "How's your father?"

"He's much better. And he told me he's very grateful for all you have done for Carla and for poor Rafael." A gentle smile graced Raúl's face. "I think Papa would not have recovered nearly as well if you hadn't been here with Carla. Thank you from all of us, Aiden."

"*Hola, hola,*" other voices called as Pascual, Felipe and Marco joined them.

"Good to see you again fellas," Aiden said as they sat down. Conversing about the drama of recent events and the afternoon's rehearsals, they filled the club with bright voices.

"Carla's solo show is fabulous," Raúl said while the others nodded and murmured in agreement.

"*Sí*, it's sad there is no more tango with Rafael. But Carla dances so well the audience will not notice," Felipe said before grinning like a love-sick fool at Raúl.

Aiden glanced over at Marco, who'd not said anything until now. "Poor Rafe. If only he'd told me what happened to him. Maybe I could've helped. He was a sensational dancer, and now it is all gone." Clearly upset by what his cousin had endured in silence all his life, Marco shook his head.

"Listen, Marco. No one really knows what goes on in families. Don't beat yourself up for not knowing your Uncle Sancho was brutalizing Rafe all those years. You were just a kid at the time too. Rafe is strong. He'll make a come-back. I'm sure we'll see him dancing again and performing the tango with Carla sometime in the future." Aiden's reassurance lifted the flailing mood and the guys in the band returned to their merry pre-show chatter.

"Come on. We must start. Customers are arriving." Marco shooed the band back to the stage. Though they scurried to their instruments, Marco hung back, his dark eyes lingering on Aiden. "*Muchas gracias,* Aiden. Thank you." Offering his big paw, he didn't say another word. Aiden accepted Marco's olive branch and shook. He returned to the stage and grabbed his bandoneón, primed it, then began to play with the other musicians joining in.

No sangria tonight. Instead, Aiden decided on tapas and a couple of beers that gave him just a light glow by the time Carla appeared on stage. In a red backless gown sliced open to the top of her buttocks, she lassoed his breath, dragging it from his lungs. Only partly restrained, some of her locks coursed down her back like long, glossy rivulets of rich oil while the rest coiled on top her head in a knot decorated with crimson miniature fans and roses. From under luscious eyelashes, her ebony eyes lifted just enough to catch Aiden's gaze as she took her opening position on the dimly lit stage. Thinking it was virtually only three weeks ago this entire Spanish adventure began rattled Aiden's logic. In front of him, posed the most exquisite and talented woman he'd even met and if he played his cards right, she'd be his. Dressed in a tight sheath of scarlet velvet which rebelliously fluttered into massive circles of frills at her knees, Carla stamped her hidden feet to the beat. With her hands coiling overhead, her body stretched taller and taller like a sunflower rising to the morning sun. Fiery, fast and ferocious came the rhythm and Carla matched every nuance of the music with her passionate performance. Her determined chin craned higher into the spotlight as she thrust and parried with the band. A cacophony of tips and taps clattered on the stage while her skirts swirled around her ankles, impishly exposing her feet's expertise at dancing flamenco. On and on she hurled herself into the dance as if she was exorcising all the pain, heartache and grief she'd suffered with Rafael, with her father, with her fears. Like a top unleashed from its spindle, Carla spun and spun until at the climax of the music, she prostrated herself on the stage, arms outstretched, lungs rasping for breath. Everyone leapt to their feet with cheers of *"olé"* and foot stamping. Everyone, except Aiden, who remained riveted on his chair, his eyes misted with emotion. Carla rose from the floor and bowed humbly. With a wicked askance glance at him, she licked her lips, burning the mist from his eyes and igniting his groin.

CHAPTER EIGHTEEN

EVEN WITHOUT RAFAEL, THE show had been a resounding success. For Carla, being back on the stage liberated her from all the trauma and drama of the past weeks. It was her safe place. The place she felt most herself — at home. Dancing the entire show solo tonight and the response from the audience proved she could have a successful dance career without a partner. Although she wished Rafael a speedy and healthy recovery, she'd spread her professional wings without him, and it felt good. More than that, she was a free agent, unshackled by the past and ready for a new life.

On saying goodnight to the band, she and Aiden strolled back to the hotel. After complimenting her for the umpteenth time on her performance, Aiden said, "I got everything sorted out today with Victor's cousin, Detective Paredes. I didn't know he knew your father?"

"Oh yes. They're old school friends." She giggled girlishly. "Everyone knows just about everyone in Andalusia."

Aiden nodded. "That's exactly what I thought." And he chuckled softly.

Before they reached the hotel's front door, Aiden stopped and turning to Carla, clasped both her hands. "I have a surprise waiting for you upstairs. I hope you don't think it's too impulsive?"

"If you've organized it, I'm sure I'll love it." She reached up and pressed an affectionate kiss to his cheek. Loitering for a moment, her lips traced a feathery caress across his. Their eyes locked, ratcheting up the sexual energy between them. She lowered to her feet, and as they entered the foyer, Carla reached for his hand. When he wrapped his hand around hers, she liked how its bulk and tender protection comforted her mind, body, and soul. Pulling closer into him, she fell into the rhythm of his step as he slowed to accommodate her.

~ ♥ ~

"OH, AIDEN, THIS IS magnificent." Elated, Carla stood at the threshold of the Sultan's Suite at the Hotel de Los Páramos. "I've never stayed in this room, but I've always wanted to." Scanning the suite, she thrilled at its decadent luxury. In front of them sprawled an oversized bed resplendent in the softest rose-coloured linen. Its feather down pillows embossed with the hotel's initials in gold thread were plump and soft, ideal for a good night's sleep. Warmed by hand-made rugs, the burgundy Moroccan-tiled floor led to the bed which was flanked either side by small hand-carved tables laid with champagne and tempting supper delicacies. Wall sconces radiated glowing fingers of amber light up the walls, bathing everything in a sensuous, rich hue.

"I hope you don't think I was eh — taking advantage . . ." Hearing Aiden trip over his words made her smile. *How sweet*, she thought. After all they'd been through, including the mounting sexual tension between then, he remained unsure of not overstepping the mark with this surprise.

"Not at all," she said seductively, taking his hand and leading him into the suite. Willingly, Aiden followed. Turning around, she lifted her leg and kicked the door closed behind them. Fanned by her newfound freedom and warm, supple muscles, Carla burned with the desire to wrap her legs around him. "When did all this happen?" she asked in an appreciative tone as she padded around the suite while he remained at ease, just inside the door.

"I arranged with Victor to bring all your belongings in here this afternoon when you were at rehearsals. And mine too."

She cast him a nod of endorsement. "Of course. Good idea. Go on."

"And Lucette and Chantelle collected Rafael's things and took them to the hospital. Your aunts seemed to approve of this change of sleeping arrangements."

When Carla looked back over her shoulder, she caught Aiden's big Cheshire grin and batted one of her own back to him. "That doesn't surprise me at all. Aunt Lucette and Aunt Chantelle are quite smitten with you. But then how could they not be? A tall, strong, handsome young man rescuing their favourite niece from the clutches of an unhappy life — what's there not to like?" She turned towards the wardrobe, a soft giggle fluttering from her throat partnering Aiden's modest chuckle. Opening the wardrobe doors, she found her clothes hung neatly and in the exact order she'd left them in the deluxe room. A grateful smile creased her face for Victor's attention to detail.

"I must say, Aiden, you certainly know how to impress a woman." On purpose, she delivered the words in a low sultry growl as she glided towards him. Slipping her fingers into the tops of his jeans, she ran them along the inside of the hip band. Because he wore his jeans so low, her fingertips touched the soft hair of his pubis, and he groaned. The tightening fabric at the zipper confirmed she'd had the desired effect. Rising onto tiptoe, she reached towards his ear. "I think I need to freshen up. Would you like to join me?"

He all but collapsed in relief. "Fuck yes."

"Then follow me." Carla prayed Victor hadn't missed any detail, and as she led Aiden into the bathroom, she silently rejoiced. One of the Sultan's Suite's most lavish features was its spa bath. Fashioned on the Alhambra pool designs, it stretched long and shallow in the bathroom rather than atop the floor as a free-standing moulded bath. Carla had no idea how the hotel pulled off such an engineering feat, but she didn't care. She was far more fascinated with pulling off another feat.

Not disappointed, she murmured approvingly at seeing the intimate pool filled with steaming water and sprinkled with fresh flowers. Infused with swirls of scented oil, the bath's fragrance mingled with the perfumed candles flickering in romantic clusters in the bathroom.

Pressing up behind her, Aiden said, "I thought you'd enjoy a hot bath after such an amazing performance tonight.

You held the audience in the palm of your hand. They loved you." Leaning in he kissed the hollow under her ear. "And I love you. Carla, you have no idea what you do to me." His hands gently encircled her petite body, beginning a slow crawl to her breasts.

Modestly stopping their journey, she said, "Not yet. Let me show you what I have to give." Behind her, she felt him shudder and his cock push against the small of her back. Yearning for him with no less desire, Carla also wanted to unleash her herself tonight. To free that secret, sexual place within her she'd not been able to express. And now with her senses heightened from the ceremony at Alhambra, the runes readings, and tonight's flamenco, Carla knew her time had come. Her body sizzled in readiness.

"I am in your hands," he said, and she claimed her power.

She pivoted slowly around to face him. "I will hold you to that."

"Oh, please do."

Carla leaned into his chest breathing him in, her arms encircling his trim waist. His masculine musk, at once fresh like the sea yet with an undertone of primal sex, raw and earthy had always intoxicated her. She ached for his cock to claim her, but she knew any great performance required discipline, timing, and control. And she wanted tonight with Aiden to be her greatest performance, and he her most jubilant audience. Tugging up his T-shirt, she reefed it as high as her arms reached and Aiden finished the task by pulling it over his head. Standing before her, his torso rippled and flinched. As if fashioned by a great sculptor, every muscle beckoned to be touched. She obliged them by reaching out and sliding her hands over his body, exploring every furrow and ridge. Tanned, buffed and muscular the V of his torso dragged her hands naturally downwards. Here she unzipped his jeans with meticulous precision, at last revealing the head of his cock, peeking out from the top of his underpants. Glistening with anticipation, it called to her to ease its pain.

"Poor thing," she purred, ignoring his cock completely, instead giving Aiden a sultry pout. Seemingly spellbound, he said nothing but swayed slightly on his feet. Gliding her fingers into his jockey shorts, she slithered this last piece of clothing down his body. Every inch of the undressing she mapped with her face only a finger width from his body. When his underwear freed his rampant cock, it sprang out and hit her lips, leaving its salty, sticky residue. She halted and looked up at Aiden. "My goodness, we are eager, aren't we?" Sensuously her tongue reached out to lick the pre-ejaculate from his cock, then circled a protracted good-bye. Aiden's head lolled, and he groaned. His obvious pleasure at her torment inflamed her groin, and she oozed with desire. Further down his underwear travelled until he stepped out dutifully, leaving him naked beside the spa. Carla shot him a mischievous smile. "My God, Aiden, your cock is beautiful." Its girth, length, and curve mesmerized her for a moment, and as Aiden flexed his manhood in anticipation, he broke free of her spell and took control.

IN CARLA'S MOMENT OF appreciation for his cock, Aiden's hand slipped under her skirt and between her legs. She gasped when he cupped her dripping snatch and pulled her closer. "You're so wet, Carla. Feel how wet I make you." He rubbed the palm of his hand against her pulsing cleft, feeling her panties soak with juice. He locked her lithe body against his own and twisted his insistent fingers under her panties.

"See how she opens up for me." Leaning closer to her ear, he commanded, "Wider my sweet. Wider." He felt her snatch splay open on his palm, spontaneously dousing him in her juice. Slipping his index finger into her folds, he slid back and forth tormenting her, but not venturing deeper. "You think only you can play at this teasing game." Provoking her, he rubbed her clit hard for a few moments until she collapsed gasping against him.

He knew she wasn't satiated, but he'd increased her appetite enough to guarantee her obedience. In his arms, she lolled like a rag doll, a delicious open-mouthed smile on her face. Taking the opportunity, he stuck his finger into her mouth. "Taste your sex, sweet Carla. Taste it."

She sucked her desire from his finger with such pleasure Aiden retrieved his digit and drew on it jealously, savouring her flavour. Wasting no more time, he repositioned her on her feet and tore off her blouse, snapping all the buttons. Underneath she was naked. Her plump breasts lifted high on her chest, nipples puckering as if cranky at their sudden exposure. Ignoring their irritation, he yanked off her wrap-around skirt and grabbing her panties in both hands so as not to hurt her, he tore the elastic, stripping her bare. Like an exquisite doll, Carla balanced on her high heel pumps, barely registering the impact of his impatience.

Captivated, Aiden gazed upon her wild, gypsy beauty. Challenge blasted from her kohl-rimmed eyes, and her entangled mane of onyx-coloured locks splayed over her shoulders shrouding her upper torso and breasts. Straining his eyes away from her pouting, elfin face, Aiden's gaze travelled over Carla's smooth, unblemished, olive skin to the neat triangle at the top of her legs. As he hoped, her mons was fully waxed, pulled high towards her washboard stomach. From head to toe, she represented not just his fantasy woman, but one of great power, talent, and presence.

Standing a full head height taller, Aiden towered over her. He could lift her in one easy movement and with her balance and strength have her legs wrapped around his neck, his face buried into her snatch where they stood. But no, that would be rushing the inevitable. Patience was a virtue which he intended to demonstrate. Facing off, their ragged breathing fell into the same tempo, and their hands flinched desperate to touch, torment and tear the other's flesh.

Reaching out, Aiden pressed his finger into her smooth slit and hooked onto her clit. "Come, join me in the bath." Like a good servant, Carla kicked off her shoes and allowed Aiden to guide her into the warm, fragrant water. Her eager snatch slid forwards hoping his finger would accidentally insert itself deep into her yearning, but he proved too cunning. "Naughty girl." He tickled her clit in punishment, and she pouted.

She slithered down beside him in the shallow water. "Would you like me to wash you?" Her hands floated on the water, brushing his cock in anticipation.

Leaning back Aiden stretched his arms along the spa ledge and got comfortable. "No. Not yet. But I'd like to watch you wash." Regarding her from under heavy eyelids, Aiden waited to see if his request would be fulfilled.

"If you wish."

"Good. But first I need to feel that gorgeous body of yours." Reaching forwards, he drew her to him, tenderly caressing her tight body. Cupping her buttocks, he pulled her on top his lap. His cock rubbed against her open snatch, desperate to penetrate but was foiled by Aiden's self-control. Digging his fingers into her back, he massaged her trembling muscles all the way up her spine to the top of her shoulders. She pressed against him and moaned in demand of more attention. He grasped her neck and finally kissed her the way he'd wanted to since their first "hello." Unleashing himself upon her, his tongue introduced itself provocatively before lashing her welcoming mouth.

Hot, insatiable and unending he consumed her, and she responded to his demands with reciprocal fervour. They clawed and grabbed at each other, devouring the other at last finding sustenance after a long period of starvation. She climbed higher onto his body and with her hands cupping his face, she tamed him into a submissive position.

Desperate, Aiden pulled away. "I need to eat you, so you need to let me watch you wash first." Without waiting for a response, he lifted her onto the side of the corner of the bath. "Spread your legs for me, my sweet Carla. And let me see what I have dreamed of."

With a demure smile, she opened her legs effortlessly on the right angle of the corner. Her cleft was even more perfect than he imagined. A thin closed line of plump pink flesh hid her womanly treasures then disappeared into a tight pucker towards her arse. With her taut, flexible body atop such a feminine delight and complimented by pert, natural breasts, Aiden sat enthralled appreciating his lover. His cock groaned to plunge deep within the glistening jewel winking from the spa's ledge as Carla's finger began to play. "You want me to wash before you eat me?" she asked with girlish innocence.

Aiden licked his lips unconvinced he could wait a moment longer.

"Very well," she teased. "Let's see if I do it right." Carla slid one finger from her clit down along the line of her sleek slit and back so delicately her sex remained closed. Lifting her finger to her mouth, she said coyly, "Oh my. That wasn't very good was it?"

Aiden tugged doggedly at his cock as he watched her contrived performance. "No, it wasn't," he agreed gruffly. "Do it again."

With a lustful smile, she pulled open her folds, exposing her inner beauty and Aiden sucked in air. Carla licked her finger and slid it ever so slowly inside herself from clit to anus, rolling her body forwards and back to give Aiden the full show. Bending forwards, her hands dived into the bath as her legs split wider apart. She cupped some water, returned upright and drizzled it over her open snatch. Aiden shuddered in anticipation at having those legs opened that wide for his pleasure. Transfixed, he thrilled watching her rub the tips of her fingers on her exposed folds, holding them open for him to admire.

"Why don't you come over here and tell me if I'm clean now?" she said impudently.

Unable to play the game any longer, Aiden pushed between her legs. The tip of his tongue found its mark and began its torment of her clit. Over and over it repeated its demanding tempo on her sweet spot. When Carla lay backwards, pulling herself open for his indulgence, Aiden opened her wider, hoisted his face on top of her and feasted.

"Oh God, Aiden. That's so good. I love what you're doing." She opened her legs wider until her toes touched the floor.

"Fuck, I love how you do that," he said between growling her folds and dipping his tongue into her slit. She tasted so delicious Aiden ravished her without mercy. Rubbing his lips hard against her slipperiness, gnawing and lapping at her folds he felt delirious. *No action sport could ever match this,* he thought. He could keep doing this for hours.

"You're driving me crazy. I love it, but I can't take any more. Finish me please," she begged, grinding her hips into his face with ferocious leg strength.

Not wanting to stop, Aiden devised another plan. "Let's see if this helps." His face disappeared, leaving her screaming snatch unattended. Sharp, hard sprays hit Carla's gaping maw as Aiden spat water into her folds. Dispensing a steady flow of liquid, he swirled it around and around licking, sucking and lapping at her. Whimpering and moaning, Carla thrust her snatch at him. "Please. Please," she cried in sexual agony.

"Soon, my sweet. Soon," came his muffled response. Licking and lapping he stoked her burn to a raging bonfire. Until, clamping his mouth over her scorching snatch he sucked at her fiercely, and she squealed. Knowing how flexible she was, Aiden wrenched Carla's legs open harder and buried his face so deep he wanted to swallow her whole. Battering her engorged clit with his tongue, he plunged two fingers deep into her and drilled her G-spot until she exploded, screaming. Sweet fluid ejaculated into his mouth and he choked trying to swallow her womanly essence. Her body shuddered uncontrollably, but he didn't stop. He wanted to please her endlessly until she could stand no more. Although his lips and tongue were bruised and tired, Aiden was like a man possessed. Lapping at her he persisted until she scrambled backwards crying for mercy from his relentless pleasuring.

ROLLING AROUND ON THE bathroom floor, Carla wasn't sure if she wanted to cry from relief or laugh hysterically with glee. With her hands wedged between her legs trying to stop the miraculous, persistent quivering of ongoing climaxes, she glowed so brightly she thought she'd catch fire. She heard Aiden splash out of the bath and lay beside her. With a cautious touch, he said, "Are you all right? Did I hurt you?"

"No. No. That was fucking amazing. I've never felt anything like that ever before. Oh God, Aiden. How did you learn to make a woman feel so alive?" She rolled towards him and threw her arms around his neck, peppering his face with kisses. Together they rolled and laughed like kids wrestling on the ground.

Aiden flopped onto his back. "I don't know. I just really like women's bodies. I like making them feel good, I like eating them and making them orgasm." A proud little chuckle slipped from his throat. He propped himself on his elbow and blasted her with his ice-blue eyes. "But with you. I love it. I can't get enough of you, *Señorita* Armando. I could eat you all day, all night and we haven't even got to the fucking yet." A dazzling, beguiling smile lit up his face.

"Are you propositioning me, Mr Bishop?

"Nope. I'm going to fuck you senseless." With that, he sprang to his feet and hoisted her over his shoulder. Dangling down his musclebound back, Carla tittered, enjoying the view of his tight buttocks flinching with each step he took towards the bedroom. At the foot of the bed, he lowered her tenderly onto the spongy mattress, and she slithered backwards making room for him.

"Wait there," he commanded, his eyes twinkling with mischief. "I think champagne is in order, don't you?" As he bent down to the ice bucket, Carla reclined on the pillows admiring his tall frame of well-developed muscles and manly endowment. His shock of wheaten hair flopping over his forehead added to her new lover's appeal. So did his piercing blue eyes which now glanced up from under brown eyelashes, scrutinizing her while she studied him. "Am I to your liking?" he asked, striding back to the bed, a glass in each hand.

"Oh yes. You are most definitely to my liking," she admitted, accepting the champagne. Wriggling in beside her, Aiden tucked a couple of pillows in place and clinked his glass to hers in a toast. Having him by her side melted her heart. At last, an indwelling peace stirred and hope brought light to the saddened corners of her soul. She sipped the iced bubbly, watching him do likewise and remembering what magic his luscious lips had just crafted, she shuddered. An effervescent ripple danced through her body.

Aiden looked hesitant. "Carla, I don't usually do this type of thing . . ."

"What? Give great head then drink great champagne?" she teased, suspecting this wasn't at all what he meant.

"No. I mean I don't usually fall in love like this," he said, taking control of the conversation. Before she could respond, he continued, "I told you yesterday, I'm desperately in love with you, and I really want us to work. But I need to know what you want. Up until now, you've not said anything about how you feel. Sure, you've given me some signals, but you've not said anything. I know I'm asking a lot what with everything that's happened but . . . You asked for two days until the ceremony with your Aunts was over. So here we are?"

The entreaty in his eyes and sincerity in his voice touched her spirit. He was right. She had asked for more time, and he'd obliged without reservation. He'd organized the Sultan's Suite for their first night together, allowed her to make the first move and proceeded to pleasure her without any reciprocation on her part. And here he was baring his heart and soul to her in the hope she too wanted a real future together. Her lips curved up in a loving smile. She took his glass and placed them both on the bedside table. Propping herself on the bed to mirror his position, she said, "Do you remember the runes reading I did for you?"

Aiden screwed up his mouth. "Sort of. But what I remember most is wishing for us to move onto new beginnings, together." A hopeful smile creased his handsome face.

"Well, when I was with Aunt Lucette and Aunt Chantelle last night, I threw the same runes as you did, plus one extra which signified harvest."

"And?"

She traced his cheekbone with an affectionate touch. "Aiden, it was the sign I was waiting for. The ceremony wasn't just about seeing if I had the gift to read the runes, but also to see whether there was a destiny for us. Together."

"And because you threw the harvest rune, that's the sign?"

Carla watched him struggle to understand. "It wasn't just that. Aunt Lucette pulled the harvest goddess card as well." Realizing what she was saying only confused him, she waved her hands in the air. "Forget about all that. It's like the Spanish fable you read about the king, the magic mirror and the shepherdess. She married the king and became queen because she'd lived a good life with no blemishes. Well now is my harvest time. Now I will reap all the good I have sewn. You are my harvest, Aiden Bishop. My king. And I am destined to be your queen. Of course, I love you. We were meant to be together."

Without a word, he bundled her into his arms and Carla surrendered to a long night of bliss.

CHAPTER NINETEEN

SUSPENDED ON HIS TIRELESS arms and mesmerized by the euphoric expression on her face, Aiden plunged his cock in and out of Carla's indestructible sex at a leisurely rhythm. With each deliberate thrust, she moaned in obvious delight. The sphinx-like smile which appeared on her face an hour or so ago, still lingered as the pink-hued rays of dawn crept into the Sultan's Suite. Having submitted to him all night, her muscles lay slack and battered, but Carla was insatiable. "Keep fucking me, Aiden. I love it. In and out. In and out. Oh, God. If only you had two cocks. You could fuck me with one, while I suck the other," she moaned. Her tongue sought out Aiden's imaginary second cock in mid-air and proceeded to lick and suck it in an intoxicating demonstration. While her pummelled cleft loosened with more juice, Carla's wanton fellatio display reenergized Aiden's cock.

"I wish I had two cocks too, my sweet," he said, thrusting stronger. "Here, give me your legs." Carla obeyed. Aiden pulled them up around his neck, grabbed Carla's waist and rebalanced his weight on his knees. In a threatening growl, he taunted, "Let's see if we can't make that sweet, greedy, little snatch of yours just that little bit happier." With a wicked smile, he slammed into her. She gasped. By now Aiden knew her thresholds, and he'd just crossed one.

"Fuck," she cried.

"Absolutely," he countered and drove a hard, fast tempo into her. She squealed with delight, clutching onto his forearms riding the rhythm with him. Her frame seemed too small to tolerate this type of pounding, but she obviously loved it. Aiden had unleashed himself on her all night, and she never faltered. In fact, the more he gave, the more she wanted. For him, he'd met a physical match. Possessing the same stamina, determination, and competitive spirit as he, Carla was the lover he'd hungered for all his life. Clenching onto her, he hammered hard until his chest heaved for respite. Rolling off, he lay prone on the bed gulping a lungful of air.

"Poor darling, you must be tired. Here let me." She shimmied across the bed and retrieved the last of the champagne. "Sit up and drink this." She handed him his glass and stacked some pillows on which he reclined. Sculling the last mouthfuls, he smiled proudly at his cock which still stood at attention, though purpled and reddened from the night's action, awaiting the next adventure. When Carla's face descended, Aiden stretched back to enjoy another head job.

"Whoa," he said. "That's great." With her mouth full of champagne, she'd engulfed his cock in one swift movement. Like an ice pack on an injured limb, the chill removed some of the burn from his penis. But Carla's great technique didn't slake its hunger for more. Rolling her tongue up and down his shaft and swirling the tip on the head of his cock, Carla played with him mercilessly like a cat with a mouse. Throwing her legs either side of him, she jumped on top, sucking voraciously without breaking rhythm. Swallowing his cock down into her throat, she worked on him ruthlessly. With arms and legs spread wide, Aiden received Carla's grand manipulation abandoning all self-control. Just as he was about to come, she spun a one-eighty turn, lowering her snatch into his face. Aiden's tongue speared into her slippery slit, and while she sucked his cock to distraction, he lapped in a frenzy. With faces buried, they orgasmed simultaneously, drinking each other's essence once more.

Sprawled across his groin, Carla panted like she'd run a marathon as did Aiden. Gazing down at her black, sex-matted hair, she looked so deliciously spent. Not at all like the sexual powerhouse lover with whom he'd spent the last six hours making love. A spontaneous smile lifted his cheeks, and he exhaled a contented sigh. "Come up here, my sweet." Not waiting for a reply, he pulled her up beside him and raised her chin, so they lay face to face. "Carla, hypothetically, what would you do if I asked you to marry me?"

Tilting her head, she pursed her lips and regarded him. "I'm not sure. I don't find the idea of marrying you in the least objectionable." She giggled, and Aiden tweaked her nose. But as her eyes cast upwards, he stilled. *She's listening for her mother's voice,* he thought. "So even though it'd seem crazy to everyone else, I guess I'd seriously consider it."

"Good to hear. I'm pleased I'm not the only one in this bed who wants to get married someday."

She batted a soft punch to his shoulder and scolded, "You know I've wanted to get married for years. I just didn't have the right partner in poor Rafe."

"And now you do?" He rubbed his shoulder in mock pain.

"Yes, I really think I do." She pressed her face into his chest.

"Carla, have you heard the saying fools rush in where angels fear to tread?"

"*Sí?*"

"Well, since I'm being the fool, do you want to have children someday?"

"Oh yes. It appeared in my rune reading at the coast. The bird rune foretold of something new, a pregnancy or project . . ." Her voice faded away. Though Aiden remained still and silent, he had the answers he wanted and didn't need to play lawyer any longer.

"Anyway, we have a lifetime ahead of us," he said nonchalantly.

"Yes, we do, don't we?" she replied, burrowing deeper into his embrace.

"Time to get some sleep, my sweet." And just before Aiden drifted into a blissful slumber, he murmured, "*Que duermas bien, mi amor.* Sleep well, my love. *"*

THEY SLEPT THROUGH UNTIL noon, had a quick tapas for lunch and then Aiden ran off to organize a couple of things. Or so he said. What else he was doing Carla had no idea? But she didn't care. She knew whatever secret business Aiden was taking care of was not the same as Rafael's secret business.

"*Trust, mi querida. Trust.*" Isabella's voice echoed in her mind as confirmation. Knowing her relationship with Aiden would be based on trust and not secrets, she smiled, slow and contented. Sipping a coffee, Carla now waited for him at the hotel's café, trying her best not to fidget. Uncomfortable yet surprisingly sexually stimulated by the heat emanating from under her panties, Carla found it difficult to quell the restlessness between her legs. Never had she experienced such a lover. Nor had she loved such a man.

"Carla." Aiden's cheery voice called from the café doorway as he strode towards her. Pulling out a chair, he scuttled it close and kissed her cheek. "I have something to tell you."

Carla smiled, admiring the sparkle in his blue eyes. *He was such a boy at times*, she thought. "Okay. What is it?"

"You know how I said I'd be staying in Spain for at least six months?"

"Yes?" Uneasiness pricked at her skin.

"Well, I'm going to go back to Australia in four weeks' time." He seemed so pleased with the news, Carla couldn't respond. "And you're coming with me. I want you to meet my mum and dad."

"What? I can't go to Australia in a month."

"Yes, you can. You're only dancing here for another two weeks. I called Uncle Domingo, and he told me that the renovation of Sevilla Flamenco is taking longer than expected, which is usually the case with renovations. So, you won't be starting back there 'til early July. I've booked us tickets to go back home for a few weeks to meet my parents. Your father said he and your brothers will look after the Ferrari, so everything's sorted. I know I should've discussed this with you. But damn it, Carla, I love you, and I want my mum and dad to meet the woman I'm going to marry."

Carla stared at him, stunned. Inside her a whirlpool of emotions began to whip, thickening into a gluggy, confusing mass.

"*Trust, mi querida. Trust,*" her mother silently guided.

"Oh, Aiden, what can I say?"

Aiden grasped her hands. "For a legal eagle like me, this impetuous behaviour is right out of character. But you told me we were destined to be together. And I agree. Let's go back home, meet my parents, spend a couple of weeks there and then we'll come back to Spain. You have a huge dancing career ahead of you here, which I'd never jeopardize. And I'm sure with all the contacts your family has, I can work out some kind of career for myself in Seville. What do you say?"

Carla scanned his face and found only love, passion and commitment. She looked down at their hands, clasped together. Everything she'd wished for, hoped for, was coming true in front of her eyes this very minute. What was she waiting for? How many more signs did she need to know Aiden was the man for her?

Enough, she thought. "Of course. I'll go with you to Australia and meet your parents. I love you." She hugged his neck in a tight squeeze, letting go of her past relationship doubts, suspicions, and insecurities.

"Terrific," he cheered. "Because if you'd said no, I'd really be in the shit." A cheeky smirk lit up his face.

"Why's that?" Carla laughed.

"Because what would I do about this?" Aiden jumped to his feet and ripped off his shirt. There tattooed on his right shoulder, in the previously vacant rose next to his mother's name was *Carla*. "You're the second great love of my life, and I intend to marry you. You're with me forever."

And as he shot her one of his champion smiles, Carla leapt up and kissed it from his lips.

THE END

STAND-ALONE CONTEMPORARY ROMANCE FEATURING STRONG HEROINES AND PAGE-TURNING PLOTS

TEMPT ME

One woman . . . Two men . . . Threesomes change everything

When Michele Johnston, a forty-two-year-old ex-dancer from the Moulin Rouge gets divorced, she leaps into her new world of singledom with unbridled passion.

Aided and abetted by three vivacious girlfriends, Michele embarks on her steamy, erotic adventures, but gets more than she expects when mysterious yacht captain Mark Miller unleashes her wanton desires.

Further complicating matters, debonair Greek businessman Nick Stavros arrives on the scene and falls madly in love with her, promising the happy-ever-after ending. But will she give up her newfound freedom? Will she choose one man over the other? Or can she continue loving them both?

Tempt Me is the first stand-alone Contemporary Erotic Romance in Diane Demetre's genre-busting series, Steamy

Secrets. If you love strong heroes, hot sex, and feisty heroines, don't miss this page-turning love story with a twist.

EXCERPT

Squeezing her way through the nightclub crowd, Michele made for the bar where she stepped nimbly into a space just vacated by a large Negro man.

"I must try one of those as well," she mused to herself, watching his tight buttocks retreat.

Leaning across the bar to be heard, Michele ordered her poison. The service was fast, the vodka and tonic cold and the music hot. With all the accoutrements to suit the scene, she settled in to scope the room, enjoying the buzz of sexual energy.

It took only thirty minutes before an extra drink arrived in front of her. The bartender pointed to the big guy at the other end of the bar who tipped his glass and smiled. She accepted his offering with a reciprocal gesture. Her drink patron stood nearly a full head height above everyone else and was built like an Arnie Schwarzenegger double with a twist of Crocodile Dundee about him. Accentuated by his casual clothes, his face and manner had Aussie written all over them. After an initial assessment, Michele gave him only fleeting attention as she'd already chosen her mark for the night; the young bartender with the trim body, aquiline face, and gelled hair.

The night progressed, and another couple of drinks arrived compliments of the titan, who remained fixed as if supporting the other end of the bar. She acknowledged each drink with a gracious smile, which he returned with the unwavering stare of a wildcat, mouth curled waiting for its prey to make a move.

While the bartender showed initial interest in her flirtations, he disappeared at the end of his shift leaving her advances unrequited.

Nothing new there, she thought, *God, what's wrong with me?* Feeling the familiar sense of rejection left over from years living with her husband, she sculled her drink and turned to leave.

But there he stood, her drinks benefactor, wearing an inscrutable expression as he blocked her exit. From a distance he'd looked a solid guy, however up close he must've been virtually a hundred kilos of pure muscle.

With a smile twitching his lips, he initiated the conversation. "You're the horniest thing I've seen in years. Why are you chasing pencil dicks?"

His brash opening remarks pinned her to the spot and, as a half-smile flitted across her face, she took a closer look at this man with the roguish sense of humour. He wouldn't be classed as typically handsome, but his sheer presence and blunt approach caused her skin to tingle. Impeding any escape, he flashed a wide, white smile, and waited for a response. His eyes, a vivid marine blue, twinkled with life experience and his collar-length soft brown hair framed his sun-tanned face. He encroached into her personal space, towering over her with the promise of a real man, and he smelt good. The scent of masculine musk mingled with the bittersweet overtones of a world-class aftershave triggered a positive response in her brain.

"Thanks for the drinks. That was very generous of you. And your name is . . .?"

"You can call me Mark. And you are?" His voice was like the breath of a friendly dragon, warm and playful.

"Michele." Her initial obligation to be polite since he'd spent money buying her drinks had softened to casual interest. "Tell me a little about yourself, Mark."

"Not much to tell really. I'd rather talk about you."

"Either you're very chivalrous or very secretive. I suspect it might be the latter. You don't give too much away, do you?"

"Not only good looking but clever as well. What is it I can do to make you choose me instead of that gay bartender?"

Shit, she thought. After all she'd been through, she'd chosen a carbon copy of her ex-husband. Why hadn't she'd seen it? But it wasn't too late to save the night. "Well, I guess you can buy me another drink, Mark."

~ ♥ ~

TEACH ME

When destiny beckons, what is a girl to do?

At twenty-four, Samantha O'Brien scores her dream job as a dancer at the famous Moulin Rouge, only to arrive in Paris to find her well-laid plans in disarray. Fortuitously, Sam is rescued by the eccentric, tarot-card reading proprietress of Hotel Hollandaise, who cautions that Paris is for lovers, but not always love.

As Sam launches into her new career, she suspects that the show's super sexy, Sicilian stage director, Tony Di Falco is more than just a creative genius and hard taskmaster, leaving her to wonder whether secrets are best shared.

Meeting Philippe Lacroix, a struggling, young artist in Montmartre saves Sam from imploding under the pressure. He introduces her to the city of love, captivating her with his angelic good looks and sensuous touch. Yet the mounting attraction intensifies between Sam and Tony, and their tense, sexually charged relationship threatens to overwhelm them. But the show must go on.

Filled with backstage bitchiness, tough rehearsals, a sprinkling of cocaine and the French addiction to cigarettes,

Sam grapples with her new life. Then without warning, her destiny changes literally before her eyes, and she learns that even in the most romantic city of the world, you don't find love, love finds you.

Teach Me is the second stand-alone Contemporary Erotic Romance in Diane Demetre's genre-busting series, Steamy Secrets. If you love strong heroes, hot sex and feisty heroines, don't miss this page-turning love story with a twist.

EXCERPT

By the time Philippe opened the second bottle of wine, they'd devoured their baguette and the sun was setting, stroking the sky in Monet-inspired colours.

"It's getting cold out here. Let's go inside, Samantha." Grabbing the wine and glasses, Philippe walked indoors while Sam cuddled Jasper to her chest and followed.

"Come on, Jasper. Time for your dinner," Philippe said.

At the sound of the magic word, Jasper sprang from Sam's arms onto the floor where he was promptly fed a bowl of dry cat kibble. While Jasper chewed through his dinner, Philippe sat on the side of his bed. Aside from a rickety table and two chairs, obscured by pencils, crayons and sketchbooks, the double bed, bedside table and a wardrobe were the only other pieces of furniture in the room.

"Sit beside me, Samantha." Assigning their wine glasses to the bedside table, Philippe shimmied back onto the bed using the wall behind him as a backrest. When she settled in beside him, he said, "I would like to paint you. A real painting, for my exhibition. Would you sit for me?"

"I guess so." She was surprised that he wanted to include a painting of her in his exhibition.

"*Très bien.* Let's begin now." Philippe sprang off the bed and dashed to the table, where he rummaged around for the right implements. Finding a large sketchbook and several charcoals, he cleared a chair and dragged it in front of the bed. "You are my queen of the can-can. Like the famous dancer La Goulue. Here, I will arrange your pose."

Philippe fluffed the pillows for Sam to recline on, and she wiggled into place with a giggle. With great care, he clasped her arm and tucked it under her head as support. Trailing his hands over her body, he manoeuvred her this way and that, edging slowly to her hips. The strength and gentleness of his touch as he rolled her forwards to lay on her side ignited a subtle warmth in Sam's groin. His hand cupped her bottom, rolling her back a little to just the right angle, and she wished he'd dig deeper into her from behind. Taking her top leg, Philippe cupped her knee, bending it to drag across in the foreground. For the final effect, he reached to her other leg and pulled it straight beneath her, running his hands down her long limb to her ankle.

"There, that will be a good starting pose I think," he said. "Are you comfortable?"

"Yes, I think so." She was anything but comfortable. Moist and ready, her sex flamed. Her nipples yearned to be teased and her arse screamed for grabbing. The seam in her jeans bit hard into the folds of her cleft. She began to unravel.

"Are you all right, Samantha?"

"Yes. Yes. I'm fine." But her dilated pupils and shallow breathing betrayed her.

She was certain Philippe suspected what she was feeling because a lazy lascivious smile graced his angelic face. Michele sensed his wild, artistic spirit swirl around her like an unpredictable tornado. Yet he remained calm and lowered his sketchbook and charcoals to the floor. Resplendent in a flowing white shirt and low-slung cargos that matched the colour of his delinquent golden hair, he fixed her in his gaze and strolled over to the bed. Gazing down at her, he moistened his lips and exhaled with a slight purr. "Perhaps I can be of assistance?"

AUTHOR BIOGRAPHY

Diane began her career as a schoolteacher before moving into the entertainment industry as a choreographer, director, event manager, dancer and actress, working in television and live theatre, and managing multi-million-dollar productions.

Following her onstage career, she spent many years as a stress & life skills therapist, keynote speaker and presenter, appearing on national radio and television under the pseudonym of the Goddess of Love.

For her outstanding contribution to the arts, Diane was awarded the 2019 SBAA International Women's Day Leader Award for Leadership in the Entertainment, Creative Arts and Media Industry.

She is an award-winning author of contemporary, genre-busting romance, suspense and mystery novels. Her intuitive insights into human behaviour are woven into her casts of characters, heightening the intrigue in her storytelling. Set in exotic locations, her stories are packed with emotional punch and feature empowered heroines who live life to the fullest, much like the author herself.

Connect with Diane

https://dianedemetre.com/

AWARD WINNING AUTHOR

> " . . . Dare to dream bigger than ever before, dare to forge our own path no matter how hard the challenges. But most of all, dare to be you and let the chips fall where they may. We are all warrior women with gossamer wings . . . It's time to roar! "
>
> — Diane Demetre

Winner of 2019 SBAA International Women's Day Leader Award for Leadership in Entertainment, Creative Arts and/or Media Industry.

Diane was nominated as a finalist in the ARRA Awards 2018 for Favourite Romantic Suspense, for her novel *Retribution.*

In 2017 Diane won the Romance Writers of Australia Emerald Pro Award for Best Unpublished Romance Manuscript.

ISLAND OF SECRETS

Two love stories separated in time. Two women following their dreams. In a paradise littered with painful secrets, will love turn the tide?

1973. Cecilia "CiCi" Freemont has a restless soul and the voice of an angel. Leaving her privileged upbringing behind, she chases her dreams to the sandy beaches of an unspoiled Hawaiian paradise, Harbor Island. But life takes an unexpected turn when she falls for the island's young heir-apparent and her newfound adventure becomes too much to bear . . .

2017. Investigative journalist Tina Templeton has dedicated herself to the pursuit of truth. But when she inherits Harbor Island, her career plans take a confusing twist. Managing the sprawling island estate is tough business even with the help of aging cabaret singer, CiCi Freemont. Especially when a massive ecological disaster threatens to destroy her beautiful beaches — and the responding coast guard captain steals her heart.

As the investigation into the disaster reveals a 40-year-old mystery that could change their lives forever, will Tina find love among the secrets, or will CiCi's painful past dash her dreams on the rocks?

Island of Secrets is an epic love story. If you like generations-spanning drama, characters with hidden pasts, heart-warming romance and intrigue, then you'll love Diane Demetre's powerful novel in paradise.

~ ♥ ~

RETRIBUTION

Winner of Romance Writers of Australia Emerald Pro Award 2017.

**She's a ballerina with a dark secret.
He's a retired sniper with a tortured past.
Will they find love or fall prey to a stalker's deadly game?**

Professional ballerina Jessie Hilton wraps her battle scars in satin pointe shoes, but there's a deeper hurt that haunts her sleep. When a handsome man steps in to save her from a mugging, something about her hero makes her heavy heart leap. Though her career can't afford distractions, he may be her sole source of safety when she gains the unwanted attention of a relentless stalker.

Ex-sniper Brad Jordan survived his tour of duty, but a tragic accident cost him the lives of those closest to him. With his faithful border collie Whiskey by his side, Brad gets a second chance when he protects the beautiful Jessie from danger. When the ballerina's stalker grows more brazen, Brad's tactical training may be their only weapon against tragedy.

Will Jessie and Brad survive a deadly game or will the assailant destroy their chance at love?

Retribution is a stand-alone romantic suspense novel. If you like tough-as-toe-shoes heroines, second-chance romance, and page-turning plots, then you'll love Diane Demetre's heart-stopping saga.

PRAISE FOR DIANE'S WORK

An exciting and erotic read A refreshing genre-busting story of a divorced, older (I hasten to add by society's standards not mine) heroine who is determined to embrace her singledom while simultaneously casting aside her self- and societally-imposed sexual repression through casual erotic encounters. Diane Demetre offers a story that challenges our pre-conceived notions of what "women of a certain age" should or should not be doing and she does this in an empowering manner. The heroine embraces and cherishes her female friendships and though this aided in the flow of the plot, it also highlights the importance for women of having encouraging and supportive female companionship. Most importantly, we see the heroine herself allow the experiences of her new-found freedom to shape her own future thus enabling her to escape the repressive nature of her pre-divorce life. All in all, an erotic and exciting read sure to captivate and thrill readers of any age.

— AusRom Today

I found this to be an amazing read and I adore the author's writing style. I was captivated by the setting, the characters, the Romani culture and the story line twists and turns. A fast flowing novel with just the right amount of eroticism thrown in. I fell in love with one of the lead characters (Aiden Bishop) very quickly and the relationship between Rafael & Carla had me wondering what would eventuate next. Well done Diane Demetre.

— 5 STARS, Robyn Powers

" This is the third book I've read by Diane Demetre and I was absolutely delighted! What a great read. It has everything: a great story line mixed with sensual exploration; mystery; spirituality and wonderfully complex main characters. Couldn't put it down. Loved Aiden – just gorgeous and every woman's dream. Looking forward to the next book. "

— 5 STARS, Deborah Bispham

" Demetre paints vividly the atmosphere of Paris and the Moulin Rouge with such detail that it adds yet another layer of intimacy to the story. A wonderful read that we highly recommend. "

— AusRom Today

" I bought this book and wow what a read! To every young woman it's a must! Life lessons learnt in an amazing story told! Though I had other things to do, I had to finish this amazing story! Bring on book 3! "

— 5 STARS

" A well-written erotic romance with its share of twists and suspense. Love the characters and the way the author describes Paris and behind the scenes of the Moulin Rouge. "

— 5 STARS, Peter Brady

" Michele, a former pro dancer, has finally extricated herself from a very unsatisfying marriage, & is ready for a chance to kick up her heels, sexually & emotionally. Intent on a one night stand, she finds, instead, Mark, a most inventive & attentive lover, something she has never experienced before. As she falls in love with him, against her better judgement, she finds that he has way too many secrets that threaten to derail their fledgling relationship. By the time Nick inserts himself into her life, insisting he is just her type, despite her thoughts to the contrary, Mark has disappeared & bad people are after both him & Michele. Under Nick's protection, Michele finally figures out what she wants from life, in a very good

heroine's journey. There's an abundance of very hot sex, & the love of a good man.
— 4.5 STARS, Alberta, ManicReaders

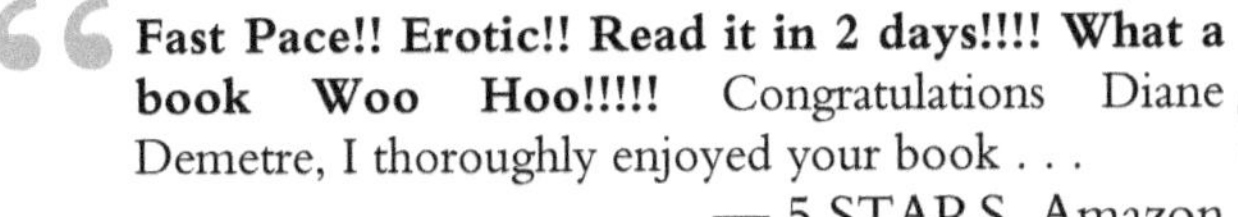

Fast Pace!! Erotic!! Read it in 2 days!!!! What a book Woo Hoo!!!!! Congratulations Diane Demetre, I thoroughly enjoyed your book . . .
— 5 STARS, Amazon

DIANE DEMETRE

www.ingramcontent.com/pod-product-compliance
Lightning Source LLC
Chambersburg PA
CBHW021314190726
48288CB00003B/838